M000209127

Otranto

Otranto

❧

Maria Corti

Translated from the Italian
with a Preface by
Jessie Bright

ITALICA PRESS
NEW YORK
1993

Translation Copyright © 1993 by Jessie Bright

L'Ora di Tutti Copyright © 1962, 1977
Feltrinelli Economica SpA Milan

ITALICA PRESS, INC.
595 Main Street
New York, New York 10044

All rights reserved. No part of this publication may be reproduced, stored in a retrieval system, or transmitted, in any form or by any means, electronic, mechanical, photocopying, recording, or otherwise, without prior permission of Italica Press.

Library of Congress Cataloging-in-Publication Data
Corti, Maria.
 [Ora di tutti. English]
 Otanto / Maria Corti ; translated from the Italian with a preface by Jessie Bright.
  p. cm.
 ISBN 0-934977-29-1 : $12.50
 1. Otranto (Italy)--History--Fiction. 2. Turks--Italy--Otranto--History--Fiction. I. Title.
PQ4863.070713   1993
853'.914--dc20   93-32681
                                                  CIP

Printed in the United States of America
5 4 3 2 1

Cover art: Alexandra Eldridge

ABOUT THE TRANSLATOR

Now retired from university teaching, Jessie Bright
lives in State College, Pennsylvania. In addition to
Otranto, she has also translated *The Woodern Throne,* a
novel by Carlo Sgorlon, published by Italica Press in
1988, as well as short stories by Sgorlon, Vitaliano
Brancati, and Mirella Ducceschi.

PREFACE

It is unlikely any serious Italian reader would fail to recognize the name Maria Corti. Even a glance inside the dust covers of her recent books reveals a list of redoubtable literary accomplishments. For example, Bompiani, the publisher of her latest novel, *Cantare nel buio,* mentions that in 1990 she received the Premio della Presidenza del Consiglio dei Ministri per la letteratura, a distinction with no direct counterpart for an American author – the President's literary prize? Other fiction awards noted in parentheses after the titles of her four previous novels, including *Otranto,* winner of the Premio Crotone in 1963, are still only part of the picture. Her academic publications include annotated editions of Cavalcanti, Vittorini, Fenoglio and Ennio Flaiano, as well as many other scholarly works, which have earned her an international reputation as a linguist and semiotic critic. In addition, she has served as editor and co-director of important literary reviews and has written commentary for national newspapers.

Although these achievements obviously represent a long and productive career, no biographer should forget to mention another perhaps equally important aspect of her life: her role as a university professor, first at the University of Lecce and then at the University of Pavia, where she has been well-known and well-loved for many years. At an age when some professors have retired or become empty imitations of their earlier selves, she was still visibly enjoying her research and especially her students, still radiating energy, curiosity and interest in people, places, language, ideas and events. She is a public figure in the most positive sense of the term – sought after by and responsive to thinking people both in Italy and elsewhere. Even before the fall of 1989 when all European eyes turned toward the east she had played a part in the cultural and literary life of Eastern-bloc nations.

Born in 1915 in Milan, she belongs to the generation who had to deal with Fascism, war, civil war, the postwar boom and the decade or more when Italian institutions themselves were threatened by terrorism from both right and left. Living through similar times could make a thoughtful person bitter, cynical or indifferent, but anyone who knows Maria Corti's life and work would probably guess that these vicissitudes, observed and reflected upon by her lively critical mind, merely increased her passion for social justice. She remains acutely aware of contemporary issues, and her creativity has not diminished. Now retired from teaching, she lives in Milan and continues to write. In fact, the Italian reader, particularly if she is a woman, might see Maria Corti as an inspiration.

Now for the story. Is it a historical novel or isn't it? The author says it isn't, or at least it isn't a traditional historical novel. In her forward to the 1989 Bompiani students' edition she concedes that the bare bones of the story are indeed based upon historical fact, at least as much as historical fact can be determined, and some of the characters are indeed real people: King Ferrante, Duke Alfonso, Captain Zurlo, Captain de li Falconi, Francesco Caracciolo, Archbishop Pendinelli, Akmed Pasha. Furthermore she begins the book itself with an introduction to explain its historical context, but she does so in a voice that is far more lyrical than scholarly. She also notes in the 1989 preface that one of the tasks of modern historians has been to separate reliable data from the cloud of legend and myth that surrounds these events. As for the prevailing religious interpretation, she includes it in her last chapter in a cleverly ironic contrast to both the literal historical view and her own more significant vision of what happened. Thus Corti is not trying to recreate or invent a panorama of a particular era on a grand scale. Hers is a much more modest effort than *Gone With the Wind* or *War and Peace*.

Yet she apparently intended the story to symbolize a different historical event than the one it portrays, an event that didn't happen until almost 500 years later: the resistance to Nazi oppression during World War II. The link between that struggle and the siege of Otranto, familiar to her from childhood, began to ferment in her imagination after the war, "like bread when the baker adds yeast," as she put it, and when the jurors awarded her the Premio Crotone she was gratified that they too had read the book as a statement about the resistance.

Another contrast with the traditional historical novel lies in the multiple points of view – the same story told by five first-person narrators, four of them witnesses and participants, the fifth a commentator who wasn't there at the time but looks back on the siege from the perspective of a year later. This technique is not, of course, original with Maria Corti, but it particularly suits her because it forces the author to think about differentiating each voice from the others. She welcomed such a task maybe partly because it would challenge even her unusual linguistic gifts. To begin with, she had to confront the chronological problem. She wanted the voices to sound authentic, but she did not want to make her characters speak in the archaic language of a regional dialect of the fifteenth century. With her knowledge and skill she probably could have done so, but then even Italian readers would need a translation. Instead, she paid close attention to register and identified each voice by social class so their discourse reveals status as well as individual character traits. She aimed for precision as well as subtlety and succeeded on both counts. But the challenge that stimulates an author can sometimes overwhelm a translator. It may be that the nuances of the five different voices have not survived. Corti also uses a number of regional or dialectical terms, for instance the names of certain species of fish – names that add local color or even a touch of the exotic for an Italian reader. But such an effect is difficult to duplicate in American English. One always hopes, but translation is an approximate art.

There is an added dimension to one of the voices: Idrusa's. Idrusa is a woman, a woman of that long-ago time who may even be anachronistic in her implicit rebellion against another possible oppressor – not the Turks but a society that demeans and limits her just because she is a woman. A twentieth-century voice? Or an invitation to believe that there have always been women who saw their world this way?

A further consequence of using multiple points of view is that readers know how the story is going to end. Actually, Italian readers know before it even begins. American readers, on the other hand, might not have learned in school about the terrible Turks who massacred the inhabitants of Otranto in 1480, but this won't matter. The author's introduction tells them and does so in poetic prose that evokes the melancholy and mystical awe associated with the legend. In any case, knowing how the story is going to end intensifies the drama. It's like watching the amateur film of that motorcade in Dallas with the doomed president smiling and waving at the crowd. Moreover, with each new narrator the reader learns more about the various stages of the action, including the ending, and at the same time the previous narrator and the one waiting in the wings become characters seen through different eyes. And so on until the tale is finally told.

Maria Corti has suggested that her Otrantini could
be seen as a symbol of yet another oppressed group: the
people of southern Italy, who for centuries of their
history have been repeatedly invaded by foreigners or
badly governed or forgotten by those in power in Rome.
Here again an American reader might miss the political or geographical reference, but this doesn't really
matter either. Our continent's history has its own sagas
of oppression and resistance.

Any reader can appreciate the essence of place, the
immediacy of detail – the smells, the plants, the
animals, the sky, the sea, the wind, the artifacts of everyday life – authentic images derived in part from the
author's childhood. Although Milanese by birth, Maria
Corti spent the first nine years of her childhood on the
Salento peninsula, the heel of the Italian boot, because
of her father's work as a construction engineer. When
her mother died she had to be sent to a convent board-
ing school back in gray, damp, foggy Milan, which
probably added to the poignant intensity of her
memories.

Such thoughts are appropriate because the story is
itself a web of memories – memories that tug upon the
imagination of each narrator as he or she returns to the
past. Memory is, of course, a filter, a focus, an interpreter of experience. Maria Corti notes that writers,
like painters, want to communicate a point of view, a
particular vision of reality, in order to make others
"see" what they have seen. Perhaps every artist or writer
tries to reveal truth or a part of the truth. So it is with
the narrators in this book. Each one recounts his or her
version of the truth, but truth itself continually shifts
away into the shadows. And yet the very authenticity of
the novel derives in part from this shifting and
multiple rendering of the same tragic story.

Finally, the title. The Italian title is *L'ora di tutti,*
literally "everybody's hour" or "the moment of all."
The French translation is almost literal: *L'heure du*

destin, the hour of destiny. This translation gave up the struggle, hoping to maintain at least some of the legendary associations by simply naming the place where it all happened. The author, however, insists upon the message in her original title. She puts that message into the mouths of two of her characters. In Part VI of Captain Zurlo's narrative Don Felice says to the captain, "You see, Zurlo, at least once in each man's life there comes a time to prove himself. The moment always comes – for everyone. The Turks have brought it to us." For Maria Corti this story of the siege of Otranto is an example of how not only individuals but an entire collectivity or community can sometimes react to oppression with heroic resistance, even against overwhelming odds, in a way no observer would have thought possible. Captain Zurlo sums up her thoughts by referring to one man's deeds: "I still remember one of the fishermen...a fine young fellow...whose obscure existence had nurtured a heroism one couldn't have foreseen. He died without a word, after single-handedly cutting down a whole crowd of Turks. Such acts are possible for humble men caught in the act of destiny, but this is something types like Don Giovanni Antonio de Foxa will never understand."

Simply on the literal level this novel can be read as a sort of history or chronicle of tragic, senseless, needless violence. Yet for all its sadness and injustice it affirms a positive and even noble vision of the potential of ordinary people. A vision that has sustained its author and can perhaps give hope to a thoughtful reader.

State College, Pennsylvania
August 1993

Otranto

♣

INTRODUCTION

Along a path made by countless bare feet among the reeds and grasses of the Idro Valley the women come down to Otranto at dawn, carrying baskets of chicory and *caciotte* cheeses; their eyes are large and dark, their shiny hair tangled, and their bearing proud. As the soles of their feet spread unharmed on the path, they gaze steadily toward the sea, in the fixed dry-eyed stare of generations of Otrantini, who have lived their lives watching for the African scirocco or the northerly tramontana, the winds by which they order their thoughts and daily activities. Reaching the city walls they put down their chicory and cheeses at the foot of Alfonso of Aragon's tower, and abruptly begin to shriek, trembling inside their black dresses as though suddenly possessed by an oracle, screaming in the faces of passersby:

"Chicore-e-e, chicory, fresh curly chicory!"

At this point, should a stranger be present, he will stand there in the shadow of the tower, his feet glued to the pavement, staring at their violet black eyes and dark skin, and asking himself in perplexity: "Greek blood? Or Arab?"

"Otrantini blood," answers the ancient chant with which the women sing their babies to sleep:

sangue otrantino,
saporito come menta e petrusino,
sangue forte e fino,
contro il turco malandrino.

Otrantini blood,
pungent as parsley and mint,
strong blood and fine
against the wicked Turk.

1

INTRODUCTION

Seen from the sea Otranto still resembles a fortress, with its bastions looking straight down on the water, but behind its empty abundance of walls and towers is a marvel of narrow white passages winding up and down, of tiny white houses and larger buildings made of tuff. In these narrow streets historical events bounce back like ripe apples from one century to another and catch up with us: here stone cannonballs fired by the Turks five hundred years ago support the steps of houses or, placed on either side of the entrance, decorate the threshold of the barber's "salon" and the post office. When evening comes young girls sit down beside the cannonballs, girls with the same eyes and hair as the chicory vendors, and call to each other from their doorways, talking about the boyfriends "slaving away in Switzerland." Meanwhile an old woman passes, tugging a recalcitrant half-naked child by one arm, and as he stamps his little feet in rage she yells at him in dialect: "Better watch out, the Turks'll carry you off to sea!" And the little boy stops stamping his bare feet and begins to cry in the monotonous prolonged wail of the Salento Peninsula.

In the center of the minuscule city one conspicuous street climbs upward, gradually widening, its stone pavement worn smooth by the black shoes of seminarians: at the top is the piazza of the cathedral. Resting upon the rock with all the weight of its Romanesque walls, the cathedral is the heart of the domain of Otranto, because They are inside it, on the right at the front of the apse, like the stone of a fruit. Every year on the fourteenth of August, men, women and children come from all over the Salento to pay homage to Them, arriving in their cars just the way they flock to international soccer matches. They all picnic on the beach with great quantities of melons from Brindisi, while the brown muscular fishermen make their way gradually along the sand, their heads bobbing to the rhythm of their steps, offering baskets of mussels and calling out:

"Candies from the sea!"

To mark the occasion the band plays *Nabucco* or *I Lombardi alla prima crociata* – The Lombards on the First Crusade – the street vendors sell hazelnuts and *copeta*, a remarkably sweet dough that is strangely hard and resists the knife, yet flakes into delicious layers at the touch of an eager hand. A treat worthy of Them.

Better to go and visit Them on an ordinary day. They can be reached by crossing the long naves of the cathedral, where one shouldn't have feet in the first place, but some kind of wings instead, to hop like a sparrow between the two enormous trees of life blooming in polychrome limestone chips in the floor, and so avoid adding to the wear on the prodigious mosaic. Dear Don Pantaleone! In the year of grace 1165 you came down from the Basilian Monastery of San Nicola di Càsole, where you had studied the bestiaries and learned the beautiful stories of Alexander the Great and King Arthur. You arrived and took charge of the Norman workmen, and now here, just to the right of the gate to Eden, King Arthur on horseback wrestles with the cat of Lausanne, and there Alexander dressed in purple and crowned like Charlemagne, sits on the rumps of two griffins backed up to one another, and graciously holds out meat or palms of glory to both of them.

The mosaic extends to the threshold of the apse where They customarily sleep behind the fragile glass of the ossuaries. The author of this book must justify having awakened Them and imposed this labor of memory; we don't know whether such a task be more painful for the dead or for the living. Indeed it was in this cathedral that some of Them found refuge, some killed themselves, and all knelt down to serve their God, stunned and overwhelmed at their fate.

There are two ways to approach Them, one, so to speak, as a tourist. The stranger who arrives in Otranto and stays a short while listens as the guide recounts the ancient story of courage and bloodshed, so much bloodshed. He furrows his brow, asks for clarification, stares through the glass at the tiny piles of scapulae, tibiae, femurs and skulls, lost in thought for a moment or two. Then he departs, with an unreal rhythm like the cadence of a fable in his soul, the rhythm of the ancient local chronicles:

In the year 1480 after the salvation of the world by Our Lord Jesus Christ, in the year 22 of the reign of his most Serene Highness King Ferdinand of Aragon over the Kingdom of Naples, in the Pontificate of Sixtus IV, under the Holy Roman Emperor Frederick III, the German Caesar; in that year Sultan Mohamet, Emperor of the Turks, undertook the siege of the city of Otranto by force of arms and overcame and conquered it, with the memorable massacre that ensued; in that year numbered 2730 after the edification of the aforesaid city (founded in the year 415 before the edification of Rome, the year 1250 before the glorious nativity of Our Lord incarnate, during the reign in Italy of Fauno Re, son of Pizo; in the time of Mercurio Hermes, the wisest of men, inventor of music, in the time of David, King of Israel, that is to say near the time of the birth of Moses, with respect to which antiquity has created this difference, that for every year in the computation of these times there exist several variations).

But let's stay longer in the ancient realm of Otranto, let's go down at twilight to the port, towards the pier, during a northerly storm when the fishermen sit crosslegged on the ground, their skin darkened by the sun, quietly watching the sea, waiting in reflective silence, like their loyal friends, for the fury to pass.

It's almost like opening a window on a secret place, a place apart. Then things change, time falls away, the fable is no longer possible: it is They whom we have before us, still the same fishermen, except for a detail or two or the momentary hubbub surrounding them; the same small men with their exquisite capacity to behave well in the hour of destiny.

We nod a greeting to them. They answer:

"Good afternoon to you," and fall silent again: a pure silence that expands around them like the clear light of dawn spreading over the hill called Minerva behind the city. It is from that silence that the ancient voices come forth, trembling within the brilliant youth that was their lives. We feel as if we have happened upon a felicitous moment and move away from the pier thinking that the substance of the chronicles has not turned from lava to stone, but is still warm and alive, here in this horn of Italy, *sus la senestre corne d'Ytaile*, and today's fishermen have simply replaced the others halfway through the voyage.

PART I

Colangelo the Fisherman

It was sunup and the morning air was cool when I went down to the harbor from the old city. The friars in the Monastery of San Giovanni, who wake up from sheer piety, were singing in the choir. And the sea crows were calling back and forth to each other, till they all got together on top of the Serpe Tower. Then they pointed their beaks in the same direction, spread their black wings and flew off toward the water. Later while I was setting my heavy lines they came back to the tower in a flock, looked straight up at the sky and burst out squawking. Otranto's houses, surrounded by gardens, followed the hill down to the sea, where monasteries marked the city's limits on both sides, San Giovanni to the west and San Francesco to the east. My house was on the hill in the old borgo, where ordinary folks lived, fishermen or storehouse workers. But from up there you could see past Rocamatura, a point of land sticking out into the sea to the west, with little inlets and landings and sand dunes. For me there was no place like Otranto, a fine city, rich and pretty to look at; provincial capital she was, and mistress of a lot of farms. There was no trade on earth the Otrantini fishermen wouldn't be ready to take up when the tramontana whipped up the breakers so they couldn't fish: they'd make pottery and ironwork, crush olives in the presses, pick grapes up on the plateau, collect wood, anything.

That morning was a Friday: the twenty-eighth of July of the year 1480. Once I got down to the lowest rocks right near the port I rolled up my breeches, because with the tramontana every wave was sending out spray as

7

it ·filled up the holes in the rocks and sucked away any water left over from the wave before it. I jumped barefoot from one rock to another all the way to the base of the Serpe Tower, where the rocks themselves had made a nice inlet and the water stayed really calm even during northerly storms. That's why I usually set my heavy lines there: it was a good place for sea bream. They'd show up every morning at first light, when deep water fish get an urge for something new.

Once I'd set my lines, I was tired from bending over, so I straightened up and looked to see what the weather was doing: out toward the strait the sea wasn't calm any more. Up on the cliff the wild fennel bushes were twisting around and the tops of the oaks were tossing in the wind. It looked as if things would get worse for sure; the tramontana in these parts never dies down in the daytime. The spray was hitting as high as the magnetic rocks up by Cucurizzo, right to the foundation of the Serpe Tower, which overlooked the whole strait. There weren't any houses right near the tower because that place was haunted. The dead used to come back at night from the sea to the shore; they'd climb out on the rocks and wander around in the weeds, sort of moaning. This story about our coast got started a long time back, when Otranto and its territory were ruled by Maria of Enghien and a snake actually lived up there in the tower. One night when there was a storm this snake wound its way up the tower walls, stuck its head through the bars of the little window at the top where the light showed the sailors their way and marked the harbor. A snake doesn't really know anything so it drank the oil in the lamp right down to the last drop and then stretched out on the stone in the quiet of the night to digest its meal. A Venetian galleon that happened to be passing through the strait hit the rocks almost at once. The Venetian merchants disappeared in the waves but they couldn't find peace at the bottom of the sea because their dead eyes and their dead feet still wanted to finish the voyage. So every once in a while at night they'd come up to take a walk along the coast and remember how nice it used to be to be alive.

To be honest, I've never seen large snakes or vipers around here that would drink oil, and that morning my fisherman's experience led me to think somebody else's cursed throat must have drunk the oil from the lamp and that somebody else was the devil himself. Ever since he fell out of heaven he's used his angel's wits to ruin folks' peace of mind.

The air was cool that morning even for July. It was coming in from the sea in a damp breeze and blowing the rose mallow and fennel bushes every which way so I thought I might as well go back to the port and take in my lines. There was no use even talking about fishing that day.

I remember perfectly well: I was just leaning down along the side of the port to pull in my lines and all at once I saw it. In fact that other day on the western wall when the curved blade of the Turkish knife passed right between my ribs, that moment was dull by comparison. I was leaning down, as I said. The boats tied up along the pier, some of them freshly painted, making others look faded by contrast, were bumping and banging against the biggest rocks because of the rough sea. Boys were jumping around in them, naked and soaking wet, having fun as kids always do. In the midst of all this, old Mastro Natale had put his nets together in a single pile, tucked them under his left arm and gone off slowly toward the level place beyond the reach of the spray. There he sat, crosslegged, his bare feet turned up, just thinking. He was the best as far as thinking was concerned and all the fishermen honored him for it.

A hundred paces from the port Procomio da Malcantone was coming back with the catch from his trotlines. His boat was bobbing up and down, fore and aft: he couldn't make it into the harbor. But since it was now in no danger and Procomio was the only one of us who had taken a cargo of fish that day, the other fishermen including myself, Jesus forgive me – we were enjoying the show from above. That's what envy will do, taint men's hearts when they're generous by nature. Procomio, his eye on the closest waves, couldn't look out in the distance without risking his cargo; so he was the last to see the thing that morning – I was the first.

They certainly weren't merchant galleons; the shape of their sails was clear right away and little by little on the crest of the breakers you could see the crescent on their hulls: Turkish galleys right there in the middle of the Strait of Otranto. They seemed to be heading for Brindisi but the waves were battering their prows and turning them west toward the scirocco. All of them, galleys of different sizes, galliots and lighters, thrown together in confusion, were floundering about in the midst of the strait. Now and then they'd disappear but the force of the waves would heave them up again on the breakers and all the while white foam was spreading faster and faster over the entire strait. In a matter of minutes sky and sea were covered by a gray vapor, like smoke, and every once in a while silent lightning flashed through it and gusts of wind blew it apart, just enough for me to see ghosts of galleys hanging out there in space. I stood on tiptoe, shading my eyes with my hands; again I saw the galleys get back on course. I put my whole mind on trying to work out the distance and how long it should take them to get out of the strait, but I got lost in my figuring because with the heavy seas their maneuvering was so slow and disorganized. Turning toward Mastro Natale I noticed Cola Mazzapinta standing on one of the rocks in the harbor, then Nachira on another, Alfio da Faggiano and Antonello d'Alessandro on two others, all of them stock still with their eyes fixed on the strait. And the surf rolling back in the wind till you could see cowries and sea urchins on the bottom; and the sea crows flying around frantically. Then there were twenty, then thirty of us on the rocks, nobody talking; all of us together but nobody saying a word – that had never happened before. But the sun soon burned off the fog so our eyes could now see the dreaded crescents very well, as they appeared and disappeared at regular intervals. When a big wave broke on the rocks it meant that a moment later we'd see them. They weren't making any headway now. They were completely off course, just tossing about in the same piece of water. We wanted to believe they were busy trying to maneuver the rigging of their square sails but when our eyes met for an instant we all read each other's thoughts: "With a sea like this, who could get through the strait?" Then, one by one, the prows turned toward Otranto and little by little as they got closer we could tell the large galleys from the galliots, and the lighters from the smaller galleys plowing straight through the waves ahead of the others.

At that moment Procomio finally made it into the harbor with his cargo of fish and when he turned his boat toward the wind and saw them, such a sight was so far from his thoughts that he let out a yell. Then he turned toward us, waving his arms and shouted again: "Ahoy! Turks!"

We were off in a flash. All of us running and shouting at the same time.

Alfio da Faggiano was yelling: "To the countryside, get the livestock and shut them in."

"Nossir," shouted Cola Mazzapinta, who didn't have any livestock. "First bring the boats inside the walls."

Nachira said no to that, the thing to do was clear out the farmhouses and put our goods in a safe place. Things were in a state of confusion when we happened to see some Spanish soldiers with one of their officers in the smaller piazza.

"Let's go ask the officer," shouted Nachira. "Maybe he'll know what to do."

We rushed up to him even as he was starting toward us. When we were close enough we quieted down to hear what he had to say. He crossed his arms and shouted: "Did you see the Turks? Did you see all those galleys?"

"We sure did see them," said Cola Mazzapinta.

The officer seemed to be angry at us. "What are we going to do now? There are more of them than of us and they're better armed. What do you expect us to do? I'd really like to know what we're supposed to do."

"The devil with it," said Cola Mazzapinta. We looked at each other in silence, then took off again at a run. At that moment we heard the voice of the town crier: "By order of the Captains of his majesty the king, Don Francesco Zurlo and Don Giovanni de li Falconi, everyone is commanded to assemble in the main piazza. Everybody in the main piazza."

Those were tough orders, and different from our ideas: we thought the first thing to do should be sink the fishing and trading boats to close off the harbor, our beautiful shiny boats, all newly caulked; then bring in the livestock and provisions from the country, and last poison the wells. We obeyed all the rules set down by the captains but when the wind brought most of the galleys in at Fogge Point and the Turks set about hacking at the rocks with pickaxes to prepare a landing, you could hear them as far away as the olive grove at San Nicola di Càsole, just to give an idea of what a furious racket mere pickaxes could make in the hands of those cursed devils.

Colangelo II

It wasn't long before the Saracen herald showed up in the city with his interpreter at his side. The crescent flag preceded them, then a bunch of flame-colored banners, all to the sound of tympanums and flutes. We were crowded into the terraces near the piazza in such numbers that everybody had to push and shove in order to see; all that foolishness of tympanums and flutes didn't mean a thing to us. The herald's clothes were white with short sleeves and the turban on his head had two feathers, one on each side, both loaded with pearls that hung down to his ears. When he got to Captain Zurlo and the Gentlemen of the Council, he stopped, straightened up, stuck out his chest and bowed.

"Take a look at what that fellow's wearing," said Antonello d'Alessandro, grabbing my arm.

"Be quiet," I answered, "Who cares about clothes at a time like this?"

"But what's the poor devil thinking of, going around all decked out like that?"

"They're pagans," I said, "they're not like us. Who knows what they think about?"

"But look at that business on his head with the pearls. Would *you* wear it?"

"Who the devil cares about that now. We're talking about war here."

Everyone but Antonello was all worried and nervous. He just watched every move with curiosity as the herald made a kind of opening speech and Captain Zurlo listened with bowed head until the Turk finally got to the point. He had, he said, a two part message: first, Akmed Ghedik Pasha wanted the city; second, all men were born first to God and then to death and therefore if we resisted we would meet death, but if we handed over the city without a fight we'd have two choices. We could either leave with our women and children and go far away, wherever we pleased, or we could stay as subjects of Akmed Pasha and honor Mohammed, the true prophet of God in all the countries of the world.

When the herald came to the end of his speech there was dead silence. No one spoke for several minutes, as though we were all in a dream. We aren't a very excitable people. But then suddenly the crowd seemed to catch fire. First it was a muttering among folks standing next to each other; then, little by little, shouts began to ring out: "What's this about going away? What's this about becoming pagans?" Then we all started to talk at once, like at a wedding supper – everybody wanted to have his say.

Nachira's voice was shrill: "Why should we be the ones to die? What if they die instead?"

"I say Otranto is our home," shouted Antonio De Raho, "and this isn't something *we* decided. The Good Lord put us here and we aren't budging."

One shout followed another until they turned into curses, calling the herald kin to dogs, bats and whores. The Turk just stood there motionless and calm, his arms crossed on his chest, letting us know we were nothing but so many flies to him.

But then Captain Zurlo cut us off by waving his arms, and the Gentlemen of the Council Antonio Lubelli, Lanzillotto Fragà and Ladislao De Marco held up their arms too. A moment later the piazza was silent again.

Captain Zurlo raised his voice – usually he spoke in a low, familiar polite way so he sounded more like a kindly gentleman than a soldier. He was brief and so calm I was dumbfounded; he might have been talking about a city five hundred miles away. He told the herald Otranto was subject to His Serene and Catholic Majesty King Ferrante I of Aragon and if Akmed Pasha wanted to rule it he'd have to come and take it by force of arms. Then he'd find out whether his majesty would consider giving up Otranto or whether, more likely, he'd hold onto it, consigning its defense to his valiant son Don Alfonso, duke of Calabria, whose military exploits were well known throughout the entire world.

The herald listened thoughtfully to the interpreter's translation, frowning now and then like a friar who hears fishermen cursing as he passes by the port.

Captain Zurlo finished his speech. Everybody began shouting all over again and waving their caps in approval. It was Saturday, the twenty-ninth of July. The sea, still riled up by the tramontana, was flinging little silvery fish onto the beach, so hard it left them stunned. For the first time in my life – and I'd always been perfectly healthy – I felt all funny and weak in my legs, in fact through my whole body, like I'd been beaten up.

"Antonello, I said, "this is war."

"No, oh no," answered Antonello. "We're gonna be in real trouble if we start thinking that way."

But I was saying to myself: "If we could just go back to yesterday, if only today hadn't come and those damned Turks had left us in peace."

A moment later the main gate closed behind the herald.

"Raise the drawbridges," shouted Captain de li Falconi. Old Don Felice Ayerbo of Aragon, *adelantado* of the Spanish militia followed up with: "Lower the outer gates and lock them."

But that wasn't the whole story: a fine lot they were, those Spaniards – it just goes to show how you never have enough time to find out about people. Here they were, these soldiers who'd swagger through the streets with their noses in the air, wearing fancy cuirasses and leather belts and bandoliers, who'd go out coot hunting in season and treat us fishermen like servants – they called themselves the noble militia of the Viceroy of Brindisi, but that night at dusk, over the walls they went, as nice as you please, letting themselves down with ropes of braided hemp and rushes. So much for them. Because of them I found myself the next day up on the tower with a crossbow and arrows, doing guard duty along with other Otrantini fishermen. We had a new trade.

In late afternoon, when the light was fading from the terraces, the Turkish herald came back. "That fellow's done for," I thought to myself. And he was, thanks to Pieri di San Pietro, who later shot him with his crossbow from atop the walls. The setting sun touched the sea, and when the tide turned the waters grew calm. This was the time when every evening up to now, our women would watch for boats out on the water and the younger ones, sitting on their doorsteps, would begin to sing.

Antonello d'Alessandro was standing to my left and Cola Mazzapinta to my right when the three of us, peering out beyond the moats, spotted six mortars and two cannons. They had taken them off the ships disassembled. The barrels were in one place, the carriages in another, with those cursed Turks darting around like bats, trying to get them ready for use. At the sight of all that artillery Cola Mazzapinta almost went crazy, like he was going to leap down from the walls and grab them: "Ahoy! Seven pieces! When Duke Alfonso gets here it'll be like a St. Nicholas party chasing those stinking bastards back into the sea."

"What an idiot," said Antonello.

Cola Mazzapinta, staring into the distance, went on raving: "We'll run them right back to their own damned country, we'll drive them out of here for good!"

"Don't get carried away," said Antonello. "Calm is what we need now."

"The fact is, they have seven good sized pieces of artillery and we don't even have one," I said. "All we've got are a few crossbows on the ramparts and a bunch of light muskets."

"You're a coward," yelled Mazzapinta.

"I don't see why," I said.

"You're scared. You're a coward because you're scared."

"When those Turks attack...," I began, but Mazzapinta didn't let me finish. He came right up and shouted in my face, "We aren't going fishing, Colangelo. You keep saying, 'Well if the scirocco shifts to the north, or if the tramontana lets up or if it blows harder instead....' You've always got an 'if' somewhere. I'm telling you when they get back to their heathen country they'll have to call on Mohammed himself to put them back together again."

As for me, those seven pieces of artillery down there at the foot of the walls did nothing to stir up my fancy. At nightfall when the stone of the top circle of the double walls turned white in the moonlight, the Turkish galleys turned white too – like ghost ships. I could make out every one of the rocks where I always tied my heavy lines to catch groupers in deeper water, as well as my nets and surface lines for mullet. I caught myself thinking that with this moon the groupers should be biting – I guess I hadn't changed my ideas to fit our new situation.

The soft splashing sound of the ebbing tide reached my ears, a homey sound for me. Of course I wasn't really out there listening to the sea, but a part of me was, a part that didn't believe what had happened. Time passed. I stopped a minute in my walk along the walls. Though the sky was above and I could see the moon I felt like I was in a cave or a prison with no way to tell what time it was and what other people in the world were doing – in a place where your thoughts could only look backward. Pretty sad. And it was one of those sticky summer nights when you're always thirsty. What was going to happen to us?

Suddenly Cola Mazzapinta and Antonello and I turned to look at each other. We'd all heard hoofbeats, hoofbeats on the hill, like the ghosts that wandered out there at night were now on horseback. Then from every direction we began to see horses galloping towards us across the moonlit countryside. Their backs looked like waves and they swirled around like eddies in the tide. We just stood there bewitched, looking down at them from the bastions, until Cola Mazzapinta spoke up: "Now what's going on?"

As for me, the longer I watched, the more convinced I was that they were demons.

"Those aren't horses," I said.

"Oh come on now," answered Antonello, "What do you mean, not horses? Let's not lose our wits completely. They could always be mules."

"Mules?"

"Yessir, mules. Take a good look at that bunch over there, the ones just plodding along."

"I'm going to find out," shouted Mazzapinta and took off barefoot along the bastions, leaping over crossbows in his way. It wasn't long before he came running back all out of breath: "They say there are 600 head," he called, "the Turks unloaded them ten miles up, at Roca di Castello, and they're getting them together on the beach so they can ride out and plunder the farms." He went on, still out of breath. "They say Captain de li Falconi went out by the north gate late this afternoon to get ready to meet them four miles from here at Frassanito Point."

"We're going to be eating horsemeat," said Antonello.

"You've got a lot to say, don't you," I snorted. "They'll be attacking at dawn." Those who heard me instinctively looked to the east, but it was still night despite the moon. We stayed there leaning on the outer walls, imagining all sorts of things, but not really understanding what they were. We stared into the darkness as if it was a lid that might be lifted off us from one moment to the next. We were like crabs that contract and stiffen up in their little space on the rocks when they sense an oar in the water.

Antonello broke the silence: "Is anybody thirsty?"

"And what if we are?" said Mazzapinta.

Antonello disappeared in the sentry box and came back out holding up a jug in the palms of his hands, as graceful as the archbishop carrying the reliquary with the bones of Saints Cosmas and Damiano during a procession.

"Look here, wine from Ugento," he said. "Those wretches down there, by God, they don't even know there's such a wine in the world."

"How'd you manage to bring it up here?" I asked.

"Never mind how, just drink. It'll do you good." He passed me the jug, and I took a hearty draught. Then the others drank eagerly in a kind of hurried guzzling that made me think of algae being sucked back by the undertow.

"How about you?" said Antonello to Vincenzo Pasca. "Aren't you drinking?"

"I don't want any," answered Vincenzo. He had stayed off by himself leaning against the sentry box.

"Don't want any?" Antonello was amazed. "What's gotten into you?"

"Look at us, staring death in the face and you're thinking about wine," said Vincenzo irritably.

"The hell with the Turks!" shouted Mazzapinta. "Here's to Otranto!"

"To Otranto!" we repeated in chorus, but in lowered voices. Like an oath.

"But I'm telling you we're in terrible danger. Don't you understand?" Vincenzo persisted.

"Don't make it worse than it is," answered Mazzapinta. "Captain Zurlo says the Otrantini've got what it takes to defend the city for a few days and since the Otrantini are us, with God's help we'll hang on till Don Alfonso of Aragon gets here and takes over."

Mazzapinta wasn't one to bother with difficulties, especially the ones that came from serious thought.

Nobody said anything else. We just gazed into the distance. From our place on the walls that night everything looked different. Take the harbor for instance, or the port and the curve of rocks that ended at Rocamatura: their outline was clear enough but it was like a world you couldn't enter no matter how much imagination you had. A thin fog began to come up from the water.

"Look," said somebody. "What's that black thing coming up here?"

We all leaned out to see. "Christ!" someone yelled. It was a huge owl.

We went back to our places. Some settled down and stretched out; others remained standing. An hour or so went by in heavy silence.

All at once Vincenzo stuck his head out over the wall and asked, "What are they up to now?" But just for something to say; his nerves were on edge.

"Forget it. Go to sleep," answered Antonello.

"I can't sleep," said Vincenzo, almost offended.

"Well then let the rest of us sleep."

"I can't believe for one minute that those cursed bastards will win," said Mazzapinta, "but I wish it wasn't so damned dark." Nobody answered him. I think we were all trying to understand something in that silence, maybe life itself. But nothing made any sense. Even God was far away, beyond the darkness. Maybe he wasn't happy either and couldn't help us.

"Over there, over there!" said Vincenzo.

"What?"

"A shadow, a big one. It moved."

"Come on now."

"Damn it, it moved." He was angry now.

We all stayed put, as if to say, "so who cares if shadows move."

"Hey, where do you think they'll start?" somebody asked in a low voice.

"I'd say the main tower," answered Mazzapinta.

We thought this over for a few minutes, without speaking.

"We've never seen them up close," said the voice that had asked the question.

"Angelo Calé saw them in Rhodes," answered Nachira. "He says they're born to battle and always ready for a fight. He says when they hear their tympanums they rush to attack and spread out all over."

Another general silence.

"How about that," Mazzapinta said suddenly, "and yet they've been beaten so many times."

"He says they get double wages for every head they cut off," added Nachira. It seemed to me that as they talked the walls were sinking lower and lower, and so were we, until we'd find ourselves face to face with the Turks.

"What's that supposed to mean?" snapped Mazzapinta. "When they cut off a head they grab it by the hair and go off and present themselves to their officers?"

"How should I know? Maybe officers take their word for it."

"Who knows...," said Mazzapinta.

Vincenzo, who was the most nervous of all and couldn't stop looking down from the wall, suddenly tensed up: "Look at that, something big coming this way! Right over there!"

"They're moving one of the guns," I said. For a moment all eyes turned toward the dark shadow; then once more there was nothing to see.

A heavy thud. Then silence again. Somebody laid down; somebody else stood up. We tried to guess the time from the position of the moon and stars.

Antonello came up beside Mazzapinta. "How come you've shut up and stopped making plans?"

"It's the damned dark," muttered the other.

Another thud, at the foot of the wall, like a boulder falling into the water. Then, off and on, more noises.

"You can tell they aren't sleeping either," said Antonello.

"That dark spot on the other side of the moat," said Nachira, "it wasn't there before."

A few seconds later Vincenzo, still on edge, grabbed Antonello's arm and said, "If I was a king I'd abolish all wars."

"So where'd you get the idea of yourself as a king," asked Antonello.

"To hell with you," shouted Vincenzo, "You make me sick." Then he added glumly, "A lot of us are going to be dead before this is all over."

"Shut up and go to sleep," answered Antonello, then raised his voice: "It's time to get some sleep."

It sounded like a good idea and we all settled down. But when things had been quiet for ten minutes, Vincenzo spoke up again: "I'd like to know why there have to be Turks on earth anyhow. What good are they?"

None of us answered, but a Neapolitan on the other side of the sentry box called out: "What's the matter with that fool?"

The dampness pressed down on us and I put on the padded jacket my wife Assunta gave me. More time passed, everything so still it was like another world. Nothing moved except the night mists coming up from the sea.

"And to think that maybe right now," I said to myself, "somewhere in some town in the world somebody's playing games like backgammon."

Vincenzo couldn't settle down. Suddenly he grabbed Mastro Natale's arm – Mastro Natale was the oldest and wisest of the fishermen – and blurted out: "With that damned artillery they'll breach the walls and kill us all, one right after another, before we know what's happening."

I was close enough to see Mastro Natale's bewhiskered face in the moon light: he looked as if Vincenzo had merely bid him good night.

"Did you hear what I said?" said Vincenzo anxiously.

"You do love to talk, don't you," answered Mastro Natale.

Vincenzo lost all control: "I can't just sit here and wait for God knows what."

The old man seized him by the shoulders: "All right then," he said in a terrible voice, "if you can't stand it we'll throw you off the walls."

That restored the silence. Vincenzo began to pace back and forth. Some of the fishermen remained standing against the stone of the inside walls, while others were squatting down, but nobody could sleep.

Even the stars got into it, sending down a light that was sinister somehow, or was it just my imagination?

Then we heard the scraping sound of shoes on stone – no fisherman of course, since we never wore boots or shoes of any kind. "Somebody's coming," said Antonello.

In fact, Don Felice Ayerbo of Aragon, *adelantado* of the Spanish militia, appeared at that point, followed by his servant Teodoro. He was the only Spaniard who hadn't run off from Otranto. People said he stayed because he was in love with one of our women, the beautiful Idrusa. He was coming to inspect the walls; as he approached we all stood up. He stopped, then announced with great gusto: "Otrantini, these bastions of yours are the bastions of all Christendom."

We looked at him, speechless. What could we say?

After taking a look at the crossbows and counting the muskets, Don Felice entered the sentry box, and came out again. Then, taken with sudden fervor, his voice full of passion, he said: "Remember that you are the very Pillars of Hercules of the Adriatic."

"We're *what*?" asked Antonello.

Don Felice paused in thought, then raised his arms: "Prepare yourselves, my good men, prepare yourselves. Dawn is upon us." And he went off, his servant following behind him.

"What was he after?" asked Mazzapinta.

"He wants us to be ready," I answered.

"Well now, that's news," said Mazzapinta.

Nothing happened for a while. We were quiet; there was nothing left of all that busy arguing and talking we'd carried on before. Everybody was either sitting down or stretched out full length. As I squatted under the battlements I suddenly realized I was tired and my back ached. It seemed to me now that my own dear Assunta and my little Alfio weren't inside the walls at all, but far far away instead, beyond the sea in a thick fog, and now and then, through that fog, I'd seem to catch a glimpse of Alfio's black curls or my wife's face, or the kitchen table or the cistern, nothing in the right place, everything all mixed up.

Feeling sick to my stomach I got up, and instinct led me to Mastro Natale. There'd been only one other man anything like him in Otranto, and he was dead: my father. They were men of the old stamp, with an old-fashioned toughness. When a storm came up they didn't give way to a lot of nervous talk like the others did. They didn't curse, they just looked at the sea, as though they understood how it was upset and wanted to break out of its barriers.

"Scared?" he asked me.

"Well maybe," I half answered. We stood there beside each other for a few minutes, not talking. I could just begin to see the outlines of things and that meant the night was nearly over.

"It's almost dawn," I said.

"No need to get too worked up," he replied, "that's a good way to get yourself killed."

To the east it was getting lighter little by little. I knew it was only a matter of minutes before that brightness spread over the whole sky.

"It's important to think before we act," he said, "and do nothing without good reason."

To which I replied: "We've never killed anybody."

"Best not to look them in the eye...," said Mastro Natale then interrupted himself. "If you look into their eyes," he began again, "you'll lose your nerve. They'll seem to be men just like you, because even pagans are made in the image and likeness of God. That's the thing."

At that point Nachira shouted, "They're starting to move!"

"They are, they're moving," shouted others.

We all rushed to lean over and look out toward the moats. Black spots were moving about in the gray spaces touched by the first light of dawn. In the same instant the Turks let out a yell accompanied by the sound of drums. I swear by Saint Basil I was a brave man. My ears were used to the crash of the waves and the sound of thunder over the sea, but that yell...oh no, that yell was like something altogether different, something too dreadful to imagine, even though a yell was what it was. Nobody could take his eyes off the foot of the walls. It was the pit of hell down there.

Once their mortars were in position the Turks began firing from the limestone heights fifty paces east of the walls, from San Francesco's hill eighty paces southeast, and from Rocamatura. The first shot came from Rocamatura, where the vegetable gardens and storehouses were. The ball grazed the Garbotti's house and kept right on going as far as the smaller piazza, almost to the center of the city: it was solid stone, about ten palms in circumference and could have weighed two hundred pounds. When it landed it sounded like thunder. More followed, shaking the earth so hard it was like the houses would fall in just out of fear itself. Meanwhile the Turkish mortars were hurling stones into the sky, which fell back onto our streets and piazzas. Even you people wouldn't have believed it was a human being who first thought up those infernal objects – it had to be the devil himself. And he'd done his work well; those cannons and mortars left no room for improvement. While all this was going through my head Vincenzo had been racing furiously along the parapet. All at once he staggered and dropped to his knees, an arrow from a crossbow stuck in his neck. That's the way it happened. A moment later he fell full length, his eyes looking wildly around. Mazzapinta rushed over to him. I didn't move, just stayed where I was, leaning against the inside wall of the sentry box, sick at the thought that Vincenzo was dying and dazed by the noise and the shouting. Vincenzo's arms twitched momentarily like he was trying to come back to the world of the living, but he didn't make it. So that's how death scaled the walls – it had singled out Vincenzo himself. This event nearly did us in and we'd have been more than happy to boil every Turk in oil, even though so far it was only a cannon and mortar attack and we didn't have the artillery to respond. Every once in a while it seemed like something more was going to occur. The captains took to walking along the inside passages on the walls, but then nothing happened. Back and forth they went, but still nothing, nothing happened at all.

Colangelo III

That first day Captain de li Falconi ordered three or four of us to go down for water. When I got to the smaller piazza, the piazzella, where the first Turkish

26

shot had landed at sunup, I saw a group of women and old men standing and gazing straight at the stone cannon ball, so fascinated and bewildered they couldn't even move. The whole piazzella was mute. Then suddenly three Greek women came out from an intersecting street, wearing reddish petticoats and scarlet kerchiefs tied at their breasts. The kind of women whose life work is making men happy. They quickly crossed the piazza and when they reached the cannonball, exchanged a few words and abruptly began to dance. Stamping their feet in rapid steps, they lifted their bare arms in a winding motion like snakes – a real pleasure to watch. Now and then they'd really get carried away and fall right down on the ball and embrace it. They'd quickly stand up again to resume the dance, their eyes still fixed on the cannonball like they wanted to eat it up. One of them, the leader, a real blooming beauty cried out: "*camela, càlaza, ghiema,*" their words for "fog, hail and blood," and at that point they all stopped stock still, like they were lost in thought. Then the leader turned and asked for oil and flour. She was so sure of herself that people obeyed at once. The three of them mixed the flour and oil and spread it on the cannonball. Suddenly they were dancing again, spinning like tops and flushed with the effort. I couldn't help thinking of red roses blowing about in the tramontana; their breasts were bouncing around inside their dresses, their curving hips shaking in the dance. "What the devil are they doing?" I wondered. By sheer reflex I almost said, "If you three go on like this somebody'll grab you and pull up your skirts." They kept on dancing. My thoughts came apart just watching them. Then abruptly they stopped.

Surprised at the sudden end of the dance, the Otrantini just stood there transfixed. Then curiosity won out and little by little they came to themselves.

The woman who had led the dance turned to me, "You," she said, "come here."

I did as she said. Cristoforo Rio was passing by on his way to the walls with a big jug of water on his back.

"You," she called to him as well, "come here."

Cristoforo put down the jug and came over.

"Dig a hole over by that palm tree," the woman ordered.

We dug the hole for her while the old men and the women who'd been in the piazza dragged the cannonball over to us. We buried it. Then the head woman drew herself up and held out the palms of her hands to get our attention. She told us in a ringing voice that from now on the Turks wouldn't be able to do anything to the city and so we should feel perfectly safe.

This made quite an impression. Like when the archbishop told us at mass that Saints Cosmas and Damiano had performed a new miracle. It was clear that people were pleased. I looked at Cristoforo: "You know, it's really true – women don't understand any-thing."

His eyes were fixed on the head dancer's legs.

"Hm'm," he said, "they give you ideas." Then he got hold of himself: "But I should be getting back to the walls," and he hurried off with his full jug of water. I moved away myself. As I turned into the main street I looked back at the three Greek women. They were squatting at the base of the palm tree by the cannonball's grave, looking calmly around with their violet eyes.

Before I went back to the walls, I made a short detour down the little alley called Crismatico, where I lived. When I entered the kitchen I was startled to see blankets and pillows and olive oil jugs on the table and boxes of linens and grain on the floor – everything sitting around as if it wasn't even a kitchen any more. Not very nice to see.

"Colangelo!" cried Assunta, and my little boy ran to hug me.

"I'm just here for a minute," I said. "I can't stay. What's going on?"

"I'm burying our stuff in the cortile."

"There's no use doing that. Don Alfonso's soldiers will be here soon and it'll all be over." I looked carefully at her: she'd changed a lot in forty-eight hours. I figured this kind of thing was pretty hard on a woman's heart. She didn't have the kind of courage it takes to hold out for very long and forty-eight hours of struggling with the idea of war had changed her very soul.

Then the little one spoke up: "Are you scared Papà?"

"No, not me."

"Why not?" He was amazed.

"Because we're going to win."

"And then there'll be a procession like on holidays?"

"That's right. There certainly will," I said.

"What about the ones who get killed," he asked in his little voice.

"Well...they'll go to heaven."

"With all their weapons?"

"No, they'll leave their weapons here for the others."

He thought a minute, then said: "You aren't going to die, are you?"

"No, no, I won't die."

"Do they wear white clothes?"

"Who?"

"The ones who go to heaven."

"I guess so," I answered and the little fellow was quiet, almost absent.

Assunta was watching me, pale, like a woman who's a little bit afraid of her husband. There was something about the room, something strange that made it hard to talk. All at once she said, "What's our life coming to?" Then, making almost no noise she busied herself, looking for something, finally producing a packet. She gave it to me, saying, "I got it ready in case you came. It's sardines in oil."

"Make sure you lock the door at night," I said.

The boy was listening, spellbound. All three of us were quiet for a minute. We didn't know what to think or say, like our heads had stopped working. At last I said, "Well, I'll be going." I couldn't even bring myself to kiss them; I fled without another word, like I was choking, like something was stuck in my throat. At the end of the alley I looked back. Assunta and the little boy stood in the doorway watching me. I waved and then turned and dashed away in desperation.

I saw women and old men busy burying jars of oil, woolen cloaks, trousseaus and all those things people usually keep in their best chests of drawers. The old men were bent over breaking up paving stones and hacking away to dig the holes, while the women quietly filled them up. I stopped running, paused a minute to watch, there in Via dei Santi Quaranta. Every now and then the old men would straighten up to rest their tired backs and stare down at the ground they'd broken with their hoes.

Then it was like I could see before me everything that made up our lives until that moment. Fishing in our beautiful boats strong enough to withstand the scirocco and the tramontana, coming home in the evening with our nets slung over our shoulders, the steaming plates of chicory waiting for us: it seemed like inside all this, our life ever since we were born, there was a kind of sweet music, wonderful music that was suddenly playing in my soul and at the sound my soul itself wanted to run away and plunge into the sea where my boat had come to rest. I wondered what was happening to me. I was freezing cold even though it was a hot day. Just then the group of women and old men came up and gathered around me. When I turned to look at them I was struck by their silence. Then one of them, Salvatore di Muro, a little old man leaning on a cane, spoke up in a shaky voice:

"Excuse me but...how many dead?"

"Only one," I answered.

"Who...who is it?"

"Vincenzo Pasca."

"Poor boy," said the old man.

"God rest his soul," said the women in a chorus.

There was a boom.

"That's another cannonball," I said. "You'd better get back to your houses. Here, one of them could land right on your head." Then, "Good luck to all of you," and I set off again at a run. But looking back I could see them still standing there quiet and thoughtful, following me with their eyes.

Colangelo IV

In the general confusion of those first days only one thing was clear: Don Alfonso's militia would be coming from the highlands to liberate us. Captain Zurlo had sent messengers right away to Lecce, Brindisi, and Naples, where men could hardly be going peacefully on with their lives now that they knew about our terrible situation. In those very days the wind was blowing steadily from the plateau, tossing soft fuzzy flowers into the air, like signs of things to come. So we waited, but the Turks weren't waiting for anybody and they continued to batter the walls from morning to night with cannon and mortar fire. As yet they hadn't tried to scale them. On the fourth day, while we were busy with the mortar attack, Antonello came right out and said it: "You know, we're beginning to look a lot like one of those siege stories that you see painted in palace halls, with castles and fortresses and galleys and huge colorful tents."

"So what?" I said irritably.

"Well, let's try to look good," he answered calmly. "When those fellows come up here, who knows what'll happen, but for now we can look good."

"It seems to me it's time Don Alfonso got here," I said, "time we were done with this job of guarding the walls."

Antonello sat down on the stone paving and set about eating a cucumber. Then, looking at me with his always somewhat mocking eyes, he said: "You might as well take things as they are, Colangelo. Here, have a cucumber," and he took another one out of his pocket and handed it to me. Then he added, "Take life as it comes." As for me, only once during the siege was I able to take life as it came, and that was the morning of August fourth, at dawn. When I started out that morning to climb up to the main tower to relieve Cola Mazzapinta, I felt a curious well-being in my blood. I'd spent four hours of the night in my own bed in Assunta's arms. The tight bond with my wife, the peaceful sleep of my child, had revived in my heart certain cheery reasons I had forgotten for hoping Don Alfonso would soon appear. I walked along with a light step, scanning my surroundings and studying the sky. The scirocco had replaced the ill-fated tramontana that turned the Turks off course in the first place. With this in mind I counted the days until the full moon – sometimes it changes the weather and brings in a fresh sea wind at first dawn. But when I got to the tower I swear by Saint Basil, my thoughts changed from white to black. The Turks suddenly began firing, and we had only one mortar. First we saw white splashes, like in offshore storms, except the splashes were coming from land instead of water and were followed by a terrible din. Then, as the air cleared, we could see the Turks. Under cover of light mortar fire they were filling up the moat and dashing madly back and forth to throw up ladders and ropes against the walls, meanwhile going through all sorts of odd motions with every part of their bodies – bending over backward, straightening up, waving their curved blades.

Then they began to scale the walls, armed with scimitars, light muskets, short pikes, and hatchets hanging from their belts. They crept upward along the stone in groups, their felt *zàrcolas* on their heads, all facing the same way like sprat when an oar cuts through the algae. Some of them, who'd already carried out massacres in other places had big feathers in their *zàrcolas*, as insignia. The wildest of all were the so-called daring ones, the *delli*; they had two wings on their heads to show that they were fast, furious and quick of mind. And there really was something about them that implied even their shadows could kill people. Right from the start nobody could make sense out of what was happening. I don't know how many minutes or even hours passed before I realized I was no longer at the post Captain Zurlo had assigned me. I had moved toward the Porticella and the other Otrantini, following the same impulse, had moved in from the west and the north to where I was, leaving a whole section of wall undefended. At the same time the *delli* and the *azzappi*, Turkish archers wearing quivers of arrows on their backs and short colorful skirts open to the waist in the front so they could move quickly and skillfully – these had massed below us and were now climbing straight up in single file along ladders and ropes hooked to the narrow ledges partway up the walls. Good God! The Turks had pulled down a piece of the wall itself and opened a breach. Only a few feet now between us and the enemy, but when I realized this, instead of being scared I was seized with excitement.

"Move it! Move it!" shouted Captain de li Falconi, "Get both sides covered!" When we threw the first Turk off the wall his eyes bugged out and he shrieked the whole way down. God knows we weren't used to seeing people tumbling head over heels down the walls – it was quite a sight – but the instinct for self-defense led us to kill others, and we were all of us yelling our heads off. So were the Turks, especially when their pikes went home. Meanwhile mortars were firing and the whole section of wall was mass confusion, uproar and dust from the tufa, the soft rock the walls were made of. Then out of the void came raging demons with huge glistening wings, urging the Turks onward. I crossed myself because in my crazy state of mind I had forgotten what the *delli* were. I thought any minute they might fly right over our heads to attack us from behind. But instead of Turks behind us we heard Captain de li Falconi's voice: "We either win here today or we're all dead ducks. Have you got that?" he shouted.

I caught sight of a mortar in our midst; how or when it got there was anybody's guess. Captain de li Falconi was still shouting, "Fire! Fire!"

Stirred by his presence and the mortar itself, we bounded into action. Back and forth we ran, all taken up with killing and not being killed. Our enemies were countless and so were their reinforcements. The only reinforcements we had were our guardian angels, who certainly helped us but didn't take over for the ones who fell. On the north corner near the small port I saw Turks shooting flaming arrows, a regular slaughter, killing among others Michele Leondari and Angelo Maiorano, one of our commanders. But I could also see that they were sorry they'd done it because Angelo Maiorano's men all reacted as if they were bound to bear witness in public for the two dead. They killed a squadron of *azzappi* and grabbing two Turkish banners, made short work of turning back the assault. Nobody paid any more attention to musket balls or arrows: the minute a Turkish *zàrcola* came in sight everybody did his job with the sureness that I guess comes from instinct, and in three hours work, despite the fiery air at our backs, we closed the breach. At that point the Turks started sliding down the ropes to the foot of the walls, where the *dellì* – those wings still on their heads – were jumping every which way like a bunch of rabbits hopping around in a farmyard.

At last we could wipe away the sweat and turn toward the city.

"Damn! That was something," said Mazzapinta.

"Well, we're still alive," said Pieri di San Pietro.

We were alive all right. But the ache in my heart left no room for the pleasure of being alive – it was regular storm of pain that drowned out everything else. Near me were four bodies left as they had fallen, covered with blood and tufa. "No hope for these poor devils," I said.

"Neapolitans. Captain Zurlo's men," answered Pieri.

We lined them up on the ground and crossed ourselves.

Just then Antonello came up, limping on a wounded leg: "Aha, there you are," he said when he saw me. "Not bad. I thought you were dead."

"Filthy pigs!" shouted Mazzapinta. "Did you see how their first move was always to cut off heads with those damnable curved swords?"

Captain de li Falconi appeared: "Are there any wounded here?"

"No," I said. "These are already dead."

"Things went well," he said. "You're good soldiers. Now, back to your posts." With this he moved on, but none of us returned to our places. We were dead tired and dazed, except for Antonello, who was hungry and simply had to have bread.

"Anybody happen to have a loaf handy?" he kept asking.

Two Neapolitan officers went by shouting we'd won a victory, like we couldn't see that for ourselves. But that's the way military men are; all they care about in the world is being able to shout that they've won.

"Mosquitoes," grumbled Antonello.

Finally we went back to our posts and two Neapolitan soldiers carried away the dead. The Turks didn't mount another attack, but we stayed put, rooted like poplars till evening. It was really hot up there on the walls, and everything was still. Only the sun didn't quit. It made me think of when I was a boy and in the hottest days of summer I used to spend hours by the city wall, listening to the birds and waiting for lizards to come out, claws spread, and slither along the stones. Now all animals had left our domain and there wasn't even a bird to be seen in flight.

Another Neapolitan officer came by to make an inspection. In the tract of wall where I was there were few soldiers – we were almost all fishermen and wool trimmers. So he looked at us sternly, said nothing, and then moved on.

"I've never understood," said Antonello, "why officers have to walk that way. Why can't they just walk the way everybody else does?"

"Listen, Antonello," I said, "do you think we'll make it next time?"

"God willing, we'll be able to repeat today's performance. Duke Alfonso will be pretty happy if he can win without even a fight."

"D'you think he'll come?"

At that Mazzapinta spoke up: "Why on earth shouldn't he come?"

"Why are you so sure?" I asked.

"Because we need help."

"That's not a reason."

"If he doesn't come we'll hold them off by ourselves," answered Mazzapinta. He'd been given to grandiose plans ever since that first night when he'd looked down from this same tower at the seven pieces of artillery unloaded by the Turks and leaped to his feet all fired up.

"If you'd quit seeing everything the same way," I said irritably, "maybe you'd be able to see things as they really are."

"What's all this 'things as they are' and 'things as they aren't'!" he shouted. "I tell you, to the east and south the walls have the sea itself for a moat and wanting to take Otranto from that direction is like wanting to lay siege to the moon. To the west and north there's us and any one of us has as much of a body as a Turk, and besides our souls are in the grace of God. Anyhow we're fighting for what's right and they're in the wrong and when somebody's in the right things are just bound to work out better, don't you see? That's what happened today at the breach."

"How about weapons?" I replied. "Where's our artillery?"

"When are you two going to knock it off?" said Antonello. "Do you know you're beginning to give me a pain in the ass?"

"Can't anybody even talk things over?" I said.

"Talking things over now is a lot of nonsense," said Antonello. "Better to get some sleep while we can."

Colangelo V

That day at sunset Akmed Pasha sent another herald to offer us peace and ask us to be slaves. His mind was like the pools of the Alimini Marshes – they only reflect what passes over them, clouds and flights of coots. He reflected what he'd been seeing from his tent for quite a while now, a breach in the walls. So he sent a herald on horseback, with a white flag on his lance, to the bank that surrounded the moat. From there the herald shouted that Akmed Pasha was ready to offer a truce under the same conditions he had demanded the first day. But Captain de li Falconi answered from atop the walls that those conditions were absolutely unacceptable, so the herald turned his horse around and went back to his camp. Night fell and the becalmed sea looked sound asleep under the full moon. All at once somebody jumped into the moat from the Turkish side. We noticed right away from up on the wall because the smooth water was like a mirror in the moonlight and we could see ripples moving toward the city. A man was swimming across; before long we could make out the motions of his arms and legs. It would've been a good joke to leave him bobbing up and down forever, but Captain de li Falconi thought we'd better help him along, so two Neapolitan soldiers went to meet him, grabbed his arms, and pulled him out just like they would a swordfish. Antonello and I and the other fishermen had gone down from the tower to the outer gates to get a closer look. A small crowd had gathered. Who was he? A renegade Christian.

He stumbled as he came out of the water and, still out of breath, said he'd swum over just to give us some advice about what to do. Well, he had a lot to say, as he stood there, glancing this way and that in the torch light. He was the kind who always knows how to make cowardice look like heroics. The Turks had us outnumbered, he said. They had plenty of supplies, so they could starve us out if they wanted to, since it was obvious Don Alfonso, the duke of Calabria, was never going to get here to rescue us. Everybody knew his majesty King Ferrante, the duke's father, didn't have the money for horses and men and all it would take to move the army. In Naples even the itinerant dried-bean peddlers knew these things.

We were astounded at first, thinking he was out of his mind, but he kept on talking, as calm as could be. He said we had no artillery to use against the enemy unless you counted those little iron pieces that were only

good for killing rabbits along country footpaths, and
we had no gunpowder either, whereas the Turks had
enough to take not only Otranto but Brindisi too.
Otranto was just a big net and we'd be hooked and
hauled out of it one by one like so many fish. Besides,
he added, fate had been against us from the start: the
northerly storm got worse just as the Turkish galleys
were passing through the strait and it died down once
they were anchored at Fogge Point. At this point the
fishermen, already impatient to get their hands on him,
interrupted with boos and whistles.

But nothing bothered the renegade. He waited for the
noise to stop and then went on unruffled: "It's merely a
matter of arranging things so you don't all have to take
leave of this world. However, if that's what you really
want...." A new burst of whistles prevented him from
continuing and Captain de li Falconi broke in:
"Silence!" he shouted. "Back to your posts, all of you!
What's going on here?"

Indeed what was going on? His words restored the
silence. I don't know what the others felt at that
moment but for me it was like a horse galloped right
through my very soul and overturned everything that was
there. Then odd things started happening to me. I went
back up on the wall to my post and even though I was
wide awake I had a dream: The moon got whiter than
ever and dropped down right over Otranto. But instead
of the city there were only walls, crumbling away but
still intact enough to show the outline of the houses.
Everything was quiet. It really seemed like the silence
of death until a gust of wind came up, then, after a
minute, another one, stirring up the dust, and finally a
furious gale from the north that drove white clouds of
tufa ahead of it and whistled in an eerie way and broke
apart the remaining walls of the buildings. Just as suddenly as it had come up the wind died down, the clouds
of dust disappeared and nothing remained but a few

scattered blocks of stone and one lone black crow hopping from one to another. And there I was, walking along among the blocks. The crow, busy sharpening its beak on a stone, let out a squawk, then when it saw me coming flew quickly away. Now I was the only living being left. I looked around and all at once there in the distance where the terrain sloped upwards toward the borgo, I saw the blackened hood of a fireplace. When I approached I saw a clay pot on the ground. I picked it up. "Why it's mine," I said. "It's the one Assunta uses to make fish chowder." Only when a shadow dimmed the excessive brightness of the moon did I see the shape of houses reappear bit by bit along with the orange groves and the old part of the city, divided by the black ribbon of the Idro, where it crosses before it reaches the sea, an arrow's flight away from the port.

I shook myself. Beside me Antonello was sitting on the stone pavement, his elbows on his knees, his head between the palms of his hands.

"Antonello," I said, "you know what I saw?"

"No, what?" he said, not moving.

"The end of Otranto."

"The *what*?" he said, raising his head.

"Our city completely deserted, the houses fallen down, everything gone."

"Where? What the devil are you talking about?"

"We're going to end up like Stigliano, Pasulo, Quattromàcine, completely destroyed by the Turks. It was like I was dreaming but I was awake."

Antonello put his head back in his hands and said, "Now go back to sleep and have a better dream."

"Antonello, that's how it's going to turn out. Wait and see. We *will* end up that way." That said, I forgot Captain Zurlo's orders, the breach in the walls, my post on the tower and took off and started down the steps. Antonello stood up and came after me, shouting: "What's gotten into you? Did you get bitten by a tarantula? Cola, listen to me. Don't go down. What are you running for? Come on now, get back to your post. We'll be in great shape if anybody can go off anywhere whenever he wants to."

Then I could no longer hear his voice. I was running through the streets. When I slowed down I was in my own neighborhood near Vicolo del Crismatico. Otranto looked deserted. I stood there gazing at the city, thinking it was as pretty as a neat and perfect little woman – the white stone it was built from was porous but strong; the walls looked grand and noble – I was born here and God had seen to it that my wife and child were born here too.

"So," I said to myself, "is there nothing that can be done? Is everything hopeless?"

"Did you come from the walls?" I started at the sudden sound of a woman's voice to my left. I turned around and by the light of the moon in the deserted street I could see her tall slight figure wrapped in a black shawl.

"Yes I did," I answered.

"Any news?" she asked.

"No," I stammered, "no news."

"So why were you running from the walls?" she said. "I've been following you for some time and you didn't even notice."

At that point I recognized her voice. "You're Idrusa," I said.

"Yes, I am. But why were you running?"

"I just felt like it," I said, "just wanted to be in the streets, to look around."

"Look around at what?"

"The houses, the streets," I said, annoyed.

"Oh Jesus, can't you see enough from up there on the walls?"

As rigid and unfeeling as a salted fish, I stood there looking at the beautiful delicate Idrusa, the loveliest

41

woman ever born in Otranto and all I wanted was to be alone and continue on my way through the streets.

"Good-bye, Idrusa," I said.

"There's no point in going home," she answered. "There's nobody there."

"Where are they?" I was terrified.

"All the women and small children are living in the cathedral now," answered Idrusa. "The archbishop's orders."

"Why?"

"Because of the danger of cannon fire, those wretched balls that rain down from the sky."

"Since when? Why didn't anyone tell us?"

"Only today, while you were fighting at the Porticella. Before, we could come and go as we pleased. Now we're under orders to stay inside."

"Then how come you're out wandering around at night?" I asked.

"What do I care about orders!"

This irritated me. "You haven't changed a bit," I said.

"No," she answered.

"So why *are* you out here? Why didn't you stay with the others?"

"Oh, just because," she said.

"What do you mean, just because?"

"If you really want to know, being shut up in there, the whole thing was like the roof beams were coming down on my head."

I was amazed. I didn't know women had thoughts like that. I looked at her with sympathy. In such a moment who could appreciate how she felt better than I?

"There's something bothering you," she said abruptly.

"Good luck, Idrusa. Good-bye now," and I made as if to leave, but she took hold of my hand.

"Come home with me. I've hidden some wine. Just one glass and then you can be on your way."

"You won't have any left if you offer it to everybody you meet."

"Holy Mother of God," she said. "It's plain as day you need it."

I stood there a moment longer, all befuddled and unable to move, like in a dream. And hadn't the whole day been a dream? I woke up that morning in my wife's arms, full of hope, and then here came the Turks opening a breach at the Porticella and then somehow, God knows how we did it, we managed to close the breach. And then along comes the herald and after him the renegade Christian with his terrible stories and finally here was Idrusa offering me a glass of wine in the middle of the night.

"Come on. Never mind everything else. Let's go," she said. We moved on together. She walked without putting on airs, just let her skirt sweep along the pavement. Idrusa wasn't like other women, nobody could resist her. The thought occurred to me that she wanted to take everything upon herself: all the pain as well as all the joy in the world. Stumbling on the steps to her house, I almost fell.

"Wait," she said, "I'll light the lamp." Meanwhile she opened the door wide to let in the soft light from the moon. I watched the way she moved as she took off her black shawl and went over to the table where a ray of moonlight singled her out. Her pretty head on her white neck, her slender body – I thought of a reed in the Alimini Marshes, the way they bend in the wind or give dancing dragonflies a place to light. She lit the oil lamp, then got out a big bottle and a glass from the china cupboard and filled the glass.

"Here, drink," she said.

The wine went straight down to my stomach in the space of a breath; it barely touched my mouth. She poured me a second glass, which I drank more slowly.

"Sit down," she said.

"Things are bad," I exclaimed.

"Why? Didn't you win today? The archbishop had a *Te deum* sung."

"Doesn't matter. Things are bad. We can only hold out for a little while and Don Alfonso isn't coming."

She stared at me with amazement: "How do you know he isn't coming?"

"A stranger told us tonight. A renegade Christian with news from outside."

"That's enemy news," she said. "It could be false."

I was irritated: "Nothing makes sense any more. At first everything was clear but now it's like when big dark clouds roll up in the sky – they always mean trouble but you don't know what kind of trouble and there's no way to find out. You just have to stay put and watch the sky."

"Maybe that's how war is," she answered.

I went on, all upset: "Everybody's unhappy now. Whose fault is it? Maybe we should have thought about all this before, when everything was all right, when we didn't have these blasted stone balls raining down on us from the sky."

"Thought about it how?"

"Maybe we should have known more about life, maybe things run their course a certain way, but they might have taken a different turn. You know what I think it is? We're ignorant. We don't know the real nature of things, so we don't understand. We live like a bunch of ants and somebody comes along and steps on us and squashes us all."

"But we've been doing what's right," said Idrusa.

"Then why is everything going wrong?"

We were both quiet for a while.

"I don't even understand God any more," I said. "Like right now, for instance. If he wanted to help us he could perform a miracle."

"A miracle?"

"Sure, what would it cost him? So when *does* he perform miracles?"

"You know something Cola?" she said. "Right now you need some sleep." Then she added, "Up there nobody can sleep. If you like I'll leave and you can stay here and take a nap."

"No, no," I said. "It's got nothing to do with sleep. It's this not being able to understand, damn it."

"Well, have another glass. Wine gives strength."

That third glass had a curious effect, first warmth in my stomach, then a really strange feeling.

"It's old wine," I said. I felt lighter and lighter, as if I had wings. My mind started jumping from one thing to another, then went back to a time many years ago when I was a boy and Idrusa wore her hair in braids.

"I was just thinking," I said, "about when we used to play that stone throwing game to see who could hit the cork oak from farthest away. Remember that? You were funny. If you lost you'd fly into a rage."

She smiled. For a few minutes we didn't say anything.

"You know what, Idrusa," I said. "I've always thought you had a thorn in you somewhere, and because you couldn't get rid of that thorn you've had a life that's different from other women's."

"Maybe," she said, very softly.

The wine had given me an awful desire to talk. I kept going on: "You know, Idrusa, I've always been your friend and I even took your side when women would gossip about you. But I didn't like what I understood about you. I must have been your friend because of what I *didn't* understand about you."

"That's all a long time ago now," she said.

That blasted wine, I couldn't shut up. I said, "Idrusa, did you love Antonio?"

"Yes," she murmured and quickly changed the subject. "I couldn't stand it any longer tonight in that cathedral with the women sighing and the little kids crying in

45

their sleep. Today the archbishop preached a long sermon. He said that while the men were fighting with their weapons up on the wall we should be fighting with our prayers in the house of God. And he was right, but I just couldn't manage to pray. I kept thinking about myself, about my life – it seemed so terribly long, even though it's passed so quickly." She stood up, adjusted the wick in the oil lamp, which had begun to give off a purplish light. As if about to laugh, she said: "Want another glass?"

"Give me one."

"There, that's enough though, or you'll get drunk."

It was the dead of night, perfectly quiet, like there were no galleys, no siege, no Turks, just us two, full of a lot of bizarre ideas. When my eyes fell on Idrusa's round and perky breasts, bursting the laces of her bodice, in contrast to her tall slender body in the clinging black dress, my spine prickled. My brain, confused though it was, had this thought: "Be careful Colangelo! This is no way to act. Don't be a swine, Colangelo." Idrusa had sat down again and, paying no attention to me, was following her own thoughts. God, she was beautiful. And smart too. For instance, of all our women, would any one but her have understood how much I needed a glass of wine that night? I wanted to say something nice to her, but I felt awkward and my head was clouded. Besides I should add that she was *too* beautiful and this confused me even more. "Why don't I leave now?" I thought. Instead I stayed. The lamplight was dim but once in a while it brightened up a bit to show the whiteness of her face against the masses of black hair, the sweetness of her eyes, in contrast to her proud body – then it dimmed again. Disturbed by my fixed stare, Idrusa started, then looked back at me, astonished. She stood up. So did I and moved toward her. I wasn't even thinking any more. "Go back to the walls. It's time," she said in a persuasive tone like she was talking to a little kid, but in that instant, so close to her, a fever came over me. The blood pounded at the back of my neck; I was trembling. The table, the china cupboard, the bottle – they all got smaller and farther away and disappeared. Nothing was left but Idrusa's white body in the tight fitting dress a palm away from me, gently wavering and filling the whole room. "Go, Colangelo!" she said. She seemed sad, sickened.

Brusque and sudden, curses on my life, I grabbed her in my arms with such fury she let out a little cry. I bared her armpits, her breasts, bit her, my mouth trembling on her white flesh. I pushed her into the other room and onto her back on the bed, and she seemed to give in patiently without desire, without pleasure. I held her tight but she was far away and this enraged me. I threw myself on her – I couldn't even see her, the room was so dark. I could feel her skin warm and soft and I wanted to suck the life right out of her. Then I began to caress her, touch her breasts and move my hand over her whole body, which remained motionless, until sudden desperation pulled me back: "I'm a swine!" I shouted and, bumping first into the bedroom doorway, then the corner of the table, I rushed out the open door into the street and set off at a run all the way down Vicolo del Crismatico. I stopped outside the piazzella and leaned panting against the wall of Palazzo De Raho. I tried to catch my breath while my heart went on beating madly.

Two men went by, a Neapolitan and Old Primaldo, a wool trimmer from the San Giovanni quarter.

"This fellow isn't feeling very good," said Primaldo.

"Can't you tell he's been drinking?" said the other.

"Drinking? I wouldn't think so. He's not the type."

They came up and looked at me.

"Colangelo," said Primaldo, "what're you doing here?"

"Who me? Nothing."

"You all right?"

"Yes," I said.

They looked at me, puzzled.

"But shouldn't you be up on the walls?" asked Primaldo.

"Huh, no. I'm here."

"How come?"

"I don't know," I sighed.

"See, he's been drinking," said the Neapolitan.

"Cola, do you need anything? Want to come with us?" asked Primaldo.

"No, no," I said.

"Well, good luck then," answered Primaldo.

"Good luck to you too," I said.

After another glance at me the two of them went silently on their way. The piazza was empty again and I stood still against the wall. I didn't feel bad at all; it was like I had forgotten myself entirely. Time passed and sick of staring at the piazza, I looked up at the sky. It was the beginning of August, a season when there's a lot of movement in the sky. I saw a falling star. "A star fell," I thought. The piazza looked bright in the moonlight. "The cannonballs haven't touched it," I thought. I'd never seen it so empty in my life, the entrance to every palazzo so closed and still.

I set off again at a walk, letting my legs find their way on their own. One step led to another and I found myself in the street where the convents were and then once more in Vicolo del Crismatico. At last my house came into sight. Still standing and without a scratch. The corner of Massaro Elio's house, which stood just across the way from mine, cast a triangular shadow in the moonlight between my door and the window to the left. A pot of basil still sat on the window sill and I could smell the leaves, the smell of ragout and fish stew.

I opened the door quietly, and that far away devilish moon, lost up there in the sky, reached right in and touched Assunta's apron hanging on a nail in the wall. I trembled to see it. Then I crossed the kitchen and opened the door to the tiny cortile: there under the pergola was the copper bucket Assunta used to go after water. I sat down on the pavement and took my head in my hands. I was only a fisherman; I couldn't make judgments about anything that didn't have to do with navigation and nets. I knew things like how many hours it will take for a fish to find its way into a well placed net. But what was happening now was too much for me and I was losing my bearings. Never before the Turks came, never once before that moment sitting there in the cortile, for all that I'd sweated to become a man, learned to fish, to curse and to make love – never had it occurred to me that I was just like my mother. We had the same soul, a soul that caught on fire when faced with misfortune.

Colangelo VI

They were memories, but with no kind of order to them. Just images and things that came to mind, like coins set aside many years ago, then discovered by happenstance at the bottom of a drawer.

I saw the long rows of yellow squashes sitting on the walls of the San Damiano farm on the road to the Alimini Marshes. The cortile used to be filled with racks of figs set out to dry in the sun and there was always a turkey spreading his tail in defiance. As a boy, I used to see him when I'd come down the path barefoot on the way back from the woods. Every evening, after I cut the lowest branches of the pines, I'd tie them in a bundle, put them over my shoulder and take them down to the farm.

As I walked along, the trees would drop pine cones which hit the grass with tiny thumps. I was used to all this even though I never could figure out whether it was really the pine trees dropping them or the wood spirits. They liked to play jokes on people and folks used to say they'd turn into rays of sunshine when somebody passed. At nightfall the sun disappeared from the woods in a matter of minutes, and every evening as soon as it got dark a lot of crickets would suddenly burst into song.

It was in that wood that I saw Assunta for the first time – a pale skinny little girl who later grew into such a fine figure of a woman that you'd think God had love on his mind when he created her. She had pretty dark hair and I really felt as if I'd brought her up with my eyes. In those days she used to gather capers in the woods and I pastured goats. But I didn't pay much attention to my animals – I was much more interested in looking for capers for her, and then I'd get carried away and talk on and on, telling her all about myself.

"What about the goats?" Assunta would say all of a sudden, if she happened to look up from a bush and didn't see them any more.

"Holy Madonna," I'd say irritably. "How much grass do they need? They're bottomless!" And I'd take off after them.

God had given Assunta a nature that was retiring and quiet and modest: she was like a wildflower. In the evening after I kissed her on her fresh and innocent mouth, I'd watch her until she disappeared around a curve in the path. The farm where she lived was two hundred paces north of ours. Then, when I got home I'd milk the goats. After a year went by I began to get nervous and irritable. In the morning when I milked the goats they'd stamp about and bleat and try to get away because I squeezed their teats so hard to get them milked in a hurry. If I got to the woods before Assunta I'd sit down on a rock and imagine I was lifting up Assunta's dress until she was completely naked. Then I'd roll around on the grass, and the goats, who'd been busy pulling little mouthfuls of leaves off the bushes, would

stop and watch me, standing still with their ears
pricked up. When Assunta appeared I'd be ashamed to
approach her. The next night I'd be in such a state that
in the morning it turned my stomach just to look at the
frisella, dried bread broken into pieces, that my mother
made with barley, tomatoes and oregano.

"How come you're not eating?" she'd say.

"I don't feel like it."

"Why not?"

"How should I know!"

"You aren't hungry?"

"You can see that."

"Well, eat something anyway. At eighteen a boy has to
eat. You've got to build up your bones."

"I'm bored with eating."

"What's that supposed to mean? You must be sick."

"I'm *not* sick."

"Then eat something."

"All right, all right!" I'd take my frisella and go out
into the cortile and then, when nobody was looking,
feed it to the goats. They'd gobble it up in no time at
all, holding their heads up high and cocked to one side,
as happy as could be.

Once in a while, in those days, I just couldn't bear to
go to the woods. I'd tell my mother, "I'm going down to
the sea." On the shore I'd get everything ready to set
out my lines for garfish. Once I'd laced reeds together
crossways with silk and horsehair thread to make floats,
I'd put a little sail on every float and attach them to
the string nets and hang hooks and lines underneath.
Then I'd spread the nets in deep water and sit down on a
rock to wait. But there was no rock where I could sit
and wait in peace. I kept seeing her wherever I looked.
The next day I'd go back to the wood. There she'd be,
collecting wild fennel or looking for capers under the
bigger leaves.

"You didn't come yesterday," she'd say, quiet and sweet as ever.

"No," I'd answer, harsh and standoffish.

"Shall we go up to the Saracen Tower?"

"Let's go," I'd mumble and we'd start to walk side by side along the mule path. I couldn't think of anything to say and it seemed to me I was very unhappy. Something new and mysterious was taking away my will to live, like I was coming down with an illness. When we got to the tower we'd gaze at the cliff and at the brilliant green water down below.

"What a lot of sea urchins," she said once.

"I'll go down and get a couple for you."

"You're crazy, you'll get killed trying to climb down here." She grabbed me with both arms to stop me, so tightly I felt my blood surge and my heart started to beat like mad. I said, very low, "Give me a kiss." She leaned toward me, offering her little white face. I held her close and kissed her passionately on her mouth, her cheeks, her neck, put my hands in her hair and mussed it all up. She laughed, happy. Then one day, where the path bends on the way to Palascia, I held her so tight she couldn't breathe. She raised her eyes and for the first time looked at me differently, like she'd understood. We stayed that way for a minute or two, holding each other and looking into each other's eyes. Then I picked her up and laid her down on the grass and lay down myself on top of her. I pulled up her dress and she let me do what I wanted, just staying there quiet with her eyes closed while I kissed her all over. Only at the end when I said, "Assunta, Assunta," she opened her eyes and looked at me without saying anything. After that she got up, put her plain little skirt back on and, standing there by herself in the grass, kept smoothing her dress with the palms of her hands. I was still sitting on the ground watching her. She fixed her hair, straightened her bodice and, finally, standing still, turned to me and for

the first time since I'd taken her in my arms, she smiled
– in such a way that I wanted all the pines in the woods
to bow down to her and the sun to shine on her and night
never to come again. We started meeting regularly at
the Saracen Tower because every now and then tenant
farmers would come through the woods. When winter
came with its prolonged sciroccos or cold north winds
we'd go inside the old uninhabited tower. I'd spread my
cloak on the ground for us to sit on. We could hear the
stormy sea battering the rocks and the wind whistling
through the narrow embrasures up high in the tower
walls.

"This is where they used to stand watch, isn't it," she
asked once.

"That's right, and when they saw Saracens coming
they'd build a signal fire and then, from one tower to
another, the signal fires would carry the message all the
way to Brindisi."

"And now the Saracens don't come any more?"

"No," I said, "the last time was fifty years ago. They
raided some farms and then went on their way."

"This tower's so old. It makes you think of spirits.
Really Cola, don't you think there might be spirits
here?"

I laughed: "*I'm* here." Maybe this was why I liked
making love in the tower: because Assunta, who was
always so reserved and quiet, got excited thinking about
the spirits, and those massive circular walls with only
the scarce light that came down through the slits at the
top were scary to her so she'd hold me tight. I'd begin
to tell her one of the legends about the old tower, but
pretty soon I'd be kissing her and undoing her clothes
and lying down on top of her and the story'd be interrupted. Afterwards, when we'd go out in the open and
lean back against the wall to watch the sea and eat our
lunch, she'd say, "What happened after that?"

When winter was over, we'd stretch out on the ground in a hollow hidden between two boulders at the foot of the tower. The air smelled sweet from the camomile plants that grew at the edge of the hollow. Swallows swooped over us as I caressed Assunta's white skin and took her apple hard breasts in my hands. She was so fresh and young that holding her pretty body in my arms seemed like a miracle and sometimes I really marveled that God had made something so beautiful and then given it to me. She quietly abandoned herself to my caresses and seemed to be a woman already, closing her eyes and losing herself in lovemaking as in a dream. Then, later, she'd become a little girl again and set about counting swallows.

"They're happy too, being together. See what they're doing? Flying up and away and then back again. But always chattering. What do you suppose they're telling each other?"

When it got dark and silence seemed to come down from above, I'd say good night to Assunta and go home to the farm. I'd stop to clean off my shoes against the stones of the cortile before going into the house. My mother'd be clapping her hands to chase the hens into their coop, but there were always a few, the newest ones, that got scared and flew every which way, any direction except toward the coop, even running right at it and then at the last moment, instead of going inside, passing right by to scatter into the countryside. All this greatly delighted my little brothers and sisters.

Colangelo VII

But then one evening things changed. Maybe it happens to everybody. A day comes along that just doesn't fit the pattern of other days. That evening, sitting there in a corner of the cortile watching my little brothers throw stones at a tree trunk, I felt a sudden fear. How would I ever manage to tell them? Earlier, at the foot of the Saracen tower, Assunta had been curious. She'd asked me, "Do you like being a fisherman?"

"Sure I do, it's the family trade."

"When a man has a trade he doesn't have to be scared. Isn't that true?"

"Scared of what?"

"Of things that might happen.

"What things?"

She began to walk on ahead of me, looking at the waves splashing at the foot of the tower.

"What kind of fishing do you like best?" she said.

"Night fishing with lanterns. You wait till a fish sees the light and begins to be attracted. If you could see the fish my father gets this way – it's a specialty with him."

She asked abruptly: "Your father, is he nice?"

"Sure he's nice, but he has his bad side too, when he's crossed."

"What kind of things cross him?"

"Sometimes he gets upset at nothing. Like, for instance, my mother has all these little jars she's so proud of. One has burn ointment in it, another has a remedy for tarantula bites, another something for cuts, or against the evil eye and so on. This morning a little boy cut himself and she rushed to her cupboard and rummaged all through it but couldn't find the right jar. She found all the others but not that one. That really annoyed my father."

"So what does he do then?"

"He goes all day without talking. Like he's made of stone."

"Are there a lot of things that bother him?"

"Hey, you're funny today, asking all these questions."

She looked at me, like she was thinking very hard, then started walking around again, this way and that, ahead of me, her hair blowing over her forehead, her arms hanging down.

"Assunta," I said. "What makes you so restless today?"

She suddenly stood still.

"Come here," I said, "so I can kiss you."

She came up to me and held up her face the way she always did – she moved like a little goat. I kissed her once, twice, three times.

"Colangelo," she said in a strange voice, like she was bewitched.

"What is it?"

"Nothing," she replied.

"Well then, shall we go?" I picked up my coat from the ground.

"Wait," she said, worried. "I want to ask you something."

"*Another* question?"

At that point, instead of answering, she collapsed on my chest in tears.

"Assunta, what's wrong?" I was dumbfounded.

"Cola," she stammered between sobs. "I'm going to have a baby."

I dropped my coat.

Sitting there on the ground in the cortile, I remembered the whole scene, while my mother called lovingly, "H-e-r-e chick, chick, chick...," and dropped barley from her half closed fist. The grains bounced when they hit the ground and in their haste to get them the chickens kept bumping into each other in a confusion of flapping wings. Finally my mother placed herself directly in front of me:

"And what are *you* up to?" she said.

"I'm thinking."

"What's that supposed to mean?"

"That I'm thinking. What else?" I shrugged.

"I've never known you to do that before." She went into the chicken coop, poured water in a dish, closed the chickens inside, then came back to me.

"Look, couldn't you be watering the vegetable garden?"

"No, I couldn't," I said irritably.

She went into the kitchen. I heard her moving things around in the oven, adding a piece of wood to the fire, talking aloud. She had a habit of talking to firewood, telling it it was green, or wet, and that's why it was making so much smoke. Then she appeared in the doorway and looked out at me: "Well?" she said.

I really did want to talk, but I couldn't. There were more miles between what was going on in my head and hers than there are between Otranto and Corfu. I lost my nerve. To make things clear I'd have to tell the whole story, because the way things were now was because of a thousand things that had happened before, from the time I first met Assunta. To make her understand I'd have to describe two years of our lives. But when she repeated: "Well?" I stood up and said, just like I was reciting from memory, "Assunta's pregnant," and then waited. I knew my mother was quite a talker, like all women when they're angry – as if they thought words could change the world, if you just say them loud enough. Instead, there she stood, staring at me wide-eyed and asking: "What have you done?"

What indeed? Was I supposed to explain the whole thing from the beginning? She came out into the cortile, right up to me and said: "*You*?" After a second she began to yell: "You wretch! You miserable good for nothing boy!"

"But Mama, I love her. I want to marry her."

Lowering her voice, she repeated, "What have you done? What *have* you done?" As if I'd drowned Assunta or strangled her and buried her in the sand of the Alimini Marshes.

She shook her fists at me, shouting: "I was stupid, I was. I never thought you were like that." Then she sat down on the wall, covered her face with her hands and began to cry. At this point I stood up and started to walk back and forth in the cortile. After a while she said, "But, Assunta? How could this happen? She's so simple, so honest. Pregnant. And people – what will people say? You've dishonored her." Then suddenly, as if she'd come upon the worst: "And your father? He's down at the port fixing the boat, caulking it. You'd better go tell him about this right away. He'll kill you, he will."

Colangelo VIII

With my heart in my mouth, and taking long strides, I went down to the port. In all family matters my father, a man of few words, was the opposite of my mother. But what would that opposite be this time? I found him on the pier spreading pitch on the bottom of the boat and went up to him and said, "Father, I have to talk to you." He sensed at once from my voice that it was something serious so he put down brush and rag on a seat and waited in silence. I summoned all my strength, clenched my fists and with my eyes on the ground, not once on him, I said what I had to say. I felt my voice quiver, which confused me even more, but I managed to tell the whole story and only after I finished did I look slowly upward, first at his legs, then his belly, then his chest until my eyes met his. He looked back at me steadily with unblinking eyes that little by little seemed to turn to stone. Terrified, I lowered my own gaze. At that point and without a word, my father bent down, picked up his rag and brush and resumed caulking the boat. I didn't know what to do; I stood nailed to the spot, hardly breathing. After a bit I stammered, "Please forgive me, Father."

Without speaking he continued to rub the keel with
the rag.

"Do you want some help?"

"No." When he finished he put the brush back in the
jar, folded the rag into quarters and put everything away
in a corner of the boat. That done, he picked up a
basket of fish, tucked it under his arm, and we both set
off toward the farm, him in front, at his slow and
regular pace, me following. I could see the hairs on the
back of his neck as his head bobbed with every step. The
wagon road was full of twists and turns and at one of
them we came upon my little brothers and sisters. When
they saw him they stopped stock still, just like a bunch
of tiny wall spiders who've seen the shadow of a broom.

"Hey, back home with you!" shouted my father and
they took to their little brown heels and scooted off on
both sides of the path.

I was thinking, "But am I really as bad as all that?"
Because in spite of everything, my conscience couldn't
deny that until then I'd been a fine young man and,
except for this one failing, I still was. But other
people seemed to have taken leave of their memory and
to believe that Assunta's pregnancy meant my whole
nature had changed. "But what's life about anyway?
What's love?" I said to myself and despaired of ever
figuring out what life was or love either. By now we'd
reached the farm and we came upon something out of
the ordinary. A tall skinny type in Spanish dress,
looking much put upon at having to wait, was pacing
back and forth in the cortile with that snooty air that
all Spaniards have. He was wearing French knee
breeches, striped in three colors, a short skirt made of
blended cotton and wool, dyed green, a regular knight's
green, and shoes that laced up at the sides and had long
pointed toes like they wear in Valencia. Next to him,
my father, strong and calm and staring straight ahead,

looked like God the Father himself standing there barefoot in the farmyard.

The Spaniard said the governor of Lecce, by order of his majesty King Ferrante of Aragon, had imposed a new tribute on all his subjects in proportion to their ability to pay and he himself was charged with proclaiming it.

My father set his basket of fish down on the low stone wall, turned around and asked without haste: "What's it for?"

The skinny Spaniard appeared pleased to be asked and replied with enthusiasm: "To build a new road between Castro and Otranto. His majesty really cares about this town."

"This road, what's it for?" repeated my father.

"How do you mean what it's for? It's to go from Otranto to Castro and vice versa."

"There already is a road," said my father calmly.

"Oh, well, yes but it's old and narrow."

"So why don't they fix it?"

"It follows the rocky shoreline," said Skinny, beginning to be irritated, "and it can't really be made much wider. It's not suitable for carriages."

"We fishermen will go on using the old road," said my father, "since it follows the coast and it's the shortest route."

"Look here now," answered Skinny, "nobody's going to prevent the fishermen from using the old road. They should feel perfectly free."

"But we're all fishermen here," said my father.

"No, damn it, you're not *all* fishermen!" Skinny was getting edgy. "The ones who have carriages, what would you have them do?"

"Pay for the new road."

Skinny was so taken aback that for a minute he looked stunned. Finally he shouted: "What kind of talk is this anyway? Everybody pays the tribute. There aren't any distinctions. Everybody has to pay!" He snorted, looked around and decided to give his proclamation to my mother, who was standing in the doorway saying nothing. Then he departed. My father, tucking the basket of fish back under his arm, watched as Skinny, hampered by his fancy shoes, struggled to stay upright as he made his way up the rocky path that led from the farm up to the road. It was funny to see him trying to keep his balance: one minute he was flapping his arms in the air, the next he was twisting his feet and teetering from one side to the other – then he'd stop short, look down at his shoes, study each move, then all at once begin to wave his arms again.

"Shit," said my father, taking one last look at him before he went into the house. After setting the basket down on a bench, he slowly poured oil into the lamp, carefully trimmed the point of the wick, spreading it with both thumbs, and hung the lantern on the wall. Finally he sat down at the table to wait for his chicory. Not one word about my affairs for the whole evening. I watched him; my mother watched me and watched him, as all three of us sat and ate in silence. This silence lasted for several days and more than once I was on the point of speaking to him again. No, that was crazy. How could I think of confiding in my father? During the day he wasn't home, he was at the port. In the evening he sat and looked out at the cortile, saying nothing. So at night instead of sleeping I kept seeing him sitting there in his usual place staring stonily ahead of him and I could find no peace.

"Well?" asked Assunta anxiously the next time I saw her. "Did you talk to your father?"

"Yes."

"How did it go?"

"Fine. He's perfectly happy," I said.

"Really? He's really pleased?"

"Yes, he said you were a fine girl and he'd be glad to have you in the family."

"That's not bad at all!" she exclaimed with a sigh of relief.

"For now we'll wait a few days," I said. "Then I'll go ask your father's permission to marry you."

"All right. We'll wait a bit."

Two weeks went by. The moon waned and set; a new moon came out. During the whole two weeks nobody in our house said one word when my father was home. Complete silence. "I'm going out of my mind," my mother told me once. "And you, good for nothing – couldn't you do things in the proper way?"

Then came an evening when my mother felt there was no point in going on like this any longer – watching her husband out of the corner of her eye, keeping a wary distance as she served the chicory. She put the younger children to bed and announced, perfectly straightforward:

"All right now, it's time we settled this business about Colangelo."

My father didn't answer.

"We've got to set things right. Assunta is a fine girl," she said.

My father still didn't answer. He assumed the posture he always took when he didn't intend to talk: his body perfectly still, his eyes on the ground.

"He isn't just *your* son; he's mine too. I'm the one who gave birth to him," said my mother, raising her voice.

"You produced something wonderful, didn't you," said my father.

"The boy's always worked, cutting wood, pasturing the goats. He's worked ever since he was six years old."

"Doesn't everybody have to work?" said my father.

These answers left my mother bewildered. I saw her sit down at the table and take her head in her hands. "She's crying," I thought, but she wasn't. After a bit she looked up and said with perfect calm: "Anyone can make a mistake, do something sinful, but the Lord himself says that even while sinning a person can still be good."

"I never knew that," he said.

At that point my mother suddenly lost patience, leaped to her feet and shouted: "If we have to go on like this it'll be the death of me!" She looked around, distracted, then went out the door into the night, heading for the countryside. I quickly stood up to follow but it was hard work keeping up with her in the darkness.

"Mama, where are you going?"

"Away"

"But where?"

"I can't stand it anymore, when he gets like that and won't talk. There's nothing more I can do."

We heard a wail in the distance.

"What's that?" said my mother, scared to death.

"A cat."

"A cat? Not the souls of drowned sailors?"

"A cat: maybe he thinks there's a fox after him. You know something?"

"What?"

"Maybe he doesn't want to kick me out of the house. He'd have already done it by now if he did. Maybe he needs time. He just can't quite swallow this yet and we've got to wait. Things have to take their course."

"But why do *I* always have to wait? My whole life I've spent waiting. And him there, not saying a word. Always the same story."

"It's his character."

"I wish I was closer to death," she said. "I'd just like to lie down here on the ground and slide softly into the sea, slip into the other world and never know anything more."

"Come on now, you're exaggerating."

For a moment we said nothing.

"And you – couldn't you not act like a fool? Couldn't you just get married in the usual way? Why do you have to make trouble? Why should you think things can't happen to *you*? So much love now and then later you'll be in the same fix I'm in."

That night I really did feel like running away. If you're close to a peeled onion you cry, but if you throw the onion away your tears dry up. A quarter of an hour passed.

"Cola."

"What?"

"What's going on in his head?"

She sat down on a rock and I paced back and forth.

"Don't you want to walk a bit?" I asked.

"No. All of a sudden I'm tired."

"If worse comes to worse," I said, "if he doesn't change, I'll run away with Assunta and we'll get married."

"Has the moon come out?" she asked.

"Yes. Look behind Rocamatura."

"But where are we anyway?"

"Downhill, in the woods. You were walking fast without knowing it."

"He'll be going to bed now."

"So let him."

"But he won't sleep. I know him," she said. Then: "Maybe he wants to talk, but just can't."

"She's already changing her mind," I thought. That's the way my mother was.

"Cola."

"What?"

"Maybe the circumstances have to change so he can take advantage of them and begin to talk again."

A week went by and the moon was in its last quarter. My father was preparing his nets because that night all the fishermen were going out on a major expedition that would last until the new moon. He'd been out in the middle of the cortile off and on all day standing and sniffing the sea air. He was the best of all the fishermen from Otranto to Castro and he always took charge of the big trips out. That evening I was milking the goats in the shed, when he called me from the kitchen door: "You, Cola, come here."

It was the first time he'd called me since I'd confessed and I wasted no time in joining him.

"Tomorrow," he said, "while I'm gone, you go borrow Massaro Pietro's horse and bring the girl here with her stuff. I've already talked to her father." I was dumbfounded.

"Don't dawdle now," he shouted. "Go fetch the lantern from the boat and get the oil ready."

I'd have jumped down a shark's throat to fetch that lantern; it was a shame it was right there inside the kitchen door. My father went out in the cortile and yelled, "Ahoy!" and from the farm across the way his boatmate answered with another "Ahoy!"

When Alfio was born Assunta and I left the farm and went to live in the old borgo, and I'm sure I'd never have wanted anything more in the world, if only the northerly storm hadn't brought the Turks in from the sea, if only life had gone on in the same way instead of always changing.

Colangelo IX

I couldn't bring back that morning when I sat in the cortile; I had to return to the walls because I'd already taken too much time for myself and it was almost dawn. While I'd been traveling in my memories the moon had left my own and Massaro Elio's cortile. My legs hurt and I was bone tired, like after hard exhausting work. I just happened to take the street that led to the piazza in front of the cathedral, without even thinking about it, but when I came out by the huge main door and found it half open, I was taken with a terrible longing to see Assunta and my little boy. I didn't know if it was all right to go in at night while the women were sleeping. I approached, and noticed Father Leone da Faggiano just behind the door sitting on a bench with his head down.

"Father," I said, " could I come in and see my wife?"

No answer.

"Excuse me, Father...."

I touched his shoulder. He jumped: "Oh dear, what is it?" He'd been asleep.

"Father, I've come from the walls. Let me see my wife and little boy."

"What? *Now*, my son? They're all asleep. If you wake them they'll start crying and who can deal with them, once they start that?"

"But it's only now I can see them."

"Oh Lord, well, which one's your wife?"

"Assunta."

"Wait here. I'll go ask Father Epifani. He knows them all. I've always lived up in the Monastery of San Nicola di Càsole and I don't know you people from Otranto. Oh dear God what kind of world is this getting to be? Wait a minute, I'll see."

He hurried off toward the sacristy and came back with Father Epifani.

"Are you hungry? Thirsty?" was the first thing Father Epifani said, his beautiful voice as kindly as ever.

"No," I replied.

"How come? They're all hungry and thirsty when they come down from the walls."

"Let me see Assunta and little Alfio."

"Come with me," he said, "but be careful not to scare her. Tell her everything's going well, understand?"

"Yes, Father."

Assunta saw me at once. She was on the floor at the foot of the altar to Saints Cosma and Damiano with some other women, who were dozing off in the dim candlelight. She wasn't asleep: "Cola! Oh Cola!" she said, getting to her feet as soon as she saw me. I kissed her on the forehead because I was ashamed to kiss her on the mouth in the house of the Lord. "Be quick," said Father Epifani, "you can't stay here at night," and he moved away. We stood there looking at each other, full of emotion. She touched me lightly, running her hands over my vest.

"You're all dusty," she said.

"It's tufa dust, from the stones," I answered.

"Even your hair," she said.

"You two are staying here?" I asked.

She nodded yes and I suddenly thought about what the renegade Christian had said.

"But you can't sleep here," I said.

"Little Alfio's sleeping," she answered. "See?" He was lying on my coat, which was folded in half, his curls falling lightly over his face, but he twisted and turned in his sleep, probably sensing that he wasn't in his own bed.

"What's he got in his hand?" I asked.

"A candle," she said, "but he thinks it's a sword. He likes the church candles so much that yesterday he sat down on the steps to the communion railing and ate one." I thought, "She looks pinched and haggard, like she's aged," and the others looked the same way, even the young ones sitting on the benches cradling tiny babies in their arms. Then Assunta began to cry, not shaking or sobbing, just gently, softly weeping the way she always did.

"Don't do that, Assunta."

"I'm scared for you."

"No, don't worry," I said. " A person can tell when he's going to die. Let's say you're walking along with a friend and all at once a veil drops between you and him; or else you're sitting on a terrace and you suddenly feel all cold and you shudder. Some even hear a voice. But none of these things have happened to me." I took her chin in my hand. "Wish me luck?"

Assunta thought for a minute, dried her eyes and quietly put a hand in both of mine. Then little by little, first from her mouth, next her cheeks, finally from her eyes, a little smile appeared.

"Good God," I said to myself. "What was I doing tonight with Idrusa? What a wretch I am!"

"Wait, I'll wake up Alfio," she said.

"But then if he stays awake?"

"No, he'll go right back to sleep," she replied. Alfio opened his eyes when she picked him up and then quickly closed them again. He had indeed gone back to sleep.

"Alfio," I said. My voice roused him and he opened his big black eyes wide, recognized me and began to smile, then laugh. What a pleasure to see. I wished I could've sat down right there on the floor and played with pebbles with him the way we did in the cortile. Assunta put him down.

"Come here," I said.

He stood straight up in front of me and asked: "Is there war where you are?"

"Yes."

"All I hear is shooting," he said. "Does it come out in different colors?"

"No, you can't see anything," I said, "just smoke and dust."

"And when the war's over, what then?"

"We'll crawl out from behind our defenses and stand up."

"I don't know when it's going to be over," he said, shrugging his shoulders. He was a funny little fellow when he got to thinking. He always wanted to know how things were made, when they happened, and I used to wonder where such a little boy got all that curiosity.

As I looked at Assunta standing there in front of me I thought: "This is how two people suddenly sense they're man and wife." I wanted to say something but I couldn't. Even though I had the right words in my head to comfort her and give her courage, those words kept getting on the wrong track and never found their way out. All I said was, "Good-bye Assunta."

And she said, "Good-bye Cola." We gazed at each other for a moment; then I kissed the little boy's head and walked down the center aisle toward the door.

"Who knows if I'll ever see them again," I thought. At the door Father Leone grabbed me by the arm to stop me.

"Are you going back to the walls, my good man?"

"Yes."

"We're not doing badly, are we? It's true, isn't it, that those pagans are really taking a beating?"

"They are for now."

"I should think so. With all these prayers we're saying."

"But maybe later we'll be the ones taking the beating."

"Us? Enough of that. Not very likely, I'd say."

"I'm going now, Father Leone."

"May God protect you. But be careful just the same. It only takes a moment to die. Make sure you do things right."

"Good-bye, Father."

"Good-bye young man." He ran after me. "Excuse me, what's your name?"

"Colangelo."

"Good. I'll mention you in my nightly prayers. We don't have time to pray in the daytime. There are a thousand things to do. Dear God, what a world we're living in. For a week now around here it doesn't seem to be the same place at all."

"Good luck, Father."

"Good luck to you, Colangelo."

It was still night, darker than before because the moon had set. When I got back to my post on the tower the men had dozed off with their backs against the outer walls. Except for Antonello, who saw me coming.

"Well," he said, "did you get the fear all out of your system?"

"Yes."

"Did you get anything to eat?"

"No."

"What an idiot you are," he answered.

"Antonello," I said. "I've done something really lousy."

"All right, let's hear it. Another dream?"

"Anything but a dream. I bumped into Idrusa and she took me home for a glass of wine and I ended up pushing her over on her bed. I forced her against her will."

At first Antonello didn't answer. He'd been sitting with his legs extended; now he bent them and hugged his knees in the circle of his arms. After a minute or two he said: "Really lousy is right."

"I went a little crazy tonight and then I'd had too much to drink."

"Still lousy."

"I don't know why I did it. I've known her since we were kids and I never even thought of such a thing before."

"Idrusa isn't *that* kind of woman," he said. "Women gossip about her, but it's because they don't understand. Women just never understand each other."

I stretched out beside him.

"Go to sleep," Antonello said. "We'll have plenty to do here at sunup."

"What about the renegade Christian?"

"Captain Zurlo gave him his freedom to go back to the Turks. If he'd stayed here we'd have made mincemeat out of him."

"But what did he expect? Did he think we'd open the gates and hand the city over to the Turks?"

"Maybe. Or maybe he only wanted us all to go as crazy as you did."

"Still, if I'd been in Captain Zurlo's place I'd have killed him."

"Right. And that way you'd have let the Turks know we're scared."

Colangelo X

These being days of scirocco, clouds formed at dawn, outlined in yellow by the rising sun. The evening of the eighth of August a rumor spread that the next day the Turks were going to concentrate their forces against the western tower, expecting to enter the city from that side and finish us off. To those of us watching from above, there seemed to be even more of them as they went about their preparations. Beyond the moat a road ran parallel to it for a while, then turned away at a right angle, climbed to the Sanctuary of the Virgin of the Sea, then descended steeply to Rocamatura Point amid the sands and olive trees. All along this road men on foot and horseback were hurrying back and forth from one group of tents to another, transporting mortar barrels and bases.

"Looks like the night before the big Saint Nicola's fair," said Antonello.

"If we had mortars," answered Mazzapinta, "we'd make short work of their whole camp. Or if Don Alfonso showed up. Think about it – what if he showed up right now? What if all of a sudden we heard the sound of hundreds of horses' hooves and then out of the distance came the banners of the Royal House of

Aragon with their scarlet bars against a silver background?"

"You're a poet, Mazzapinta," said Nachira.

"Cross my heart, it'd be a wonderful sight."

Because the scirocco was still blowing, a misty fog was rising from the sea toward nightfall. It would cover up pieces of road, then uncover them again so sometimes it seemed to be traveling along by itself but then other times it was the tents that seemed to be moving. When Captain Zurlo came up to inspect the walls in person, accompanied by the sound of trumpets and by Captain de li Falconi, the patches of fog had slid away from the land and gathered over the sea, and the red ball of the setting sun appeared tired and sad as if it was bringing bad news of things to come. Captain Zurlo looked everything over carefully, giving lots of orders. After he decided on the exact spot where the only heavy fire-power we had – one mortar – should be positioned, he also told us where to locate our three crossbows. The truth was we had few light arms left and we were running out of ammunition for the muskets.

Looking at us one by one, the captain said, "We have to keep our wits together and remain very calm. No getting carried away. You've got to be careful not to waste any shots. If we make it through tomorrow there's still a chance things will come out right."

He fell silent for a moment, then said, "I know some of you have the idea Duke Alfonso and his troops aren't going to get here soon enough. But if you hang on and don't give up you'll be giving him the time he needs. Are we all agreed on this?"

"Yessir," we answered in a chorus, gathered around him and standing at attention.

"For now settle down as comfortably as you can and try to sleep. All along the walls only those on guard duty will stay awake."

He looked at us again, one by one, and said, "I've got a lot of faith in you, more than in the real soldiers. For now take it easy and rest." He turned around and both he and Captain de li Falconi disappeared from view.

We were all at our posts before dawn, ready for the fight, crouching behind the tower battlements. Yet perhaps two hours went by and the Turks hadn't made their move. The sun was already high and we were still waiting there, peering this way and that and straining our ears to listen.

"What are they doing?" asked Mazzapinta. "Can anybody figure out what they're waiting for?"

Nobody replied.

For some odd reason he said at that point, "Ten men could hold the tower."

Still no sound. Time was passing and from the position of the sun it was clear that it was almost three hours since sunup. Antonello now seemed entirely taken up with plugging a tiny hole in the inside wall of the sentry box, stuffing it carefully, one piece at a time, with tiny stones he found on the ground. When he came upon a bigger piece, he'd take out all the ones he'd already used and start all over again.

Nachira was using a cloth to polish the blade of a long lance, which he'd then turn round and round to see the reflections. Mazzapinta, who'd unearthed a leather waistcoat from some unlikely place, put it on like a cuirass and was patting it with his hands. Antonello was still busy with his pebbles, some as big as mussels. He took them out, then put them back. A swallow began to fly in circles above us – maybe he'd once had a nest in the tower and the silence had lured him back.

"He's looking for his nest," said a voice.

"*Fusci, fusci, bedda mea* – Run away, away, my beauty," said another, the words of an old song of Otranto.

Then nobody paid any more attention to the swallows
and faces became serious and thoughtful again.

"What are they waiting for?" repeated Mazzapinta.

That's what we all wanted to know. Shut in by the
walls and cut off from the world, we couldn't get a full
picture of things: we didn't know that among the Turks
it was rumored that Duke Alfonso was on his way from
the interior. The rumor had about as much substance as
a wisp of cloud but the Turkish army was waiting to
attack until their scouts returned. About five hours
after daybreak, with the sun almost directly overhead
and their artillery massed on the embankment, the Turks
piled into the moats to the sound of their drums and
then began to climb the walls like ants. If we'd had
enough gunpowder and boiling pitch the next day we'd
have been able to go back to fishing for groupers and
bream. But as soon as you sent one of them flying
downward with a couple of sword strokes to your right
there'd be another climbing up on your left. When they
fell they'd twist around in the air, then plunge into the
moat, so fast you didn't even get a chance to see their
faces. Except for one – I remember him well. One
shoulder bleeding, he'd disappeared from the parapet
of the tower and tumbled all the way to the bottom, I
thought, but he hadn't. He'd caught hold of a tangle of
ropes and climbed back up, until there he was in front
of me, hanging by his hands from the ledge of the
battlements. "What's he up to?" I thought. "What's he
trying to do?" I rushed forward but quick as a hare he
bounded onto the bastion. "I'll get you now," I thought.

We found ourselves locked in an embrace and for a
moment our faces were close enough to get a good look
at each other. He was breathing hard with his mouth
open and his jaws trembling, but the eyes, those black
eyes fixed on mine had an expression that was sad and,
damn it, beautiful. For a moment it seemed like we
didn't know what to do. I looked at him and he looked

back at me – until I gathered all my strength, closed my eyes and pitched him off the tower. I staggered away and covered my face with my hands. I couldn't breathe for the lump in my throat and in that instant I wanted desperately to be alone, far away from the walls, the shooting, the dying, just to be alone on the rocks by the sea. Instead, there I was right in the midst of the worst of the assault. At that point I saw Mazzapinta, his imagination all fired up as usual, waving the naked blade of a scimitar he'd torn out of a Turk's hands and shouting: "Take that, Castilians! Take that, Aragonese!"

"What's gotten into that one?" said Cristoforo Rio.

"He's lost his head as usual," I said.

By half past noon the stones were on fire, the tufa sizzled with the heat. I was melting, my eyes were clouded. I said to myself, "I'm about to die." Then I quit thinking altogether, even about death. Any idea would've turned my stomach.

Then up the walls came a dense mass of shouting Turks. When they fell they came right back again. It was the fiercest attack of the day, so hard to combat that Captain de li Falconi called in the few soldiers he had dispersed along the walls to east and west and assembled them all on our tower. For more than an hour the battlements swarmed with Turks and Otrantini, Otrantini and Turks; they struggled hand to hand, crowded together so nobody could tell who was winning or losing or what the devil was happening. I felt a sudden surge of enormous strength – I don't know where it came from . – and besides I'd found an ax that belonged to a dead Otrantino and used it to dispatch a good number of Turks to the next life. When I ran out of Turks I still kept rushing about with the ax in my hand like in a dream. At nightfall on the ninth of August the western tower, which had sustained the heaviest assault, was still in our hands. All my comrades gathered around me and began slapping me on the back. I didn't know what they wanted and, when they began telling me I deserved special credit for the victory, I was amazed. Later I was sitting by the sentry box eating a frisella with sardines in oil, while men were taking turns carrying off the dead on their shoulders. I was hungry. Captain Zurlo and Captain de li Falconi passed by on their usual evening patrol of the walls to count the dead and the living and keep track of weapons.

"This fellow here put up a magnificent fight today," said Captain de li Falconi, pointing at me.

I stood up hastily, holding my frisella in one hand and the jar of sardines in the other.

"What've you got there?" asked Captain Zurlo, smiling at me.

"Sardines sir,"

"What's your name?"

"Colangelo."

"Are they good, Colangelo?"

"To my taste they're the best, sir," I answered.

"You fought like a champion," exclaimed Captain de li Falconi, "and with only an ax."

"Bravo," said Captain Zurlo. "When you've finished eating, go on down from the walls. You're at liberty till dawn. Are you married?"

"Yessir."

"Go see your wife. Tell the monks you have my permission."

"Thank you sir."

"And then get some sleep. We'll have a lot to do tomorrow." Turning to Captain de li Falconi, he said in a low voice, "We don't have enough men here."

"Well, they're all we've got now." Watching them go off muttering to each other like two visitors leaving a room with a death bed, I lost my appetite. I sat down and put my head in my hands.

"Saying your evening prayers?" asked Antonello.

"Here," I answered, handing him the jar of sardines, "You finish them. There's no sense leaving them for the Turks."

"What's wrong?"

"Go ahead, eat the rest of them."

"Oh-oh, I get it. You're going off the deep end again like a real idiot. You're an odd one all right. You fight like a hero all day and now look at you."

At that I wiped my face with my hand; I was all in a sweat. "I'm going down," I said. "The muskets are in the sentry box. The spare lances – I don't know where they are. Look around for them yourself."

"Go ahead, be off with you," he said.

When I got to the stairs I turned to look at him. He'd sat down, arms folded, and was looking up at the sky. I was going to shout back to him: "I really am an idiot, Antonello. Not you though. You've kept your head on your shoulders. You're always at your post," but he spoke first.

"If you find some bread or a frisella bring it back. How can anybody eat sardines by themselves?"

"All right," I said and started down the steps.

At dawn the sun was buried behind mountains of clouds. When I got to the wall there was already a sense of battle in the air.

"Did you have a good sleep?" shouted Antonello. "Those bastards got up early this morning."

"You know what I brought you?" I said. "A *tarallo* cookie."

"Where'd you get that?"

"Assunta had some for the little one."

Antonello took it in his hand and looked at it before he ate it. "Takes me back a long time." Then: "When we could buy them every day in the cathedral piazza we never gave them a thought."

A shrill whistle nearly split our ears as a musket ball whizzed by a few inches away.

"Here we go again," said Antonello.

"Look out!" I yelled. It was an arrow, but he was quick as a cat and he'd already gone down on his knees then sprung back to his feet a bit further on. It began to rain bullets and arrows and we had all we could do to jump in and out from behind our defenses like grasshoppers. I saw Antonello on his knees again but this time he didn't get up; he stayed there hanging on to the wall with both hands.

"What is it?" I yelled, running over to him.

"A ball in the stomach," he said.

"Antonello!" I cried out from sheer emotion.

He looked straight at me. "Sh-sh-sh," he said, "this is no time for tragedies."

"Wait, I'll carry you down. Hang on," I repeated in anguish. I lifted him by the armpits and propped him against the wall under the stairs and ran off to look for water to bathe his forehead.

"Wait, I'll take you down. Wait," I kept saying, panting, but he paid no more attention to me. He seemed hardly to know he was there on the wall beside me – he was all taken up with something else far away that I couldn't see. "Antonello! Antonello!" I cried, shaking him. He didn't speak, but made an effort to look at me for a moment, then quickly returned his gaze to that far away thing, completely absorbed. Then his eyes stopped moving. He was dead.

"Watch me Antonello!" I yelled. "Watch me!" and I raced along the battlements hurling stones downward and throwing myself on the Turks climbing up. Grabbing a short sword from a dead man I held off the Turks from a good piece of the wall, fighting for an hour with a fury that bordered on madness. No longer aware I was married or had a son, I imagined I was going to liberate the walls all by myself and the cathedral too and the whole of Otranto. Instead when the Turk stuck his knife into my back I fell to the ground in an instant. How little we get to do when we're alive. What terrible hopes we sometimes have.

Captain Zurlo I

When Ferrante I of Aragon, king of Naples, elevated me, Francesco Zurlo, from the outlying Capuana district to be governor of Otranto as the representative of his oldest son Don Alfonso, duke of Calabria, a restless bellicose man, hated in many parts of Italy; when this occurred Akmed Pasha was bathing in the waters of the Kubuk or the Sakarya Rivers and had never heard the name of Francesco Zurlo, nor had Francesco Zurlo ever heard of him. But there was indeed an Akmed Pasha, and from the day of his birth he carried the seeds of the pain and sorrow he would bring to me. I was a slender man, but strong; indeed had I been governor of Francavilla instead of Otranto my life would have been considerably longer and King Ferrante would have felt neither more nor less regret if the actual governor of Francavilla had died in my place. Naturally the matter has little importance with respect to the sad and sorrowful history of grief in the universe, but in context I cannot avoid reflecting upon the fact that my nomination came about simply by chance, and this, because it reaches beyond my understanding, affects me even more than my fate itself.

It all began on a beautiful sunny morning when the sea breeze enticed me to go out for a walk. The skies over Naples were alive with birds and nothing in the streets stood still; in fact the whole city echoed with the sounds of life. Then all at once a trotting of horses, people rushing to their doorways: here was the king. Don Ferrante, as devout as all the Aragonese, never failed to present himself to God every day in one of the innumerable churches of the city so that the Neapolitans would be constantly reminded of his extraordinary piety; he was arriving with his coach and four to hear the first mass at Santa Chiara. Seeing him lean out from the coach and then slowly descend, impassive, in front of the church, I said to myself: "Good-bye, morning walk. Now I've got to go to mass." I made a bow; his majesty nodded a greeting, lowered his eyes and entered the church. All through the mass he remained motionless, kneeling on a red satin cushion, his thin lips whispering the responses along with the acolytes, toward the officiating priest. When he raised his eyes from his missal to focus on the tabernacle, the pallor of his gloomily solemn face stood out in the half shadow of the church. It was then that I made a discovery: there wasn't another face in the entire kingdom that could produce the frigid cold that emanated from the king's; not even the face of a corpse, which would have possessed the advantage of recalling human fragility and the tenuousness of life. Don Ferrante's face suggested something like fate or destiny, with all the chilling aspects of that sort of correlation.

The priest hunched his shoulders, then threw out his arms, and said, "*Ite, missa est,*" and quickly brought his hands together as though to catch some tiny flying creature.

"What do I do now?" I thought. "Slip out quietly and continue my walk? Impossible. But why in the devil did I come this way today?"

Meanwhile the barons of Santa Chiara, having learned of the king's arrival, were already in the piazzetta so that his exit from the church produced general bowing. Brancoccio spoke for all of them in paying his respects: he said it was absolutely impossible to express the intensity of desire with which one awaits the arrival of the king, this cause of unforeseen felicity; hence that morning when the new sun had entered Santa Chiara it had kindled sparks in the hearts of all these, his most faithful subjects, grateful that his majesty had sacrificed a small fragment of sleep in order to honor the district of Santa Chiara with his presence. The immortal virtue of the king had graciously condescended to reside among mortal men, unworthy and insignificant though they be, and no outpouring of mere words could ever suffice to explain this beneficence or express its attendant public joy. The king was fumbling with his fingers inside his striped cloak as he studied the barons' faces, regarding them as basically a good thing, fully appropriate, but at the same time deserving of secret disdain. Finally he invited all present to a hunting party. Ferrante I's passion for the hunt and for raising game animals was famous; the deer and foxes in his reserves were fed like princes, to the point that certain sharp tongues used to say, "When the king dies animals will feel more grief than men."

"We have some magnificent boars in Li Astroni," said the king in his thin cold voice, "boars that do justice to our kingdom. We'll chase them out of their dens."

The barons smiled obsequiously.

The king continued: "This time my son Cardinal Giovanni will also participate in the hunt although, as you well know, he takes more pleasure in the things of the next world than of this one."

He followed his words with a tiny motion of his hand, a truly beautiful hand, tapering and regal: "Zurlo," he said, "what are you doing off there in the corner?"

"My humblest respects, your majesty," I answered. Someone moved aside and I found myself on the king's left. He scrutinized me: "We've seen very little of you at court," he said.

"Your majesty, I have been outside Naples in the fiefs of Casarono and Bagnolo."

"Bagnolo?" He fell silent for a moment, with that coldly dreamy attitude peculiar to calculating natures. Then he said: "Your lands are close to Otranto."

"Yes, sire," I answered.

"A lovely pearl of our realm, Otranto," he exclaimed.

"An excellent harbor," I answered.

"Years ago I used to hunt coots in that area," he said, "on Lake Alimini. That's near Otranto, isn't it?"

"Four miles away, your majesty."

"Alimini! The name itself is like saying, 'Hundreds of coots in a single day!'" he exclaimed. He returned his gaze to me, his face once more impassive: "The Turks are in Rhodes, you know."

"Alas," I said.

"It's said they will soon be in La Valona."

Silence. He turned away, saying coldly: "Where is my coach?"

While someone motioned to the servants to bring up the coach he favored me with a frigid smile: "Providence has placed you before me today, Zurlo, to remind me that you are the man best suited to be sent as my governor into that territory."

I was stunned.

"You seem not to accept the honor very cheerfully," he said with an ironic glance. But in the depths of that look I read simultaneously: "Be careful, *ego sum dominus*." Was I mistaken or was he thinking of the ancient offenses of our family, friend to the Angevins?

"I'm merely astonished, your majesty," I answered.

"You will have time for your fiefs as well," he said, then added: "Come to the palace one of these days. We'll have a chat about it. *Videbimus et cogitabimus.*"

He moved away from us, got into his carriage, and bid us good-bye with a fluttering of his eyelids accompanied by a sigh. Once the wheels were turning rapidly the carriage disappeared in a great racket behind the corner of the Monastery of San Francesco.

It was a stroke of bad luck, and so ended my pleasant outing on a sunny morning. I turned back toward home, already preparing myself to tell my wife and children what had happened and to impart the completely unexpected news.

I had three children, a boy and two girls, who were already grown by that time. The oldest, Cosima, was, I can truly say, a quiet girl with a steady temperament; she never raised her voice and politely agreed with everyone, yet always managed to do what she wanted. Thus I used to compare her in my mind to one of those tranquil streams that sparkle in the sunshine as they make their way slowly through rocks and woods to the sea with no urge to uproot trees, flood the countryside or turn into raging torrents. She wouldn't even disturb a twig: for her, living was simple, orderly and enjoyable.

Isabella, the youngest, however, always wanted the opposite of what everybody else wanted, and since she didn't care one bit about other people's desires she often found herself surrounded by discord. In addition, every now and then she would suddenly decide to devote herself body and soul to one thing: training a dog, for example. Then, when the family would sit down together at mealtimes it was impossible to talk about anything except her dog. She passionately described his progress, how the animal had learned to obey a command to raise its right ear and lower its left one, or else raise its right ear and right paw at the same time. If seemed as if Isabella's entire self overflowed in concern for that dog.

"She'll change as time goes on," my wife would say, to excuse her.

"But why so *much* time?" I wondered.

Another of Isabella's peculiarities consisted in always doing things at different hours from everyone else: reading at night, for instance, and sleeping in the daytime.

"It's because she's an intelligent girl," said my wife. "Intelligent young people are always a little high strung and tend to do things on impulse."

I answered irritably: "Well then, intelligence is superfluous if it doesn't even identify the hours when mother nature intended people to sleep."

"There's no talking to you," my wife replied tearfully. "You have such a mania for arguing about everything...."

"But why, my dear, do you get so upset at any sort of discussion?"

She looked at me resentfully: "Francesco, you don't love your children."

Despite the peculiar nature of my wife's logic, the children confided in her about everything, in me about nothing.

Sometimes though, to be truthful, Isabella would be taken with sudden fits of tenderness in my regard. She would come into my study, hug me and kiss me, then sit on my lap, tall and gangly as she was, and mix up all the papers on my desk out of curiosity to look them over.

"How nice it is here," she would say, or perhaps: "How odd you are, father mine, so pedantic," and her voice had the same tone as when she rumpled her dog's coat and made little kissing noises, saying: "What cute little crooked legs you have, my lovely little beast." The diminutive dog would look at her through the hair hanging over its eyes and wag its tail. I have to confess that in those rare moments I was happy: a father's love is of an ineffable sort and hence the cause of secret sorrows and joys.

Giovanello was in the middle as far as age was concerned, but his nature leaned more toward Isabella's than Cosima's. In the evening he would get together with others of his own age in the gardens of the Capece house in the shade of the oaks to talk. They had decided that the world should be completely transformed and therefore they needed to discuss one problem every day; thus they pounced on problems as if they were candied fruit. Later, when he came home all enthusiastic, the sight of his family, none of whom were doing anything to transform the world, left him profoundly irritated.

Sometimes he came directly to my study and said: "Listen to me, please. I have to talk to you."

"Very well," I would answer. "Ten minutes, because I have things to do."

Then he would begin explaining the results of his conversations at the Capece's, emitting pronouncements every bit as hasty as they were inaccurate, on any and all issues confronting the world.

"You and your friends," I intervened at a certain point, "want to build a Castel dell'Ovo without even knowing how to build a cabin. You know what you should do, Giovanello? Get interested in our vineyards or, if you prefer, the olive groves. Start learning, for instance, how to treat diseases of grapevines."

Giovanello would get all red in the face, leap to his feet and begin pacing back and forth in the room in long strides:

"You know what you lack, father? You are very intelligent, and when someone talks to you, you take the ideas one by one out of his argument, set them apart, see if each one follows logically from the one preceding and if it doesn't, you immediately point out the error. But you lack one thing; you aren't interested in anything new."

"You are young, my boy."

"It's not a question of age; it's a question of believing the world can renew itself, that it will get better, that all men will ultimately find some good on this earth. This is the only thing I want to work for."

"It does you great honor that you aspire to bring about men's happiness," I answered, "but your not wanting to learn how to compute the yield of an olive grove, for instance, or cure diseases of grapes when we are proprietors of olive groves and vineyards – this seems to me to be totally unreasonable."

Other times Giovanello would complain for weeks that he was bored with Naples, that he wanted a change of place, wanted to see other ways of life, other kinds of people. "A person has a feeling there are places waiting for him," he would say. Therefore when the king decided to send me to be governor of Otranto, Giovanello was absolutely certain the place waiting for him was Otranto. He began to wander irritably about the house, saying that it was obvious to everyone how I still treated him like a boy and couldn't be convinced that he was now a man and as such perfectly able to come with me to Otranto. He was talking from sheer excitement, without a shadow of reflection.

One day I told him plainly: "No, I'm not taking you with me."

We were in the garden, sitting in the shade of a cedar of Lebanon. He leaned toward me, his face both flushed and sad: "But why is it anyway that you don't want me? Why?"

"Giovanello, in that area all sorts of things might happen any time; you have no idea of the dangers right now."

"What dangers?"

"The Turks, for example."

Whereupon he raised an arm and shouted: "All the better!"

"Allow me, if you will," I answered, mastering my annoyance. "Why all the better? You only have one life, just like anyone else."

But my son always paid attention exclusively to what he himself said. "I'm coming with you," he replied.

I found myself thinking at that moment about how children grow up with an intolerable rapidity. At the beginning they are objects to be cleaned up, caressed and put down somewhere; then all at once they are starting off cheerfully on their own toward all kinds of foolishness and it's as if everything their father and mother have done for them is wasted and the past is a collection of useless and empty acts. My fifty-year-old heart rolled down the slope of these thoughts and closed up tight, so that when Giovanello set about insisting: "I'm coming with you; I want to come with you," I finally answered:

"Oh, all right. If you want to come, then come." It has to be noted that in major decisions we are never really totally present; only part of us makes the move to decide, and that part isn't always the brain.

"You'll let me come then?" he asked, as if he weren't yet sure or maybe for the pleasure of hearing it again.

"Yes, although I remain opposed in my own mind. But on one condition. If the Turks appear in the domain of Otranto, you depart immediately for Naples."

"The Turks!" repeated Giovanello, ecstatic.

Captain Zurlo II

We started out on the long overland carriage trip. It was June, which meant we had the advantage of long hours of daylight, although we had to constantly squint against the sun and the blinding whiteness of farm buildings along our route. When the hills and the rounded mountain peaks were behind us, when villages sizzled in the heat of the endless plain, we knew we had reached Apulia: Apulia, with its red earth and olive groves, whose shriveled leaves were covered with white dust; with its long stretches of stony ground that God must have designed on purpose so that cicadas, crickets and mole crickets might bask motionless in the sun with legs extended and daze the countryside with their metallic song. At sunset the cicadas seemed to struggle for a half hour or so before submitting to the final silence. And the hearts of the peasants echoed that struggle as they denied the peace of the dying light and filled the air with chants of eternal sadness. They traveled the rural roads standing up in their *sciarabàs*, heavy wagons built up high on both sides with wooden boards that creaked and swayed as they bumped along. Every now and then the drivers would interrupt their chant to shout "E-e-eo-u!" and whip their sleepy mules, who'd shake their heads in response, with a jingling of harness bells.

"Good evening to your lordships," they would say when we passed, and as they addressed us tired smiles would brighten their faces, smiles that tugged against something harsh and troubling. The mules raised their heads to look at us, then fell back into their sleepy pace.

At dawn the next day still the same sights: red earth, olive groves, a few vineyards, patches of dry stony ground. We seemed to be following the same road as the day before. Giovanello was quiet, groggy from the heat and the bright sunlight.

Low stone dry walls marking property lines ran through the fields in front of us. Around farm buildings, the gray of olive groves alternated with the tired green of prickly pear, in its perennial cactus immobility. The buildings themselves, all of them whitewashed, might have been taken for deserted, if it hadn't been for the occasional bunch of peppers hung on a door to dry, and now and then a dog who came out of a farmyard to look at the carriage, not sure if he should bark or not.

"Giuseppe," I called to the coachman, "Shouldn't we be catching sight of the fortress of Trani pretty soon now?"

"About two hours, Don Franco," he replied and we all fell silent once more.

The sky seemed to press us down with a hood of light; it was even hard to believe that clouds might still exist.

"This country is an inferno," shouted Giovanello all of a sudden.

"Your lordship," responded the coachman, "the sun is good here, the sun is a friend: such figs it makes, such wines!"

"But a person could die of this heat," said Giovanello in disgust.

"You don't know these figs," the coachman insisted in his drawling voice. "People here live on them. Eat them fresh in the summer, dried in the winter. Everybody here is poor and in some towns they hardly seem like men at all – more like creatures halfway between man and beast. The sun is all the riches they've got, your lordship." Giovanello listened, but shook his head in irritation.

At last the fortress of Trani came into view. It was surrounded by palms, its grandiose walls proudly ready to repulse all brigands from land or sea in the name of Giovanni Antonio de Foxa, *adelandtado* of the Spanish militias and a less than perfectly loyal subject of his majesty King Ferrante. As we approached, an officer on horseback came out to meet us, wearing an iron gorget and carrying a mace. He had a long thin face and olive skin; his eyes and neck reminded me of an owl. He stopped directly in front of us, frowned, welcomed us to the fortress where, he said, we would most certainly enjoy the benefits of Don Antonio's hospitality. Meanwhile his horse, brought to a sudden halt, snorted and sniffed the air.

"We wouldn't want to miss this pleasure," I answered. "We are exhausted and we would really appreciate four walls around us and a bit of shade."

Without a word, the officer waved his right arm as though to give an order to an invisible troop, and moved away. We followed. A moment later, after leaving the carriage and horses at the guardhouse and passing through the gates on foot we found ourselves in an outer courtyard flooded with sunlight but with not a soul to be seen. Silence everywhere. We entered the inner court with its grandiose architecture, it too deserted in the heat of the sun. I strained my ears to listen for voices from within the castle: nothing. Still the same sinister quiet broken only by the sound of my own steps and those of Giovanello and the officer, who had not opened his mouth again.

"But isn't there anybody here?" whispered Giovanello in an uneasy, almost fearful tone.

"Hm'm, well...," I answered, beginning to look around more carefully. Everything was mortally still. The officer bowed, then disappeared through a small door. Narrow embrasures at the level of the courtyard corresponded to tall windows surrounded with iron bars in the two upper stories of the castle. The sun beat down, turning the tufa of its walls to a blinding white and seeping into the embrasures. Only on the north side did the line of windows fall in shadow, resting the eyes, despite their lugubrious procession of iron gratings. From the last one hung a dark cloth that someone might have forgotten there, or perhaps it was simply a curtain fallen from its original place and caught in the grating. I noticed that at each of the four corners of the ground floor there was a small door made of planks nailed together. All of them were closed, including the one behind which the officer had vanished. Had we fallen into a trap? "What if they're going to kill us?" I thought, but the next instant I said to myself, "What am I thinking of? There's no reason for them to kill us. It's this murderous heat: they've all gone to sleep." At that moment I realized we were being steadily watched by eyes behind the embrasures: the eyes of men who by now had surely looked us over from head to foot. The really disturbing note was the absolute silence, as if we were in a prison or a cemetery. Then all at once we heard a wild cry, and in response a rattling of iron; and finally through one of the doors came an old servant clad in scarlet-colored velvet livery. "If the gentlemen please, they may make themselves comfortable in their rooms and rest," he said in a low voice. He took us through the door he had come out of, then up a wide stairway to the second floor, showing us into two solemn chambers furnished with canopied beds, damask hangings and paintings. Then he bowed and disappeared in silence.

"Where on earth have we ended up?" asked Giovanello.

"Look, it's cooler here and there are two beds. Let's take a nap and we'll talk later."

Giovanello collapsed on his bed fully dressed, then burst out laughing. "Mamma mia, was I ever scared!"

I looked at him – so different from the Giovanello back in Naples, the young man who wanted to change the world – so much the boy.

In late evening we entered the main drawing room to pay our respects to Giovanni Antonio de Foxa. A big vigorous man dressed in the rough but colorful garb of a common soldier, he was seated on a bench, his legs apart, his hands resting palm down on both sides to help support his heavy bulk. Meanwhile he was talking in his hearty unmelodious voice to a number of courtiers and a monsignor.

"Illustrious Zurlo," he bellowed when he saw me. "Welcome to Trani. This heat takes away the appetite for everything except something new. Your son?"

"Yes, Giovanello."

"Sit down, make yourselves at home. How was your trip?"

"Not too bad, thank you."

"I saw you arrive from the window. Fine looking horses, but a little heavy aren't they?"

"They're Spanish utility horses, marvelously tough."

"Must be pretty hot out there on the roads?"

"Quite. Like the ground itself was about to burst into flames."

"What news from Naples?"

"Nothing special. His majesty spends his time hunting, supervising his barons and thinking about the Turks."

"You know what?" answered Don Antonio. "I say we're under the influence of evil planets. Before long this country will be in ruins."

Giovanello watched him enthralled.

"Excellence," Don Antonio continued, "I'm telling you, every one of the Italian princes thinks of nothing but his own interests and what's worse, thinks he can use the Turks to promote those interests. They don't even know, wretches that they are, that winning with the help of the Turks is the same thing as losing." He turned to a courtier: "Bring us something to drink." The courtier made a bow and went out.

"And the pope?" shouted Don Antonio, so loud that his voice echoed in the vault of the ceiling. "His holiness may be an excellent man, but it's for sure there's too much he doesn't understand. He doesn't have the head for it; in fact he doesn't have the head to wear the tiara." He stopped and thought a moment, then said: "Paul II was the right man at the time. Yes indeed, mother nature gave *him* the spirit of greatness, but that spirit is dying right along with our century. Well what do *you* want?" he added, turning to the slight figure of a servant who had entered noiselessly and now stood before him bent over in a deep bow. An old hollow-cheeked courtier answered in the servant's place: "The tenant farmers are here, sir, the ones who want a new wall to mark the boundary of the estate."

"I already told them no," answered Don Antonio harshly. "It's a useless expense. Pretty soon now we'll have to fight the Turks and you're thinking about building dry walls."

"The present wall is falling to pieces," insisted the courtier. "It's full of vipers' nests and the peasants consider it dangerous."

"Dangerous?" Don Antonio's purplish nose expressed his disdain. "Just let them keep away from it. Vipers don't bother you if you don't bother them."

"But the little ones." The courtier spoke again in a gentle tone, "they don't understand the danger."

"Little ones!" snickered Don Antonio, looking directly at the courtier. "Their guardian angels will look after them. Ask monsignor here for the details."

"Two have already died," said the courtier with deliberation.

"Well then, that was their destiny. I can't keep track of all the peasant children who happen to die. I've got other things on my mind." He waved his arm and the servant withdrew and quietly disappeared. Then he turned to Giovanello: "It's bound to happen, Giovanello. This noble land is headed for disaster. Before long it'll be invaded, devastated by the Turks, like the plains of Hungary. And what do we have down there on the strait of Otranto? A militia, maybe? Nothing but scum. Scum that fish for a living, grow a few grapes – that's what we've got. Bah! Scum that'll drop their pants in terror."

He stood up, put a hand on my shoulder.

"For now let's go toast your health. How about some chilled Malvasia wine? A drink fit for cardinals!"

That night almost an hour after we'd gone to bed Giovanello came into my room.

"Is it true?" he said in a frightened voice. "Are things really that bad?"

"Go to sleep for now, " I answered. "Don Alfonso is only a soldier, and like most soldiers he doesn't know men very well, or like them either. He doesn't know

93

what men can do if they only wake up. Do you hear all those crickets?"

"Yes, they're serenading us."

"Well, to tell the truth, when I go to bed I prefer a good lamp and a book. But here we'll have to make do with crickets. Go on along now. Get some sleep."

"Good night."

"Good night, Giovanello."

At dawn we were on the main road once more, and the fortress of Trani soon faded from sight behind the palm trees on the horizon.

"Giuseppe, when will we get there?" asked Giovanello after a long silence.

"Only God knows, your lordship," answered Giuseppe. "It depends on so many things: the horses, the road. Here every once in a while the road gets completely wiped out by sandstorms. What storms they are too, my good sirs! Then you have to look for another route. If there haven't been too many storms this spring then we should soon be there. It's a matter of God's will, your lordships."

"So, if the road is in good shape...?"

"If it's good, tomorrow morning. At the latest, day after tomorrow, that is, you understand, if nothing happens. Of course, you know my good sirs, sometimes in this world a person can find himself in the wrong place at the wrong time – even if the road is good. Anyhow when you start to see the marshes then you'll know Otranto isn't far. And there's a special kind of chicory in these parts. This is really beautiful country," he said happily, cracking his whip at the horses.

Giovanello, sitting beside me, kept watching Giuseppe as if trying to figure something out by looking at him. "Giuseppe," he said suddenly, "have you always been a coachman?"

"Well, your lordship, I was only eleven years old the first time I drove a wagonload of hay for your grandfather, God rest his soul. I've been handling horses for fifty years now."

"Have you always liked doing it?"

"Why shouldn't I, your lordship? Horses are intelligent beasts; they understand what you want right away. I get up at four in the morning when there's barely a bit of light in the sky, then go right to the stable. The horses hear me come in and turn to look at me, then bob their heads up and down. The way they greet me gives me a good feeling in my blood, a little boost, you know, like you get from a grain of pepper. But a pleasure is always a pleasure, even when it's small. I tell you, excellence, with the help of the Lord, I've had the best life I could have hoped for."

It looked as if Giovanello wanted to reply, as if he had the words on the tip of his tongue, but instead he raised his eyes to the blue of the sky and remained a long time like that, lost in thought.

Captain Zurlo III

Except for a few palazzi belonging to the nobles, all the houses in Otranto looked alike, whitewashed and built right against each other for mutual protection from storms coming in off the sea. During this summer season they were crowned with yellow squashes that sat triumphantly along the tops of their walls under a buzzing of gnats and mosquitoes. Otrantini men were dark and muscular, with bony faces and little tendency to talk. From a certain point of view they were all identical, in the sense that when I tried to establish contact with one of them, someone else, the same in every case, looked back at me with suspicious eyes. To be sure they knew there had been a foreign governor and master of the castle long before my time, long before they themselves were born. I was simply part of the way things were, like the October rains, and there was no point in talking to me about their affairs. If they encountered me they were content to take off their caps, step aside and bow their heads. The children, half naked, half clad in rags, ran away as soon as they saw me, then stopped at a certain distance, backs against a wall, to fix me with an unblinking stare. Big eyes opened wide in amazement, they almost held their breath. If I waved a greeting to them, their faces darkened at once and they dashed away out of sight. The women were also thin, unlike those in the interior, and mostly dressed in black. They had velvet eyes and soft lips. Some of them were strikingly beautiful, the one called Idrusa, for instance. It was her beauty, in fact, that separated Don Felice Ayerbo of Aragon from his wits and good sense. She might very well have found her place in a painting if current painters hadn't been afflicted by a deplorable weakness for women covered with silken brocades. From the terrace of the castle I often watched the Otranto fishermen and their wives at work. It was clear that they had a sort of chief, Mastro Natale. One day, on the pier, I approached him, just to talk.

"How is life treating you?" I asked coming up to his boat.

He took off his cap. "Good day to you, your lordship. Things aren't bad, God willing." A swarm of little boys were running and playing among the boats, but seeing me they all stopped wide eyed.

"You have so many little ones, here in Otranto," I said.

Master Natale smiled slowly and answered, "Our women are fertile even when they get on a bit in years. They're thin and worn, but they still know how to have babies."

At that point a number of fishermen approached, making a circle around me and Mastro Natale.

"If you are in need of something," I said to them, "if things aren't going well, let me know."

They regarded me with suspicion, saying nothing.

Mastro Natale spoke for them: "Our desires are simple: that the sea give us a lot of fish and few storms."

"Very well. At any rate, be assured that I am here to serve you. If you want anything you can come to the castle."

"We thank your lordship," said Mastro Natale, while the others, heads down, seemed to be lost in thought. But not one of the fishermen ever made an appearance at the castle.

I had only one friend in Otranto, Don Felice Ayerbo of Aragon, with whom I played chess in the evening after I took care of the muster of my 1200 men in the castle courtyard. To be truthful, Don Felice didn't have the temperament for chess. Quite the reverse, he had a particular propensity for living by inspiration and impulse. Hence he didn't profit from our games; indeed he never played without being constantly distracted.

Nonetheless we were both getting on in years and we had reached that age when one needs something to look forward to at certain hours. For us a chess game was a modest focal point, like the daily rosary for women. Such actions don't need to be significant or even to affect one's private destiny. Only the young try to make all their hours meaningful and that's why they are always restless and unsatisfied. Don Felice Ayerbo was actually related to the royal family through certain female relatives and hence didn't have to pay taxes. Anyone could easily tell that he belonged to the upper ranks of the nobility simply by the way he crossed a room or picked up a fork, as well as by his confused ideas about practical things. Besides the family castles in Montesano, Patù, and Alessano he was continually

building others in the air, the effect of the heroic
sentiments that forever clogged his heart.

One evening we were at the chessboard as usual. The
huge drawing room was wrapped in shadow except for
the corner near the window where the light from the
candelabrum made our faces loom large against the
background of darkness. Each one pondered in turn, then
moved a pawn. Don Felice's left hand hung limp: the
right one slipped slowly in and out of the circle of
light as it guided the pawns. The shadows of bishop and
castle moved over the board, approached each other,
separated, grew shorter, vanished completely in the
light, then reappeared with the next move. Don Felice
sighed, drummed the fingers of his left hand on the edge
of the table, then sank back into his chair and, raising
his eyes from the board, gave me a look of admiration.
"You're a born chess player, Zurlo," he said.

"Well at least in a chess game accounts always balance," I answered.

It was his move, but although his face leaned forward
into the circle of light, it still seemed as far away as
before, held back by something.

"Anything wrong?" I asked.

He smiled, embarrassed, and didn't answer.

"A business matter?" I persisted.

"No, oh no."

"Bad news from Spain?"

"No, no. Everyone's fine, just fine."

He moved his bishop. "Your move," I said, after
taking my turn, but instead he sank back again in his
chair and furrowed his brow: "Zurlo, this will sound
stupid to you, but...well, I'd like to know now what love
really is."

"Oh Christ!" I thought.

"You yourself," he asked, uncertain, "what would you
have to say about it? You've never told me your ideas on
the subject."

"Don Felice," I said, "if we're playing chess, we should keep our minds on the game."

"You're absolutely right. So let's stop playing and you tell me your ideas."

"Now? But couldn't we finish the game first? Do we really have to interrupt it to talk about something so remote from us both?"

"But my dear friend, is it really so out of place to talk about the greatest adventure life has to offer?"

"Not out of place, but...well, be patient with me. For years now, my mind has been occupied with anything but this kind of subject. If you were to ask me to talk about wines, wools, casks, firewood, cakes even...but *love*!"

"Yes, but let's be objective," he insisted, "love is life's greatest undertaking."

"Don Felice, you always think in such grandiose terms."

"But I'm talking about so-called 'great love,'" he said with a worried air. Don Felice's conversation often reminded me of when I was thirty years younger and filled with aspirations that I couldn't even remember now without a major effort. The idea that he had retained those aspirations for his entire life was profoundly irritating to me, but my irritation was incomprehensible to Don Felice.

"I've been watching you all evening," I said. "You're not yourself today. Perhaps you didn't sleep well, or you've eaten something too heavy."

"Eaten something heavy? Oh no, I only had chicory."

"That's odd."

"It's just that I think about these things once in a while, my friend. Not about love in its low or common aspect – my thoughts are not just an old man's fantasies. I'm concerned with a 'great love': something that happens when you meet a woman and discover that the reason you were born was to love this woman. You discover your destiny."

"But can it really be like that?" I asked.

"The devil it can't. There is plenty of testimony to this kind of love. Look at history itself, if you want proof."

"Oh well, so let's admit that every now and then something surprising happens in this world, even if it's only to two people out of many thousands. The fact remains, as I see it, there have to be a certain number of conditions present and they all have to occur simultaneously. Look. In the first place the two people have to perceive each other through a kind of fog that renders them both ineffable, mysterious, vastly different from each other. Keep this clearly in mind – I said vastly different. Because whatever one of them understands about the other doesn't help at all. It's what they *don't* understand about each other that creates the effect. At this point something has to happen to get one of them out of the picture: a pestilence for instance, a death in battle, or maybe just a fatal departure, or family hatred. That sort of thing, who knows. Then the affair can shine in full splendor, can be, one has to say, a 'great love.'"

Don Felice looked at me sadly, shifted himself in his chair, then stood up and crossed the room. When he reached the window that looked out on the port he stopped for a moment lost in thought, gazing toward the sea. At last he turned and came back to the table and said: "Zurlo, I'm in love."

"Santa Madonna!" I couldn't help but exclaim.

He stared at the chessboard as if addressing it and said in an emotional tone, "Yes, I am in love. I've never seen such a woman, never experienced such a feeling. You see, all she has to do is move her hand, shrug her shoulders, fold back the lapel of her dress, and I'm overcome with unspeakable ecstasy and infinite dismay at the same time. Ah yes, Zurlo, wouldn't you yourself experience bliss and dismay if suddenly, a few paces away, you saw a creature you'd spent your entire life fabricating in secret fantasy, a being from an imaginary world? If you saw her sit down across from you, fan herself, eat a piece of marzipan, smile? Wouldn't you be enchanted with her every move?"

"Excuse me, Don Felice," I said, "but who is she?"

"A woman from Otranto; she's called Idrusa. I remember the first time I saw her. The little face of a woman framed by dark hair appeared in my study, spoke, then all at once vanished – like a vision. I tell you, if we could relive certain moments of our lives, moments we're so poorly prepared for the first time around, oh what a magnificent world this would be!"

"How old is she?" I asked.

He answered hesitantly: "About twenty."

"Twenty?" I repeated, taken aback. "The same age as my Cosima."

"Age is a function of destiny," answered Don Felice. "In the scriptures it says that Old Boaz loved Ruth deeply and that she loved him in return."

"Take it easy, Don Felice. Boaz and you – it's hardly the same thing."

"What do you mean?"

"I mean that outside the Holy Scriptures young girls don't fall in love with old men."

He looked at me with a certain displeasure. Then, gazing toward an invisible point at the other end of the room, he said: "She's a little dove, a young woman who has suffered and needs to be loved."

"As far as that's concerned, it would seem that women always need to be loved and they're all doves. It has to do with a certain masculine feeling that they know how to take advantage of with great success."

"I want to help her," he answered. "She's stymied, doesn't know what to do next. She has even thought of

killing the man who offended her. And when people
think of murder it means they can't find any other way
out: *abyssus abyssum invocat in voce cataractarum
tuarum* – deep is calling to deep by the roar of your
cataracts."

Don Felice had spoken with passion and he was now
waiting for me to answer, but I said nothing. Whatever
could I tell him? "Be careful, old friend, it's not for
nothing that a woman possesses a '*dolce leggiadretta
scorza* – sweet and lovely exterior,' as the poet says, and
love is not an ineffable torment but a very, very different matter that always leads to a certain obligatory
foolishness, in dimensions that are proportional to
one's age." Was this what I ought to tell him? We could
hear the shouts that accompanied the changing of the
guard on the castle battlements and the sound of the
soldiers who had been relieved coming down the wooden
steps inside the walls.

Don Felice, who had perhaps read my thoughts, gave
me an affectionate look and said: "One could disarm
oneself, give up, as you'd wish, Zurlo, but that's not
life, believe me it's not."

Captain Zurlo IV

Don Felice had a servant named Teodoro whom he had
brought from Naples and who, like him, was of Spanish
origin. Teodoro must have been created at a moment
when nature's fancy was livelier than usual, since it's
certain that Mother Nature doesn't always have such
variety in mind. One has only to take note of the men
he encounters in traveling, whether by carriage or on
horseback, or of those he finds at his table or signs
contracts with in business. Hence there aren't too many
general types of human beings, and a number of them
have time to turn up among our acquaintances. For me
this fact simply doesn't apply in Teodoro's case, even

though during the time I spent on earth I dealt with a good many servants. He was short and slight, in fact so thin that from behind you could see his long pointed shoulder blades under his waistcoat; he was also somewhat cross-eyed and completely devoted to Don Felice. Nonetheless he spent a third of each year in a state of peevish resentment toward his master, and consequently toward the world in general, all because of trifling offenses he believed his master had distributed in his direction during the days that made up that one third of the year. The absent-minded Don Felice, of course, hadn't the vaguest awareness of any of these supposed offenses. At such times Teodoro, once his chores were finished, would sit down crosslegged on the floor of the vestibule of the house and silently watch his master's every move. For example, he'd wait there in the hall when Don Felice had to go out and since he was refusing to hand his master's hat to him, Don Felice would absently pick up the overseer's cap and put it on instead. Teodoro would let him reach the doorsill before he simply looked up and said: "What hat is that?" Then he'd return to staring stubbornly at the floor. Or else when it was time for Don Felice to go to Palazzo De Marco to review the garrison, Teodoro wouldn't remind him for anything. Instead he'd watch on the sly from his place on the vestibule floor and, although he could see his master's back through the open study door as Don Felice sat immersed in his reading, he'd keep silent for a good while, deriving particular satisfaction from his own behavior. Finally he'd say: "So you aren't reviewing today at Palazzo De Marco?" Don Felice would stir in his chair, then, remembering his obligations, jump up and begin bustling about the room. At that point Teodoro's enjoyment reached its height. By late evening he'd still be sitting on the vestibule floor but his upper body would begin to lean further and further to one side, a

sign that sleep had conquered the pig-headed servant's
passive defense – a partial conquest however, because he
wouldn't budge from the vestibule floor even though it
meant he would get up the next morning with every bone
in his body aching, and his face a drawn mask of misery.

His heart's most secret wish in those periods was to
suffer, to inflict torture upon and do violence to
himself: he skipped meals and indeed, as I've already
said, slept on the floor. This was his way of punishing
his master. He would stare at Don Felice every now and
then as if to say: "So you think you can get away with
insulting me?" (and in his mind the offended Teodoro
addressed his master with the familiar pronoun). "You
think you have a right to mistreat me? All right then, I
won't eat – I'll die first. I won't eat and I won't go to
bed." Of course, Don Felice didn't believe he had any
right to offend his servant; on the contrary, he never
could figure out Teodoro's motive for these periodic
fits of sulking. He'd say to me: "Oh dear, oh dear!
When he gets over it this time I'm going to have to talk
things over with him; I've got to persuade him to be
reasonable."

"You expect to change the nature of a lunatic?" I'd
reply. But Don Felice, who believed in so many lovely
things, even thought it was possible to transform men
for the better.

Then the day would arrive in which Teodoro would
wake up a new person, filled with devotion, generosity
and even wit. Don Felice would notice the change the
first thing in the morning by the tone of Teodoro's
meteorological pronouncements. In fact, when Teodoro
handed him his breakfast tray, exclaiming: "Fine day
today!" or even "Nasty weather this morning!" it meant
he had recovered from the sulks. At this point Don
Felice invited him into his study and had a long talk
with him. Teodoro listened to his master with visible
enjoyment and responded that his heart was afflicted by

what had happened. To be sure his master was not blameless in the matter: let him judge for himself. For example that day when the viceroy and Captain Zurlo had come to see him and he had sent his loyal servant into the kitchen to prepare linden and camomile tea for a supposedly upset stomach, but really to get rid of a pair of ears. This was insulting, it attested to a lack of confidence. Don Felice replied that he jolly well did get stomach upsets and that was the jolly good reason why he had sent Teodoro to the kitchen. However, since Teodoro was a new man this morning and since Don Felice couldn't wait to revive their old affectionate habits, they took turns consoling each other and begging each other's pardon with teary eyes.

When Don Felice first fell in love with the Otrantini girl, Teodoro was perplexed, but he withheld judgment and showed no reaction; then he began to be enthusiastic. He had the cook prepare special sweets for the girl and took to talking about his master with glowing eyes, as if he'd suddenly discovered Don Felice's heroic qualities. From Don Felice's confidences I learned that Teodoro's bouts of ill humor had significantly diminished both in number and duration, so that their life together was mostly smooth sailing.

There was one other person who was favorably impressed with Don Felice's madness – my son.

"Oh, but this is really wonderful," he exclaimed with enthusiasm when he found out about it.

"I'm afraid I don't see anything wonderful about it," I replied. "This mélange of so called 'great love' and the Psalms of David looks to me as if he's having some problems with his circulation." But my son insisted that it was wonderful indeed and from then on he was Don Felice's friend; he often went to visit him and they discussed ideals.

Sometimes Don Felice and I took an evening walk out to Rocamatura, through pleasant orange groves whose dark green contrasted with the red earth. The view from the point was almost painfully beautiful. Otranto looked like an immense castle surrounded by solid bastions and towering over the sea.

"Who knows," I said. "This land may well fall prey to misfortune."

"Misfortune?" asked Don Felice, intent on watching two young peasant women drawing water from a well for their chicory gardens.

"The Turks aren't going to stop in La Valona," I said. "They'll try a landing somewhere in Italy. But where? That's the question."

"Oh well," said Don Felice absently, unable to take his eyes off one of the two girls, as with elegant composure, she carefully lifted the jug of water and placed it on her right shoulder, arching the other arm over her head to steady it with her left hand. Then she calmly set off, barefoot, toward the countryside. "Let's hope things turn out for the best," Don Felice added.

"Otranto?" I persisted. "Brindisi? Taranto?"

"Why Otranto? It's so small," he said.

"It's on the strait," I answered.

After we'd spent some time examining hypotheses and counter-hypotheses we found ourselves beyond the point and within sight of the Alimini Woods. Don Felice sat down on a rock, breathing hard from the effort of moving his heavy body along, and said: "You know my friend, your worries and predictions are beginning to be contagious. I really don't know whether the Turks will come or not. What I *do* know is that we are surrounded at this moment by colors, perfumes and women, and you can't even manage to be aware of any of these things for a minute because the Turks have invaded your head. Chase them away this evening, I beg you. Get rid of them." He stopped briefly, wiped the sweat from his neck and his forehead, then continued: "My friend, let's put our minds on things that matter from a distance.

For instance look at the beauty spread around us in the sunset." His eyes moved over the panorama with an expression of subtle joy.

Captain Zurlo V

When the Turks arrived in Otranto, they interrupted many things, including those long discussions for which we were so well matched. I can truly say that there is nothing more comforting than a well-tuned conversation between two such exemplary talkers as Don Felice and myself. The world outside our window seemed to have been put there by God in his goodness, just to provide a subject for our dialogues within.

But on the twenty-eighth of July in the year 1480 the world burst open our doors and came inside. When the prows of the Saracen galleys turned toward the port I was on the high tower of the castle, a good place from which to watch our destiny. I alone knew that behind the wind whipping those sails there were political factions, intergovernmental quarrels and ministerial plots – a combination that would soon change things definitively for all those citizens of Otranto who happened to be enjoying perfect health in that July of 1480. I knew it and I said it to myself, while the poor Otrantini, who didn't know anything, awaited orders.

I was responsible for 1200 men: 800 Otrantini and 400 Neapolitans, in addition to the garrison of the Spanish viceroy, an office held by the archbishop of Brindisi. These latter were under Don Felice's command, but there was actually only one thing they did well – ask the viceroy for leave. In fact, as soon as the Turks turned toward Otranto I sent one of them on horseback to inform him of the unhappy turn of events. When he arrived at his destination the archbishop discovered him with a request for leave in hand, this time on behalf of the entire garrison. The viceroy heard his message, said nothing in reply, then violently tore the request into tiny pieces and scattered them on the floor. "That will be the end of that!" he shouted in Spanish.

The next night four hours after sundown Don Felice arrived all out of breath to bring me the news that the Spanish soldiers had let themselves down over the walls with ropes and fled.

"Now," he added, "I'm the only Spaniard left."

"That's not much help. Couldn't you keep them here?"

"Eh, oh no – they ran off. Anyway what's the use of keeping cowards around and feeding them?"

"Things look bad," I said. "We don't have enough men."

"But," he exclaimed, "we have all the good citizens of Otranto, such great-hearted people!"

"Would you have them fight with their hearts? They've never seen a battle, never handled weapons."

"They'll do it; I know they will. I can already see them on the walls, firing away, pouring down boiling oil; I can see the Turks below with their heads all battered and broken." Then he added, breathless: "My friend, I feel as if I'm just now starting to live. Do you understand, Zurlo, do you know what I mean?"

"Yes, yes, I understand," I sighed.

At that moment there was a knock on the door and Teodoro entered.

"He too has stayed," said Don Felice, "the only one of my men to prove his loyalty to the king. Isn't that right, Teodoro?"

"I stayed," replied Teodoro, "because there's no way you can get dressed by yourself, as heavy as you are – it's just too difficult. With all due respect, take your fancy stocking breeches as an example – you simply couldn't get into them alone."

"Oh Teodoro," exclaimed Don Felice, abashed.

The next day, as I put on my cuirass and fastened the links of chain mail, I couldn't help but feel a bit mistreated by life, which according to my exact calculations, always acted with a sort of befuddled imprecision: the Spanish soldiers I'd so counted on were gone; on the other hand it had been impossible to get Giovanello to leave Otranto. When before the Turks had even landed I had told him, "It's time for you to pack your things and depart at once for Naples," he had balked: he wasn't going. It was useless for me to try to explain that despite his ready capacity to understand abstractions I couldn't see him heating pitch and carrying it up on the walls, or killing and skinning dogs. Besides somebody had to be on hand to comfort his mother and sisters and that somebody could only be him. "I'm not a coward," he concluded. "I'm staying here."

On the fifth day I decided to write a letter to the king, making one more desperate appeal for aid. Then I'd locate someone brave enough to slip out of the besieged city and make his way to Naples. Since the Turkish cannons had been pointed directly at Otranto for four days, I dispensed with a long preamble. I said we were running low on provisions, we had few men and if we were to be wiped out our disappearance from the face of the earth was of no importance. The real evil would be the danger to the whole kingdom, not to mention all Christendom itself and the apostolic faith of which his most serene majesty was the representative and guardian. As I laid down my pen I glanced at the portrait of Don Ferrante on the wall of my study. His majesty was wearing a red satin waistcoat edged with gold and a starched collar. He stood to the right of the throne, while on the left three ministers gazed at him with humble devotion. He, however, appeared to pay them no heed. So what was the king thinking of? To tell the truth, it seemed that with the greatest gravity he was thinking of nothing at all. I stood up and started off toward the archbishop's palace, since only he knew all the Otrantini well enough to suggest the right man for this exceptional mission.

His eminence Archbishop Pendinelli was the noblest thing in Otranto. He was extremely slight of person, with thin and delicate hands. But the hundred and ten or so pounds that he weighed were evidence of enormous stability in the midst of destruction; in fact they were direct testimony to the presence of God. And I ought to mention that the image of God held a major place in the hearts of the Otrantini. When I reached the archbishop's apartments his secretary told me his eminence was on the terrace reciting his breviary.

"On the terrace! With the cannons firing from morning to night?"

"Oh, his eminence doesn't give them a thought," said his secretary. "He's immersed in his prayers."

"You shouldn't let him do it. It's too dangerous."

The secretary raised his eyes to heaven, as if I should take the matter up directly with God himself.

There was nothing to do but wait to be received. When the archbishop came to greet me, it was with a step so light I scarcely heard him approach. "And how are things going, my good Zurlo?" he said.

"The situation is getting steadily worse, your eminence," I replied. "We can only resist for a few more days."

He raised his fingers and said in a soothing voice, "Immense faith is necessary at this moment."

"The fact is we don't have any artillery, your eminence," I answered, "whereas the Turks have some very heavy pieces. If reinforcements get here soon, there's hope. Otherwise we aren't going to make it."

"Listen my friend, if you could just for a moment put aside the idea that certain things are impossible for God, what would you do for our city?"

I snapped back: "Exactly what I'm doing now, your eminence, just what I feel I should do as governor and as one of his Catholic Majesty's soldiers. I've positioned the Otrantini on the battlements and the towers; I've got part of the Neapolitan soldiers on the walls and the rest near the Monasteries of San Giovanni and San Francesco. The Turks will attack those two points first because they're the outer limits of the city. They won't assault the port because the water's too shallow for their galleys. I've requisitioned all animals that could be used for meat, even dogs and cats, so I'll be able to ration food. Furthermore, if you like, I can predict the end of all this if reinforcements don't get here in a week."

The archbishop shook his head as if to deny my last comment, at which I nearly lost all patience, saying: "From the way you talk, your eminence, it's as if Otranto was inhabited by rank on rank of sword-bearing archangels and seraphim when in fact only poor un-armed fishermen live here."

"Zurlo, let's not get all upset. Not a leaf stirs without the will of God. Now then, how can I be useful to you?"

"I need a man who's absolutely trustworthy and extremely courageous for a dangerous mission, to carry a sealed letter to his majesty in Naples."

"Very well. Come back tomorrow and you'll have your man."

I left the palace in a bad mood, noting to myself how often conversations with saints get severely muddled. And it wasn't just that either. It disturbed me that there were so many people in the world who never really had to do any serious thinking – Don Felice for example, or my son Giovanello, or the archbishop. How was it possible that I always ended up dealing with the ideas of minds that didn't know how to think?"

The next day the archbishop was waiting for me in the loggia of his palace.

"I have found the man," he said most deliberately, in his quiet refined voice.

"Good. How old is he?"

"Twenty-seven. You will be pleased with him."

"Well then, I'd better see him at once."

"Yes, it's best that you talk to him. I've already explained what is to be done."

"Will he have the necessary courage?"

"Judge for yourself, Captain," he answered with his disconcerting calm, then moved away and opened the door to his private apartment. The door closed after him and when he reappeared he was followed by a tall young man with thick very black hair and a sinewy neck. He was running his fingers over a short piece of heavy white reed he had in one hand, but when he approached me he stopped stroking the reed and stood at attention, as if ready to carry out an order at once.

"Your name?" I asked.

"Fanciullo."

"How's that?"

"Giovanni Fanciullo."

"Ah! We'd like to know whether you're willing to let yourself down from the walls into the sea tonight, watching out for Turkish arrows, then swim across to Rocamatura. After that you'll have to use your own judgment as to the best way to reach Lecce. There they'll give you a horse to go on to Naples."

"Yessir," he said simply.

"Listen," I said, "before you accept, remember this is a dangerous mission and you might well die trying to carry it out. Think it over."

"I don't think anything, sir," was his response.

"Very well," I said. "What's that stick for?"

"It's a reed I'm going to slit then plug with wax to serve as a carrying case. Once you've put the letter for

Naples inside, I'll tie the reed to my breeches and the letter won't get wet."

"Good idea."

Quick as a leopard, the youth turned away from me, knelt down in front of the archbishop and kissed his hand, moving with a grace that was startling in a man so robust and muscular.

I began figuring the exact place on the wall where I'd order him to be lowered, between the north and the east on the sea side. I calculated the height at that point and hence the amount of time the poor fellow would be suspended in the void like a bunch of grapes hanging from an arbor – an easy target for Turkish arrows. At such a thought I instinctively looked toward him: he was standing quietly beside the archbishop, both of them wearing a faraway smile.

That night the sky was exceptionally clear, so we had to wait until the moon set before ordering the Otrantini men to lower Fanciullo. We had all been ready for quite a while; he himself waited with his naked back against the sentry box and two loops of rope closely circling his sides. The men charged with lowering him were silent, as were the others who had come to watch his descent.

"Go ahead," I ordered. "It's time."

"Does the rope seem tight enough?" asked Mastro Natale.

"Yes."

"Good luck," said Mastro Natale.

"Good luck," repeated the others, in chorus.

"Good-bye," he murmured, climbing over the parapet and letting himself go in space.

"Easy does it," I said, "easy now." The rope slid over the parapet inch by inch, held taut by three pairs of fishermen's hands. We watched him, glancing now and then at the anchored galleys and the darkness beyond. There was nothing more we could do. I thought for a

second that he was no longer holding on to the wall
with his hands; a second later I thought I saw him wave
his arm toward us. The night was so clear I was sure the
Turks must see him. All at once the fishermen's hands
stopped moving, while I was still bent over the wall. I
stood up:

"What is it? Something wrong?"

"Better to let him stop for a moment," said Mastro
Natale, "otherwise they're bound to see him."

For a few minutes there was only the whisper of our
breathing, then the rope began once more to ease over
the parapet, very very slowly.

"Now he's at the point where he'll be most easily
seen," said Mastro Natale.

We leaned out: he himself apparently knew it because
he was curled up as if to crawl into a hole. The rope
slipped on imperceptibly, guided by the three men
braced against the wall.

"If he gets hit by an arrow pull him up at once," I
said.

The farther down he dropped the more his body swung
back and forth at the end of the rope and his descent
proceeded by a series of jerks.

"We know," responded one of the men to my order.

We were all nervous now, myself as well as the men.
We were thinking that it was too late to save him, past
the point where we could help him in any way. There
were still about thirty feet to go; the rope was still
slipping slowly over the parapet, the men on tiptoe
looking downward, their muscles tensed.

"He made it," said Mastro Natale at last. All we
could see was a minuscule vortex and a slight rippling
at one point. The rope went slack on the parapet. None
of us moved for the full length of time we imagined it
would take him to swim under the water of the port a
few meters away from the Turks. I thought the fishermen
were figuring the exact number of strokes necessary to

get across those waters, which their own arms and legs were so well acquainted with. They followed him in silence. All at once Antonio De Raho said: "He's there."

Still silent, the fishermen pulled up the rope, their arms moving together in long strokes.

When I left the wall and crossed the cathedral piazza, I slackened my pace, feeling an emotion that was new for me. I wished I had been a man like one of those fishermen from Otranto.

Captain Zurlo VI

Don Felice was waiting for me at the castle, impatiently pacing up and down in the guard room on the ground floor.

"How did it go?"

"Very well. He made it across," I answered. "He'll find a horse at Minervino or Lecce and be in Naples in three days.

At that Don Felice's enthusiasm began to bubble up again. "What men these are, these simple folk. How can history keep them all in sight? What can be done to make sure their remarkable deeds reach the ears of posterity?"

"It would be enough for me if they reached the ears of the king, and he decided to send troops," I answered. "If we don't get reinforcements in a week it's all over."

A week passed with no sign of any troops, not even a shadow. The enemy assaults became more and more frequent; they had already breached the walls twice and our numbers were dwindling. Still, to tell the truth, my men were extraordinary: they had everything they needed to resist except weapons and invulnerable bodies. I still remember one of the fishermen, Colangelo – a fine young fellow who ate sardines with oil and whose obscure existence had nurtured a heroism one couldn't have foreseen. He died without a word, after single-handedly cutting down a whole crowd of Turks. Such acts are possible for humble men caught in the net of destiny, but this is something types like Don Giovanni Antonio de Foxa will never understand.

On the eighth day I was wounded in the shoulder while directing a counterattack on the west wall. The wound oozed blood for hours and obliged me to leave my post. I was in the armory of the castle when Don Felice presented himself and said without preliminaries: "I'm going up on the wall to fight."

"Why on earth do *you* want to go up there? You can't move the way you once could and within an hour they'll send you straight to the great beyond."

"I want to share the fate of these men," he said.

"Don Felice, for the love of God," I answered. "Otranto has enough troubles these days. There's no need to increase them by acts of sheer madness. What we require at this point is good sense."

He studied me with curiosity: "My poor friend," he exclaimed, "you're such a fine and sensible governor and yet you've never been happy."

I walked up to him, faced him down: "You aren't going up on the walls," I said emphatically. "You're going to stay right here and carry out your duties as commander. As master of the castle I could make this an order."

"I know what you want of me," he said slowly. "You want me to pay the ransom when the Turks enter Otranto. There isn't a Turk in the world who couldn't be swayed by my reserves of gold. And after that I should take care of my gout and eventually meet my death in a great canopied bed with wife, children and grandchildren standing around, and a bit further off, servants lined up against the walls listening to the priest recite: '*Libera, domine, animam eius sicut liberasti Danielum de lacu leonum* – Free his soul, oh Lord, as you freed Daniel from the lions' den.' Am I right?"

"Well, that wouldn't be such a bad thing," I said.

"Just so. People are always happy to see someone take his leave in such a proper and exemplary way. But this time, no." He sat down on a bench, looked me directly in the eye: "You see, Zurlo, at least once in each man's life there comes a time to prove himself. The moment always comes – for everyone. The Turks have brought it to us."

"Captain Zurlo! Captain Zurlo!" someone shouted from the cortile, whereupon Antonio Lubelli, one of the gentlemen of the council, burst in, all out of breath.

"What's happened?"

"Fanciullo's here. He's back from Naples."

"Fanciullo? But how did he make it through the Turkish lines?"

At that, Fanciullo appeared and abruptly fell to his knees in front of me. His naked torso was covered with blood and his arm was bleeding.

"Greetings to your lordship," he said panting.

"Where have you come from?"

"From Naples, sir."

"But how did you get through?"

"Yesterday during the attack on the Porticella there was so much dust and smoke that I was able to slip in among the Turks and get as far as the moat. It was full of mud so I made the sign of the cross and buried myself with just my mouth sticking out so I could breathe. The Turks passed by a few feet away but none of them saw me. At nightfall they began to withdraw toward their camp, shouting a lot strange words, full of *shee's* and *shah's* – must have been orders. One in particular had a really loud voice and some kind of wings on his head and everybody obeyed him. And then there were two or three stragglers who were playing games with their scimitars and laughing – you'd have thought they were men just like us."

"Then what did you do?" I asked.

"After that it got pretty dark and I crawled out of the mud and inched along on my belly to San Cosma's well. I remembered it had a common wall with the cellar of Palazzo Colussi. There were a lot of big rocks and sizable stones there. You'd have to see it to believe it. I climbed into the well. Luckily there wasn't much water in it and I could breathe all right as I swam."

"But the water in the well is poisoned," I said, amazed.

"I thought of that, sir, because I remembered the first day when they came you ordered us to poison all the wells. I said in my mind: 'Be careful Giovanni, you mustn't let yourself drink a single drop.' I had a dagger tied to my breeches just in case somebody saw me. I'd have fixed it so they'd take my body but my soul would already be gone. But, thank God, no one noticed me. Then I remembered the walls of the well were plastered over pretty thin and the stone underneath was the kind of soft tufa you can cut with a knife. So I got busy with my dagger scraping through the plaster. It was really damp everywhere and there was almost no light – like when you go night fishing and the sky is cloudy. It took a few hours to get through the plaster. I could already feel the tufa dust with the palms of my hands, but my arm was getting so tired I rested for a bit, doing a dead man's float in the water. Then some pieces of tufa began to flake off and I pitched them into the well and little by little the hole got bigger. When it was big enough for me to fit into I clambered up and with one somersault I landed in the cellars of Palazzo Colussi."

"You've done something really extraordinary, Fanciullo," I exclaimed.

But he said, "No sir, it wasn't that hard."

"And if the well had been completely full of water, what would you have done?"

"Oh well, sir, I'd have died. Then it would have been hard."

"Fanciullo, did you see the king in person?"

"Yessir. He agreed to see me and asked me first thing if the Spanish soldiers were fighting well. So I told him they'd fled over the walls the second night with *zuche*. He thought a minute, then said: 'What are these *zuche*?' So a courtier explained how we make these kinds of ropes out of hemp and rushes, and the king didn't say any more."

He rummaged in his breeches for a few seconds, then drew out a bulging length of reed: "Here's the answer for your lordship," he said, "but I never saw a single sign of any militia along the road, not a soldier, not even one. Nobody's coming to Otranto to help us."

I opened the reed and took out a parchment from the royal chancery. It acknowledged my letter, noting that it had been placed in the hands of his majesty the king, that he had read it with infinite and heartfelt sorrow, that he affirmed it would indeed be a shame if a city as beautiful and prosperous as Otranto should fall into Turkish hands and therefore we ought to resist with all our strength in expectation of the arrival of Duke Alfonso, who would soon take the matter in hand, would in fact already be in Otranto if he but had the wings of Pegasus and the power of Midas to transform stones into gold. Furthermore his majesty had full confidence in his magnanimous subjects, the defenders of Otranto, since he knew them to be so desirous of honor in this life as well as in the next. I handed the letter to Antonio Lubelli and Don Felice: "The king has rushed to our aid with parchments," I said.

"Oh, kingdom of Naples," exclaimed Don Felice, "breeding ground of beauty and gentle genius and always in a state of hopeless desperation!"

"Look to this man here!" I shouted as Fanciullo, after teetering back and forth on his knees, fell to the floor in a faint.

"Who knows how long it's been since he's eaten," said Antonio Lubelli, while two men lifted him and carried him off.

"As long as it's not poison from the well," I said.

Don Felice exclaimed in a loud voice: "The day of the great chanceries is over. The people who wrote these parchments are completely incapable of imagining how the matters committed to their care ought to be dealt with."

"Chanceries are the least of our worries," I replied. "The fact is that Europe is caught up in an immense power game in which we are only a pawn."

"Perhaps we are the pawn that will determine the outcome of the game," said Don Felice.

"I'm going back to the walls," said Antonio Lubelli and went out.

"However," added Don Felice, "history will render justice." Ever since the Turks had landed in Otranto, Don Felice had been all excited about the idea of history. As for me, I had other things to think about: there was almost no one left on the east section of the walls and the way things were going we wouldn't be able to last more than two or three days. In addition every once in a while I had particularly painful moments when a question, always the same one, popped into my mind: "Will Giovanello survive?" Thus that day I didn't give any more thought to Don Felice or to his resolution to go up and die on the walls. It was Teodoro who reminded me about it, running after me that evening as I crossed the piazzella after inspecting the walls.

"Don Francesco," he called, waving his arms so erratically he looked like a puppet.

"What is it?"

"I'm scared...."

"Eh, well chin up. We're all scared."

"But I'm not scared for myself, I'm scared for Don Felice."

"What's happened to him?"

"He's acting very odd this evening. He took his sacred books and put them in a little box and told me, 'I'm giving them to you, Teodoro. And I'm giving you these too,' and he handed me a bunch of gold chains. Then he said, 'Let's sit down here for a few minutes, Teodoro,' and he drank an entire flask of old wine. He's sleeping now."

"Let him sleep, and when he wakes up tell him to come and look for me at once. Tell him I need him."

"Yessir," said Teodoro. "Can we still win, Don Francesco?"

"Of course we can win."

"It's stifling though, this evening. I'd say it's going to rain, Don Francesco. We need a good shower; it'd clear out our blood. And anyway summer showers give strength. Oh and I meant to tell you something else: after he'd been drinking Don Felice said Don Alfonso wasn't going to come to our aid after all. Is that true?"

"What does Don Felice know about it?" I answered. "Get back to him now, Teodoro and don't leave him alone for a single minute. Do you understand? Not even a minute."

I saw Don Felice the following day – stretched out on a table in the castle armory, bleeding. Teodoro had come to get me in a great hurry up on the west tower where I was attending to the mortar.

"Captain, Captain, Don Felice went up on the walls and now he's dying. Please come, for goodness sake, come with me!"

"Dying?"

"Oh yes, he's been mortally wounded."

"But what did you do? Why didn't you send him to me?"

"He told me he was going to see you, sir. When he woke up he said, 'Well, how's it going Teodoro? I slept in my clothes.' He seemed to be in a good mood. Then he said, 'Everything's all right now. This little sleep was just what I needed.' Then I helped him up and told him, 'Captain Zurlo wants to see you right away,' and he answered, 'He must be worried about me. How nice all this is,' and then he went out."

I rushed down and when I reached him I found Giovanello standing by the table. Don Felice was looking at him.

"I'm happy now," Don Felice was saying, "it's all over." Then he turned to me: "My friend I beg you, don't upset yourself. Don't start in with your logic..."

"Where are you hurt?"

"In the stomach, I think."

"Is the pain very bad?"

"Bad enough."

"We're going to treat your wounds now and then transport you to your own bed."

"Don't bother, Zurlo." He was breathing with difficulty. Placing his hand just below his throat, he said, with a shadow of a smile: "I'm already dead up to here." After we moved him to his bed he fainted twice; he had lost a lot of blood. When he recovered consciousness the second time, he said, "Here in Otranto I've found happiness."

"Try to rest now," I answered.

"I wasn't resigned....You understand?"

Then he began to ramble deliriously.

I returned to the walls to organize a last counter-attack, my thoughts still fixed on Don Felice. The Otrantini had assembled rakes, woodcutters' axes and scythes; by now we were fast approaching the end. When I got back to see Don Felice at night, he was still alive

and no longer delirious. Teodoro motioned to me as if
he had something to say, so we went into the next room.

"What is it?" I asked.

"Don Francesco," he said, distressed. "He wants to
die now, but he can't."

"What?"

"Well, no, he can't. You know how it is: the soul has
to settle all its affairs before it takes its leave. Have
you ever seen how people will wait for a relative who
lives far away? The carriage finally arrives, the relative
gets out, goes up to the bedroom, the dying person
looks at him, takes one last breath and dies. It's the
same when somebody kills himself for love. He seems
to be already dead, but when he hears the woman's voice
he opens his eyes, she kisses him and then he dies."

"What the devil are you trying to say? What is it you
want, for God's sake?"

"Don Francesco, you've got to send for the woman,
the one called Idrusa. He's waiting for her."

"Did he tell you that?"

"No! But there are things you just know."

I looked at Teodoro in astonishment. He stared back
at me with determination.

"You have to send for her," he repeated. I was
perplexed. But after all....

"Go get her," I sighed, "dispatch someone to the
cathedral to tell the monks."

He ran off like a squirrel.

And Don Felice died. The following night, the last
one before Otranto fell, after I had finally prevailed
upon Giovanello to get a couple of hours of sleep, I
went up to the terrace of the castle in the prey of a
sudden urge to return to the place where he and I and
Don Felice used to sit and talk while the city slept and
the final heat of the day rose from the still-warmed
stone of the houses to encounter the cool damp of the
night. Those were good times! Although Don Felice and

Giovanello had the *idée fixe* that I didn't pay enough attention to the complex of things they called the poetry of nature, I still found pleasure in contemplating the vast space of the sky, inhabited as it was by an infinite number of moving bodies. They were wondrous to me for their pleasant order, their perfect harmony – sensations I sought in vain on earth. Besides, the idea of limpid, eternally arid space provided a startling contrast to my sense of terrestrial dampness, so prevalent during those southern nights, a damp that conferred upon our earth, this domain of men, a hint of things impure and tired and transient.

But that night, in the depth of that very night, I saw the celestial vault with different eyes, a revelation whose full meaning I couldn't quite grasp and one which challenged all my mental acuity. As I watched the wavering lights of the stars the power of the heavens overwhelmed me, as if gazing into the limitless distance would lead me to be drawn into it, *velis et remis* – with sails and oars – until I drowned there. "It's because your nerves are on edge," I told myself, "and because the end is near." Don Felice was dead. And I myself? When would I die? A few moments after asking this question I saw the ball of the earth divided in two. On one side was all of daily life's infinity of things in motion, a busy swarm of deeds done with maximum energy, then undone with the same fervor. On the other side were those few hidden things in a man's life that never mix in his daily activities because they are impossible to buy or sell, so that they alone survive those activities and form a tiny procession to accompany him to his death, along with his enlarged liver, his unsteady heart and his hardened arteries. Nonetheless, since during the course of my existence I had developed a firmly entrenched habit of rational argumentation, I told myself my state of mind had been described too many times in literature and elsewhere for me to be surprised at experiencing it. My thoughts were simply moving step by step closer to death. Besides I had to admit that my good health could still give me a small hope of postponement; *verbi gratia* a day or two. I sat down on the railing of the terrace and for a few minutes thought of nothing. Below me was Otranto, half concealed in the impenetrable night. I could distinguish the dark mass of the cathedral and the buildings along the main street, from all appearances immersed in sleep – hundreds of years old they were, these habitations where so many men had spent their lives, where so many women had woven clothes of silk and wool during the long winter days, the gold bangles on their arms jingling against their tiny looms. "Tomorrow," I thought, "or the next day, there'll be a great uproar after which the Turks will be dining, singing and falling asleep inside the walls of these houses. In the meantime I will already have fluttered away like a dragonfly, into the realm of the heavens, assuming there is a realm of the heavens that concerns us, assuming there really is Someone keeping it in reserve for us."

From that point on I stopped considering anything at all and kept my eyes focused on the dense darkness in front of me. I must admit that my thoughts that night were moving *pedibus aegris in sententiam* – with tired feet toward definition. They lacked the richness of perspective and ornament that comes when the thinker is seated in a deserted room with a book in hand and the mind, like a good lantern, carries out its normal function of casting light around itself. Still, at a certain point I began to realize the important thing wasn't what would become of me, but what I had already been. It's unlikely that the idea of what we have been makes us happy, far from it, but at least it constitutes a reference point, the only one we can hold on to as we confront the end: my wife, my children, my house in

Naples came to my mind, radiating a kind of splendor
that reflected on me as well. In them I saw the life I
had lived, but I saw it with a new tolerance for all,
almost a love for all – no longer the bright lucid love
of the past but a warm and quiet love that brought
peace. I thought of the first thing my son Giovannello
had written and signed with his own hand. He was seven
years old: "Everything is fine. I went swimming and I
made a very big sand castle. Yesterday a little pigeon
hatched." Yes, yes, everything was fine, if it hadn't been
for the sharp pang of nostalgia now enveloping every
memory. The nostalgia of departure. Then, all at once,
I was seized by a chilling blast of solitude, as violent as
a sudden gust of wind. The silence of the night became
the silence of the grave. I took a few steps along the
terrace and then behind me I heard a soft thump in the
direction of the inside parapet. I turned around and saw
a dark shapeless mass swaying back and forth in a
corner.

"Who's there?" I shouted.

"It's me, Don Francesco," answered Teodoro's voice.

"What are you doing here?"

He was sitting crosslegged on the ground, just as he
often did on the floor of the house when he was having a
fit of the sulks at Don Felice. The thump had probably
been due to his temporarily dozing off and losing his
balance. Who knows how long he'd been there, perfectly
still. I hadn't even noticed him when I came out on the
terrace.

"I'm praying for Don Felice."

"Go on now and get some sleep. Tomorrow's going to
be a bad day. The Turks may well break through."

"I don't give any thought to the Turks, Don
Francesco. With the gold chains my master left me, I'll
be able to pay the ransom. My thoughts are for Don
Felice. Can you tell me what blows he's taking now?"

"What blows? He's dead."

126

"But that's what I mean. You know how he is. He
confessed and received communion, so it's sure he won't
go to the inferno – but purgatory – eh, with that
business of the woman from Otranto, who knows how
long he'll have to spend there. Can't you give me some
idea what his punishment will be, when they'll sentence
him? Happy as he was, he'll be arriving there all
confused. But if I keep on praying then they'll reduce
the sentence. In my town people say if you pray for
somebody every once in awhile his soul gets to come
out of the flames of divine punishment and go to a cool
damp room where water drips from the walls, so the
soul gets some relief from the suffering it has to
endure day and night."

"Good," I answered. "So you want to stay here, is that
it?"

"Yessir, but you should go down and sleep because you
have a big job to do. I saw you praying earlier."

"Who, me?" I said dumbfounded.

"Eh, oh yessir. It's nothing to be ashamed of. Prayer
is man's strength."

"Well, good-bye then to you as well, Teodoro," I
answered, going back to my previous thoughts.

"Sleep well, Don Francesco," he replied, "and may
God give all of us the grace not to despair if the Turks
break through."

The next day the Turks did break through, at the San
Francesco gate. When I realized the end had come I
ordered all bells to be rung joyfully as if the
Neapolitan militia were arriving. The trick worked for
a few hours and the enemy interrupted the assault and
regrouped all their men on the other side of the moat
in a defensive position. But since nobody came, a little
before noon they launched their final attack. They
filled up the moats, and fired all their artillery at
once, but without loading it, so they wouldn't hit their
own men, simply cover them with smoke as they crept

forward on their bellies. I was on the part of the wall
nearest the cathedral by an arch of porous crumbly
stone resembling tufa – the Turks had concentrated
their major forces at that point. Here I called all the
men together who were still able to fight. It was early
afternoon. Luck smiled on us for yet a little while, the
weather too. Huge clouds began to blow in from the
southeast to diminish the heat of the sun. At that
moment Mastro Natale came up to me and said:
"Captain Zurlo, take shelter in the cathedral. The men
will need you later to arrange the surrender."

"Look, Mastro Natale, will you take charge of my
son, get him away quickly?"

"It's no use for you to die now," he answered.

"I'll withdraw with the last men left. Go now."

"As you wish, sir. And on behalf of all the Otrantini,
my greatest respect." He acted as if he were about to
sneeze. The old man was moved.

"Good-bye Mastro Natale," I said.

Then Captain de li Falconi shouted: "Zurlo, they're
coming in the breach," So I stood up and with what
voice I had left in my throat gave the last order: "Run,
get inside the cathedral. Save yourselves." While I was
repeating: "Save yourselves," waving my sword in the air
the Turks took aim, hitting me in the chest, and I went
down. I didn't feel much pain, more than anything else
just a hard blow as I fell, followed by a clouding of my
vision. "So this is how it feels to die," I thought. "It's
not so difficult. I guess I really can just slip away now.
No, it's not at all difficult."

PART II

Idrusa I

Of course I went barefoot, like all the fishermen's wives, except unlike the others, I carefully knotted my hair and held it in place with cords of bright colored silk: my desire to be beautiful never deserted me. Often I'd walk out by myself through the main gate of the city and down to the olive trees at Rocamatura, just like a little boy who sets off alone and then gets all taken up with the wonder of being alive and wanders aimlessly for hours. Looking at the olives sloping down toward the sea on either side of the rocks, with parts of their roots exposed to the sun, I'd wonder why men didn't go mad with the urge to live among the trees. The oddest thing about Rocamatura was the rounded sand dunes where white lilies grew on tall thick stems. I'd walk along, sinking up to my knees in the sand, until I reached the point, then lie down with my hands behind my head and stay there maybe for an hour, staring at a lily moving in the breeze, asking it: "What does it take to be happy?" The seagulls would be flying above the rocks, the seacrows among the olive branches. But when in my life did this begin? There must have been a mistake at some point. So I'd think back carefully over the years, one by one, searching my memory – no use. Then, little by little, I'd start to feel sad because I could no longer enjoy the olive grove and the birds flying through the air. I'd get up abruptly and begin gathering capers and putting them together in bunches: fifty big ones, fifty medium sized and fifty little ones. Counting helps a lot sometimes. When I left home to become Antonio's wife I was seventeen. Since I was an orphan my sister and brother-in-law had arranged the marriage. In those days I was consumed with the desire to be a good wife, skilled at keeping every corner of the house clean, expert at washing clothes on the terrace and making pasta. True, at night when he held me tight in his arms, overcome with a fury that made him breathe like an asthmatic, it was all a mystery to me and I'd lie there motionless, my eyes wide open in the dark, feeling sick to my stomach. But the next morning I'd be eager to begin again, cleaning and cooking and fixing a lunch for Antonio to take with him in the boat. I'd put some special treat in it, like capers from San Damiano. They were small and especially tasty because they grew between the rocks and the sea where they couldn't lose their moisture and stayed hard on the outside and juicy underneath. When he came home I was happy and I'd start to sing; but some days all of a sudden I just didn't want to see him.

In the evening after the sun went down beside the Serpe Tower, we'd sit out by the well in the middle of of our little cortile, where we could watch the sea. Antonio wasn't one to talk much and even less with me; like all the fishermen he was bored with talking to women about unnecessary things. One evening he said to me suddenly: "You know, for a while now I've been thinking about getting you another house, different from this one."

"How come?" I said, completely amazed.

"This one's damp and gloomy. I know you don't like it."

"But how can you hope to get another one?"

"I'll just work so hard I'll manage it." Looking off in the distance he added, "It'll be full of sunlight and we'll sit across from each other at the table and the windows'll be open."

"A new house," I murmured, "good lord!"

"I can tell you're not happy here. You're used to the country, the farm." He took my hand and squeezed it in both of his, lost in thought.

I cried out: "Look! Out there in the strait – a pair of fishing smacks from Brindisi."

"Really?" he said absently. He brought the palm of my hand to his mouth and began kissing it. The two fishing smacks seemed to stay in the same place. Could it be that he didn't even see them because I was sitting beside him? Didn't he hear the mule stamping and pawing with his hooves in Compare Pietro's stable?"

"Idrusa," he said softly, "do you really care about me?"

"Why shouldn't I?" I felt his arms around me. Then he picked me up and carried me into the house: "You're the most beautiful woman in Otranto," he said, "the most beautiful in the world. Your skin is white, your breasts smell like perfume." I was astounded to hear him talk like that.

We made love. I caressed his hair, his neck, his shoulders. But that night a curious thought came to me: I was like a farm, a portion of which the farmer had plowed and sown with grain that was flourishing in the rich soil, while the rest had been left to grow up to brambles and wild fennel bushes.

The next day my sister came down from the plateau to help me with the laundry. I washed the clothes first, then she put them in the big clay tub and covered them with ashes. When the cauldron in the kitchen was almost boiling, she began to pour the scalding water on the ashes with a pitcher, moving her arm in circles. The odor of soda and ashes in the rising steam mixed with the wood smoke and hung over the big tub as well as over my wash tub, and over the terracotta oil jars and the stools piled high with laundry. Then the smoke increased and poured out the kitchen door in great billows carrying the smell of burning wood. I looked up from my tub: "When you and Pietro got married, did it make you happy?"

"What do you mean, happy?" she answered, coughing from the smoke and busy with what she was doing. She went into the kitchen and began poking the stove, yelling at me: "May I ask why you put in the new wood when there was old wood left? Didn't you even notice it was green?" I went back to soaping the clothes. When she came back out into the cortile I took my hands out of the water and straightened up: "Listen," I said, "I'm fond of Antonio but I don't love him."

"Hush, don't talk nonsense," she answered, continuing to pour boiling water and wiping her eyes, teary from the smoke.

I shouted, impatient, "I don't feel anything at all when he makes love to me, nothing, nothing at all."

My sister went inside to the cauldron, added cold water, and regulated the fire by taking out a piece of smoking green wood, which she threw into a basin of water where it began to sizzle. As she came out into the cortile again she said, "That's not normal. You should look after yourself better. Take a little herbal wine in the morning with some biscuits. You need something in your stomach – it's weakness that makes the blood frigid."

I was twisting a sheet into a rope to squeeze out the water and at that I slapped it angrily down on the board and shouted: "But I don't love him. I *do not love him!*"

She came around from behind the tub and stood in front of me: "What's gotten into you?" she said, severe. "We found you a good man, prepared you a nice trousseau, made all sorts of sacrifices to get you married and now you come out with this kind of nonsense. Marriage is God's affair; you have to honor it."

Smoke began pouring out of the kitchen again, burning our eyes and irritating our throats. All that burning and irritation was beginning to go to our heads.

I shouted, "But I'm not happy. So what happens now?"

"Stop it, Idrusa. Do me that favor. Hurry up with the wash. Otherwise the tub will get too hot and the ashes will turn the sheets yellow."

I went back to washing in a rage. I could always put an end to things by killing myself, I thought, but I didn't like the idea of not being able to talk any more, or bathe in the sea – of being eaten by worms. "You know what we could do?" said my sister. "We could make an anchovy pie so as not to waste the coals."

She went back in the kitchen, shook the oven door, then took the mixing board and set to work kneading the dough, cutting up a round cheese and cleaning anchovies. Every once in a while she called to me: "Are you finished washing?"

"No," I answered.

By the time I said "yes," she'd already put the pie on the coals to bake.

"Good," she said, "we've got everything done."

"What's going on here? Is the house on fire?" shouted Antonio as he came in from the cortile. We hadn't expected him so soon and at first we didn't know what to say. My sister got hold of herself first: "The wood's green" she said, "it's smoking."

"It's not the wood," answered Antonio. "Everything here is old, the chimney too – it won't draw. We need a new house, a house with more space and fresh air."

"A house with more space and fresh air?" That day my sister was being hit with one surprise after another.

"Right, we've got to buy another house."

"With what?" asked my sister.

"I'll go out fishing day and night. I'll make twice as much," he answered, determined.

"And you'll ruin your health, which is a gift from God," she said. My sister was particularly pleased to note God's part in everything.

Instead of answering, Antonio came up to me and touched my hair in a quick caress, while his eyes said he wanted the house for me, wanted to see me happy. May I be damned if I didn't want to be a good wife to him. I swear I did. I smiled at him, and to do even better I put my arms around his neck and gave him a kiss, right there in front of my sister. She picked up her laundry to take home, looked back at me from the door and said," My dear sister, you're just like a rainbow."

Idrusa II

It was the month of September and the city was holding a grand celebration to welcome Don Felice Ayerbo of Aragon, *adelantado* of the Spanish militias to the domain of Otranto. He'd arrived by land from the interior, passing through Lecce and Minervino with his rich retinue of high officials in their crimson and black striped robes and cloaks of fine cloth. Don Felice, a heavy white-haired man, was clad in a silver cloak and carried a sword and a silken purse, while his escort of Spanish soldiers followed majestically in their short skirts of shiny armor. They knew our people didn't like them, so they tried to impress us with pomp and ceremony. That's how it happened that on the twenty-ninth of September, the feast of the so-called Doctor Saints, Cosma and Damiano, there was a grand procession on the sea to honor Don Felice. To be sure, the fishermen, who expected a tramontana, had advised against it, but the Spanish command, always suspicious of the Otrantini's ideas, insisted. There were a hundred boats on the water rocking in the wind, with the ladies and gentlemen of the city on board, dressed up in their fine clothes of a thousand different colors and reveling in the sound of bagpipes. They made a pretty spectacle out there on the sea and gave Otranto the look of a wealthy pleasure-loving city. Bobbing up and down on the waves in Mastro Natale's boat, the statues of Saints Cosma and Damiano made their entrance, swaying in the wind on their canopied platform, like two saplings hung with decorations for a holy day. Toward them and against the flat blue background of the sea came the Basilian monks from San Càsole, they too rocked by the motion of the waves, their faces peering out of the hoods of their long gray habits. All the men and women were dancing on the sea in a huge crowd, ladies with silk sleeves, blacksmiths and wool trimmers, soldiers...what a happy picture of life it all made!

Only the fishermen, sweaty from rowing against the wind and worrying about a storm, stood out from the others because of the sober distant expression on their dark weatherbeaten faces.

Antonio, who was one of the strongest oarsmen between Otranto and Cape Santa Maria di Leuca, strong enough to bring in a boat in the worst of northerly storms, was rowing the saints' boat under Mastro Natale's direction. Meanwhile I sat beside Assunta in Colangelo's boat as he kept a steady rhythm with his oars in the moving greenish water where the algae rose from the bottom and twisted around itself like eels. When we got to the caves half way to Rocamatura Point, the sea became rough and the boats began to pitch and turn off course.

"Hard to port," ordered Mastro Natale, alert and level-headed as always, standing up in the stern of the boat with the saints.

Offshore, according to a fixed law of the sea, the waves were rolling up to the point and then a moment later reversing themselves to splash back over the boats in a burst of spray. At first this delighted everybody, especially the ladies, who'd never been out to sea in the tramontana. People squealed for joy. But then, little by little their enthusiasm diminished and they began to be frightened – as if they'd found themselves in the midst of something that had nothing to do with the procession, some secret urge for violent orgy that rose from the surface of the sea.

"Is it dangerous, is it really dangerous?" the Spanish soldiers asked the fishermen.

"It's the natural course of the wind," shouted Mastro Natale, "it'll calm down when the sun sets."

"Should we turn back?" asked a frightened Spanish officer.

"No," Mastro Natale answered roughly, "right now it'd be tough to land on the rocks; some of the boats might break up. After sunset it'll be child's play."

"Are you sure you know what you're talking about, my good man?" asked the officer.

That kind of idle talk annoyed Mastro Natale and he gave the Spaniards a hard look, but said nothing.

Colangelo too seemed annoyed. He was watching the princess of Tricase's little boy, who was whimpering and hanging onto his mother's skirts.

"That little snot-nose is scared to death," he said. "He'll be a prince some day and we'll all have to bow down to him and kiss his hand."

We were close to the boat with the saints and Antonio leaned out: "Idrusa," he called to me, "the saints want to dance our *pizzica pizzica*."

"What if the sea won't keep them afloat?" replied Colangelo, but just for something to say, because we were used to the sea and we knew the difference between one tramontana and another.

"What do you mean not keep them afloat?" intervened Assunta. "Dear Jesus!"

"What if the sea doesn't like the Spaniards any more than we do?" answered Colangelo.

"Something bad will happen if we bring hatred into processions too," said Assunta.

"If I'm bringing hatred, it's because I can't stand those people," said Colangelo, and suddenly he started talking in a low voice to himself, asking questions and then answering them in a give-and-take of conversation: "Ah yes, your graces, perhaps you think so because you're all dressed up in fancy clothes, eh? But you won't last. The devil take you."

"Hush," begged Assunta in a subdued tone, crossing her fingers. "Hush now. What if one of them heard you?"

In fact just to our right was a big boat full of Spanish soldiers with an officer seated at its prow. He had finely chiseled features and olive skin with metallic highlights brought out by the sun. His dark intense eyes contrasted with the indolent pose of his body and anyone who looked at him would think of those bittersweet fruits that torment the palate with their unstable taste. I watched him closely because he was the handsomest man at the whole celebration. If he wasn't, then my destiny had already begun to confuse me.

"Who knows what far away places they come from?" said Assunta.

"Professional soldiers like living in a lot of different places," answered Colangelo. "They don't have the same tastes as we do."

"What do you know about it?'" said Assunta. "They have somebody they love somewhere, just like anybody else."

"If they did, they'd stay there."

"You can't be sure," said Assunta. "It's like with fish. Some get caught in nets and others don't."

"Not at all," Colangelo retorted. "Fish carry out God's will; Spaniards don't. The devil take them. Look at that one over there, the way he's rowing – a fisherman in the middle of a malaria attack could do better."

Assunta said no more, afraid he'd lose his temper. Like his father before him, he was pretty excitable on the subject of the Spaniards in Otranto.

As for me, I just felt it was great to be alive, there in the midst of all those ladies in their silk dresses with the bagpipes playing. Even the gray rocks speckled with black were part of life. I was seeing the world extending before me in an endless plain like the surface of the sea, all sown with beautiful things, when I noticed the Spanish officer again. He was sitting there in the prow of the boat next to us and staring at me with intense curiosity. I looked back at him, lowered my eyes, then quickly looked up again. He was still staring at me. I was surprised, then annoyed and I quickly switched my gaze to San Cosma, whose clay hands were holding a medical book and a long pen, also made of clay. At that moment our boats rounded Rocamatura Point and the Alimini Marshes appeared on the horizon, with the faint outline of the coast and the pine groves beyond them toward Brindisi.

"We've just about made it," said Colangelo. "The sea's calm past the point."

"It wasn't so bad after all," said Assunta.

People in the boats began to call out again to show their satisfaction: it's hard not to when you're in such festive company. The cheerful mood spread from boat to boat, livening up conversations and increasing the gentlemen's gallantry, the effect of which was easy to see in the sparkling eyes of the ladies.

I can honestly say that when I noticed the Spanish officer still looking at me I didn't quite know what to make of this new state of affairs. At that very instant the military trumpets sounded and sudden silence followed. Then Archbishop Pendinelli, who was born a long, long time ago, spoke up. He was a tall man and thin as a reed in the marsh, his voice feeble, his lips pale, as he blessed the waves of the sea. Gazing at length into the blue sky, he prayed to Saints Cosma and Damiano, who'd been chosen by God, he said, to heal souls as well as bodies, asking them to distribute their grace and forgive men's foolishness on this festive day. He explained that a long time ago Cosma and Damiano were famous doctors in a country called Cilicia. They took care of the sick but wanted no pay, believing that money itself was the root of all evil and thus in the universal litany of saints they were called *anàrgiri*. At this point people looked from one boat to another asking what on earth that word meant, so strange did it sound to all of them. Then the monks chanted a Te Deum of thanks and the fishermen's muscles turned the boats around while birds gilded by the setting sun flew off toward the west. I was thinking maybe once upon a time Saints Cosma and Damiano had also liked to go out and have a good time drinking and joking with women. Maybe they hadn't even said prayers or thought about God at all until suddenly one day they were taking care of a leper's wounds and they discovered the truth in that poor leper and from then on completely forgot their former life.

The Spanish soldiers' boat came up beside us again. "With the whole sea out there, we have to have them right on top of us," grumbled Colangelo.

"Oh what are you complaining about? They aren't bothering us," said Assunta.

"Not you maybe," he answered, "but they're bothering me because they don't know how to row. Look now, if I don't watch out every minute they'll be hitting us broadside."

In fact they were passing extremely close. I thought the officer was directing them this way so he could take his time and get a good look at me. Once in a while I'd give in and return his gaze, then resist again and stare off in the distance to where the setting sun shone red on the towers of Otranto. It was like a game: I looked back at him again, then at the long line of boats and the sea, where the saints mingled with the crowd and everybody, whether they knew each other or not, seemed to be friends.

It was a long way back against the evening wind, which blew in the opposite direction from the afternoon. When Mastro Natale commanded at intervals: "Hard to starboard," or "Oars on the port side," his voice rang out clear and firm, seeming to come from above that old body standing upright on the planks in the stern of the boat. All at once I wanted the procession to be over, ended years ago. So when people got out of the boats and the port was full of gentlemen and ladies, colors and banners, just like a fairy tale, I left them all and hurried off to the old borgo. When I reached my house I went inside, slammed the door, opened the big chest, took off and put away my fancy dress, then closed the chest again. I was back in my everyday black apron when the bells began to ring for the Ave Maria; I stood there at the foot of the bed listening to the sound fading slowly through the leaves of the garden, then down toward the sea, rocked by the soft air in one sad note followed by a clear chiming. Something had happened inside me and I didn't know what it was.

Antonio came in late from the tavern, excited and tipsy from wine. He held out his arms and wanted to make love right away. Afterwards I fell asleep. When I woke up the next morning and Antonio had already gone out to set his lines, I sat up straight in bed. "This life is no good," I thought. "I have to do something about it, maybe work harder." With that in mind I got up and began to busy myself with the housework. I was drawing water from the well when the idea came to me: "Embroidery!" I exclaimed to myself. I left the water bucket on the wall, and sat down on the ground by the well: "That's it, openwork on fine linen backing, just like the women on the main road make. I'll sell my work for trousseaus and help Antonio make more money." The idea appealed to me; when I was a little girl my sister had sent me to one of those women to learn that kind of embroidery. I knew the pattern for little figures of men and women and stars, as well as the stitches for other shapes, like the different kinds of pasta.

I did the necessary shopping that very day and the next morning I was already sitting in the cortile pulling threads through the backing to start my edging and eyelets. Doing embroidery left me a lot of time to daydream, and it was indeed during one of my needle's passes back and forth on the same spot that the image of the Spanish officer came to me. I recalled how he'd sat watching me intently from the prow of the military boat. That, I remember, was the first time I thought about him. Just for an instant, no more, and I hardly gave the matter any importance. After two busy months I sold my first embroidery. "Look at this," I said regarding the coins in my hand, "real money. Enough of these and everything will change."

I raced down to the port like a boat under full sail. Antonio was just pushing off to start a day's fishing. "I've sold some embroidery," I shouted from the pier, and he waved his arm in cheery acknowledgement.

"I won't be back till after dark," he answered.

I waved to him and started home, but I hadn't gone twenty paces when I turned and ran back again to the pier to hold up the money so he could see it.

"I'm going to buy more linen," I shouted.

He nodded yes as he untied the boat from its moorings.

I set off again, but a few steps further on I turned and went back to the pier once more: "I think I'll get a new dress too," I shouted.

He looked at me for a while this time, then smiled: "All right, I get it," he said. "You're going to spend it all on a dress."

Unfortunately, that's what I did. There were so many different fabrics in the store, including one flowered one, so beautiful that the minute I saw it I imagined a wonderful formal robe, split just below the bust to flare out in a wide skirt. My imagination chased all other thoughts out of my head and feasting my eyes on the damask brocade I felt really happy.

But when my sister saw it she seemed to take leave of her sanity and began to scream at me so loud that people heard her from the street and the neighbor women arrived in great haste.

"Just look what she's done!" she said, "Look at this mad woman! A brocade fit for a grand lady while Antonio's working so hard he doesn't even take time to sleep."

The women fingered the brocade and shook their heads in distress.

Only Antonio, when he returned, came to my defense. He said I lived in my own world; I hadn't yet entered the real one. But one of these days I would and then I'd have an easier time of it.

That night after I went to bed I couldn't sleep. I was unhappy with myself and felt I'd done something stupid. Antonio said nothing, didn't even move. "Maybe he's already asleep," I thought, staring wide-eyed into the darkness. My mind was all topsy turvy and suddenly out of the confusion popped the Spanish officer.

It was the second time I'd recalled him. But this time the thought stayed with me. I knew absolutely nothing about him but just the way he looked made him seem to be the exact opposite of Antonio: handsome, elegant, refined, and with a certain carefree manner. I tried to think about something else but for some reason that night nothing else would come to my mind – just the thought of the officer. Besides who was going to see him again anyway? It was a bit like being inside a fairy tale where you can go on with the story as far as you please.

"Idrusa," Antonio said suddenly.

"You're not asleep?" I was amazed.

"No, but I'm going to sleep now...I just wanted to say...." He interrupted himself, then began again: "Listen Idrusa, whatever you think about you know God's there to see into your heart and he knows about it. But that doesn't scare you or make you ashamed, does it? Because it's only natural for God to see everything."

"Well, yes," I answered. "Only natural."

"When a woman gets married," he said, "God's not the only one on earth to see what's going on in her heart, her husband's there too. And she shouldn't be scared or ashamed. She should tell him everything, just like she does with God. Am I right? What do you think?"

"You're right."

"Good," said Antonio. "Now we can go to sleep. It's late."

Idrusa III

One evening at vespers, as the sun sank into the sea, its rays now touching only the rooftops, and the fishermen in port were hauling their boats out of the water onto the cobblestones, carefully putting away their ropes, clay jugs and lanterns inside them, I was crossing the cathedral piazza, happy with my rapid solitary walk amid the palazzi, when I came upon the Spanish officer. There he stood, a few paces in front of me, just outside the entrance to the governor's house, talking with two gentlemen. I stopped, glued to the pavement. He looked at me, first absently, then more intently as though trying to recall something, not sure what. Then suddenly he seemed to remember, smiled, left his companions where they were and came over to me.

"Good evening," he said, very politely.

"Good evening," I stammered and found myself inside the world of his dark eyes, a marvelous world indeed. Had it been up to me, I wouldn't have opened my mouth again.

"I haven't seen you since the day of the procession. Do you live in Otranto?" His gaze passed over my entire body from head to toe and I felt a rush of emotion and shame.

Just then Cola Mazzapinta, who was also crossing the piazza, came up beside us for a moment, never taking his eyes off both of us, his face set in a disapproving frown. What's more, as he turned away at the end of the piazza, he directed a questioning gesture toward me, as if to say: "What the devil are you doing?" then disappeared.

"So then, where do you live?" the officer persisted.

"In the old borgo, in the fishermen's alley."

"Are you married?"

"Yes," I answered. Did it make any difference to him? Apparently not. He continued to smile and calmly went on talking.

"Do you work?"

"I do openwork embroidery on linen," I said.

"Openwork on linen," he repeated, "that beautiful embroidery with designs of little men and stars?"

I nodded yes.

"Who taught you people how to make those pretty designs?"

"They were brought from across the sea," I said, "a long time ago."

"I like them."

"They're an old custom." I'd never considered our embroidery designs especially pretty, and even at that moment I couldn't really manage to give such an idea much thought. I'd been overcome with an urge to get away. "Good evening," I said, but at that he took hold

144

of both my hands, like children do when they want to play ring-around-the-rosy. He held on tightly and I was frightened. Was it going to be simple or wasn't it, to pull my hands quickly away and give him a proper lesson? Simple things aren't always so easy to carry out. But I finally managed and then rushed off to Vicolo del Crismatico, arriving home with my heart in my mouth.

The next day in the clear cool morning light I could only be astonished at that evening's encounter. Thinking of him holding my hands tightly in his own, I was filled with doubt to the point that I could hardly believe it had really happened. I spent the morning embroidering. Antonio had left at dawn in the boat and there would be no sign of him till that night.

In late afternoon I sat down on my front steps to work on my embroidery again. All the women of Otranto sat outside their doors this way in the evening, doing their sewing, or cleaning bunches of chicory, or repairing their husband's nets, all the while gossiping back and forth from one side of the street to the other, waiting for the church bells to sound the rosary. Every woman in Vicolo del Crismatico did the same thing; even when they went back in their houses at dusk each one did the same things as every other, all as alike as waves on the sea. There were times when I found all this very dull. When they'd begin cleaning chicory the tufa of the houses looked gray, with a darker streak of blue here and there, then a half hour later it would be changing color and when the rosary began it was all deep blue. A few minutes after we went inside it would turn to the bluish black of night.

That day as evening approached while I sat working with my needle, the setting sun outlined the tops of the houses more clearly than their facades and you could see the path of the light through the air. The women were talking and doing their usual things when all at once we heard the sound of shod feet coming from the

steep narrow alley that cut across Vicolo del
Crismatico. Everyone fell silent and all heads turned in
the same direction: there in our street appeared the
Spanish officer. He was walking slowly and in the
general silence we could hear his long pointed shoes
strike the pavement at every step. His eyes, however,
passed rapidly over the women, the children, the
bunches of chicory, like the eyes of a sparrow hopping
along in a meadow. The women stared at him, speechless and obstinate: Addolorata remained motionless in
the act of bending over to reach her hands into a bucket;
Assunta stood holding a bunch of chicory in one hand
and a knife in another; Mastro Natale's wife Filomena
stopped moving, her fingers spread on her fishnets – all
forming a line of hostile staring eyes. A cat crossed the
street, then stopped to sniff at a fishy smell. The
officer approached with slow even steps, his two fingers
hooked through the leather belt from which his sword
hung down on the right and a silk purse on his left.
Several little boys tagged along some distance behind
him.

"He's looking for me," I thought.

His short skirt of bright colored silk, gathered at the
waist by his belt, widened toward the bottom in a bell
shape, catching the last light that fell between the two
rows of women standing in shadow. He stopped in front
of me, bowed his head ever so slightly in greeting and
looked at me without a word. But his eyes spoke. A
minute or two later he resumed his walk, ambling along
at his indolent gentleman's pace to disappear around a
corner, my house being the last one in the fishermen's
alley. Then all the women turned to me and kept
looking without talking, something new for them.
Whenever anything happened in our street one of the
older women would begin a discussion about it and all
the others would join in; this usually went on until dark
because every so often they'd feel like stirring things up

by starting the conversation all over again. Not that evening. I glanced from one to another but I was isolated, alone in my distress. Gradually they took up their tasks again, cleaning chicory and mending nets in silence. As the last light faded behind the rooftops where the birds flew off to the west, a flock of crows passed over us, hurrying toward the high rocks and cawing from the depths of their errant souls. The shadows deepened and left us and our street in darkness.

"Who can guess what he wanted," I said loudly.

No one replied.

"Well, what do all of you think about it?" I added.

"As for me, I don't like him one bit," said Addolorata, Antonello's mother.

Silence again. The women seemed troubled.

"That fellow's no Christian," said Addolorata suddenly, "he's a hawk looking around for chickens."

"Who's a hawk? What are you talking about?" Antonello appeared at that moment, back from a day's fishing, put down his nets in front of his door and looked at us.

"Our business, women's talk," answered his mother brusquely. He stood there for a moment by his door, still eyeing us.

"You've all got a funny look on your faces," he said. "What's going on here anyway?" and without waiting for a reply, he went inside.

When the Ave Maria rang we crossed ourselves and sat down in shadow, each on her own steps. Master Natale's wife Filomena began to recite the rosary aloud, while the rest of us gave the choral responses. But as I repeated, "*Sancta Maria, Mater Dei,*" I kept seeing the officer's skirt. It was made of cloth so fine you couldn't even tell the color; I wondered what color it would really be, seen in the full light of the sun.

Idrusa IV

The next evening the women were all in their places as if waiting for a show to begin. True, they were sewing or washing chicory in buckets just as they did every evening, but now and then one of them looked up and around. I sat at my door with my embroidery, preparing an eyelet. At the same hour, as though it were prearranged, the officer appeared again. This time he was wearing a silken cloak that contrasted sharply with our rundown street, where the houses were stained with damp patches from the salt air. The moment he came into sight all the women lowered their heads, then quickly looked up again, their eyes brimming with disdain as they focused on the cloak. As he moved along he seemed first to enjoy the scene, then to become annoyed, gazing at a point further on. That point was the door of my house. I was struck by the way he moved, so unlike the fishermen, who never went walking just for the sake of walking. When he reached my house he wasn't satisfied with merely looking at me, as he'd done the night before.

"Good evening, good luck with your work," he said with his charming foreign accent.

After he was gone, Filomena, who'd been mending nets at her door, which was directly across from mine, put them down on the step, set her ball of cotton on top of them, stuck her needle into it, then folded her hands in her lap and said to me: "Now do you know what he wants?"

The women were watching me.

"Well, if I just don't pay any attention to him, that'll be the end of it," I said.

"Excuse me," said Addolorata, "but if you didn't mean to pay any attention to him, why, may I ask, did you bring him up here?"

"I didn't bring him," I said, indignant. "He came on his own."

"A likely thing," she retorted, "a young Spanish gentleman coming all the way up the hill to the old borgo for nothing?"

Nobody spoke for a minute.

"Those folks have a lot of worries," said Filomena.

"Call it worries if you want to," answered Addolorata, who knew all there was to know about Otranto's nobility. "Take Don Vincenzo De Raho, for instance. People used to say, 'He's a real gentleman, with only the very best intentions,' but he helped himself to all the women on his estates." She stopped, then began again, "And if they were married he'd say to the husband: 'Saddle the horses, let's go for a little ride.' Then he'd take him to a festival somewhere, give him lots to drink."

"A festival where?" asked Margherita.

"Oh anywhere, in some village or other. There are always plenty of festivals for saints' days. Then he'd say to the husband, 'Here, keep the horse and the saddle and bridle too.' And what could the poor fool do then?"

"But this one here is Spanish," said Filomena. "That's even worse."

Alfio da Faggiano's wife spoke up: "My Dorotea was very pretty as a girl. It's true she had one leg a little shorter than the other because a witch got in through the keyhole one night and gave her a bad fever that stunted it. But Don Vincenzo's son took a real fancy to her. You should've seen it. Everybody knows sons take after their fathers when it comes to that kind of thing. So you know what I did?"

"What?" asked Margherita.

"I got Canon De Pasca to talk to him. You want to know how he answered? He said, 'Well father, what do you expect. We're all sinners.'"

"What did the canon say then?" asked Margherita.

Alfio's wife didn't reply.

"He did say something, didn't he?" persisted
Margherita.

"Oh well, he told him to pray for the salvation of his
soul," said Alfio's wife with a sigh. "Then afterwards,
when Don Vicenzo's son had said goodbye to the canon
and gone on his way I took it upon myself to say: 'But
Monsignor, couldn't you have reprimanded him?' But he
told me there was little or nothing anybody could do,
except pray."

In the excitement of the discussion they'd all ended
up in the middle of the street, filling the air with talk.

"So much the better," I thought. "To the devil with
them anyhow," and I went inside. "All I have to do is
not look at him and that will be the end of it," I
repeated to myself. "Just turn my back when he goes by,
or even go right into the house. That'll take care of
him." I poked my head outside for a moment. The
women were still talking but the subject had gotten
turned around. Now they were criticizing the girls of
Otranto, who instead of lowering their eyes when they
found themselves face to face with gentlemen, looked
right back at them. They were falling into bad habits.

The minute Antonio got home I hastened to tell him:
"Antonio there's a Spanish officer who keeps coming by
on our street every evening. The women say he comes for
me."

He looked at me. "So what you *you* say?"

"He comes for me," I answered quickly.

Antonio's face darkened, his cheeks quivered. I
waited, full of fear. Then he placed both hands on my
shoulders and looked me straight in the eye. But he said
nothing, just looked. After a bit he let go of me and sat
down at the table. Finally he said, barely audibly:
"Better stay in the house at that hour. Don't show
yourself at the door."

"All right," I said, "I'll stay in the kitchen." We
didn't speak to each other again for the whole evening

because when Antonio's worried about something there's no way you can get him to talk. He went out in the cortile by himself and began to pace back and forth. At nightfall Mastro Natale came into the cortile and I heard Antonio say, "I'll kill him, I will."

"Wait a while," answered Mastro Natale. "There's plenty of time for that later on."

"So what should I do?"

"Nothing, since so far nothing's happened. Just keep an eye on him. You can't kill somebody just for taking a couple of walks."

When we were in bed and the oil lamp burning in front of the image of the Madonna of the Sea cast moving shadows of the chairs and bed on the walls, Antonio moved close and held me in his arms, his muscles tense. "Idrusa," he said, very low.

"What?" I answered.

"Are you sure you love me?"

"Sure I love you? Madonna Santa, Antonio, what are you saying?" but at the same time I felt something sinking inside me, like a stone thrown into the water.

I obeyed Antonio and didn't go out on the steps to do my embroidery.

"I mustn't see him anymore," I thought, "so I have to sit all evening in the kitchen." Since I had a net to repair I spread it on the table and began to mend it, but when I heard the women fall silent at the sound of the officer's steps on the pavement, I rushed to the tiny kitchen window and hid behind the pot of basil to watch. For me he seemed to transform our poor little street into Lecce's Piazza Sant'Oronzo, then leave us behind to turn a corner and go off in search of the wonderful adventures that his life consisted of. His hands were slender, very different from the fishermen's hands, so rough and scaly like fish bones and innards or other filthy things.

What a situation. Every day I vowed to the Madonna I wouldn't go to the window, reinforcing my vow as the hours passed, so by evening I was absolutely sure I wouldn't do it. And instead there I'd be, my forehead resting against the window frame. Why is it, I'd like to know, that a person can want to do something, really want to, and then all at once, he does the opposite. The kitchen window reminded me now of Malepasso, a place just below Porto Badisco where the rocks are terribly high and if you look down to the transparent green water and the depths of the sea below, your head begins to spin and you get a terrifying urge to throw yourself off the cliff and plunge into the sea.

At that point Antonio changed his fishing schedule and one day he came home at the end of the afternoon and he himself sat down on the steps to mend nets. When the officer arrived I saw the whole scene from the kitchen window and so did all the women watching wide-eyed from the street. As soon as the officer noticed Antonio he slowed his pace and began to advance like a cat, stealthy and ready to spring. Antonio slowly placed his nets on the pavement to his left, got up, stepped down to the street and stood there without moving, his face flushed and his fists clenched at his sides. The officer put his right hand on the hilt of his sword.

"Oh God," I thought, "Antonio's got his knife. Now they're going to kill each other." At that moment from around the corner toward the piazzella came Cola Mazzapinta. He stopped twenty paces away and folded his arms. Then Nachira appeared from the same direction and came up and stood beside him. Perhaps a minute went by and then Antonello also appeared, moved up and stopped, arms folded, beside the other two. Then Cristoforo Rio and Vincenzo Pasca. Finally Mastro Natale joined the group. All six of them stood watching the officer, who now drew his sword. Antonio didn't move, just raised his head enough to thrust out his lower jaw. His face was red with anger, his lips slightly parted, his teeth clenched in a way that made me think of a wolf about to attack. The fishermen advanced together for a few steps, staring at the officer, then stopped. The women stood frozen in their doorways. For a moment the officer eyed the fishermen, then Antonio – his own face had turned pale. Then he jumped back.

At that Mastro Natale's wife held up her rosary and wailed in anguish: *"In nomine Patris et Filii et Spiritus Sancti."*

"Amen," said the women in chorus.

At the sound of their voices Antonio roused himself, then stepped backward and resumed his rigid stance. The officer looked at him, then spun around and fled into the street that cut across our alley.

The fishermen were pleased with Antonio that evening, happy with the way he'd handled things.

After that the officer made no more visits to our street and I was certain I'd never see him again.

Idrusa V

Antonio began to kill himself with work. He fished day and night. And when he wasn't fishing he'd go off with his friend Alfio into the surrounding villages to peddle shellfish. In the evening he came home dead tired and fell asleep, sometimes before I finished salting curds and straining them through reed baskets to make his favorite dish. In order to surprise him I'd go outside the city during the day to buy curds from neighboring farms. When high fishing season came, all the fishermen usually set off toward Brindisi or Castro. They'd be gone eight or ten days, perhaps even longer, if they were caught out at sea by offshore storms. When they returned their boats would be loaded with shiny fish that sparkled like jewels in the sun and every boat

captain standing with his arms folded amidst the
baskets of fish, seemed to be a king. Yet here was
Antonio saying he wasn't going.

"But you're a boat captain," said the fishermen.

"You'll have to be patient with me," he answered.
"This time I'm not coming."

"But why?"

"Because I'm not." They couldn't get any more out of
him but they all knew he didn't want to go out because
of me, for fear of the Spanish officer.

"What's gotten into you?" they persisted. "The
woman's behaved herself, stayed in the house so far and
she'll go on staying inside. The other women will keep
her company. Who ever heard of a fisherman deserting
his mates like this, for no real reason?"

"I'm not coming," he repeated.

They shook their heads.

One day when I was home alone I heard a knock at the
door and there stood Mastro Natale. The old man came
into the kitchen, sat down and, laying his cap on the
table, said, "Good day."

"Good day," I answered.

He closed one hand inside the other and looked at
me: "Sit down. How old are you Idrusa?"

"Nineteen."

"Best of luck," he said calmly. My heart was in my
mouth.

"How long have you been married? I should know, but
I've forgotten. You were pretty young weren't you?"

"It's two years now."

"Best wishes again. And you're fond of Antonio?"

"Why shouldn't I be?" I said with vehemence.

"You're sure there's nothing amiss between you?"

"Nothing at all." Nervous, I ran my hand over my
hair. He spoke slowly, as slowly as he walked.

"So," he repeated, "you're fond of Antonio." He
paused for a moment, looked around the room, then

154

added: "You know how things stand, don't you? Antonio's working his head off. Day and night are the same for him, no time off even for a drink with his friends at the tavern, just fishing and selling fish so he can get the new house. And now when he's got the chance to make ten times as much at high fishing season he doesn't want to come. How would you yourself explain such a thing?"

"He's jealous," I said.

In the silence that followed I no longer felt ill at ease, just terribly eager to talk, so much so that I shifted my position, and my chair creaked. "Go on," he said.

"I haven't done anything," I said, "but I feel guilty just the same."

"Guilty of what?"

"I'm not like the others."

He didn't answer.

"The other women are better than I am, but their lives don't seem real to me. Do you realize what they're satisfied with? Just living, that's all. I simply can't be happy like that. But the two things don't fit together. I know they're better than me but the idea of being like them makes me feel like jumping off the cliff at Malepasso."

"Have you talked about this to Antonio?"

"Oh no, but I do talk to my sister."

"What does she say?"

"That there's something wrong with my head. Tell me, Mastro Natale, do you think there's something wrong with my head?"

He looked at me thoughtfully: "It's just that it's hard to say what'll come of all this." He picked up his cap and began to turn it between his fingers. "Because in the end my dear, you've got a husband to cook and wash for, you've got a house to clean and nets to mend. That's just life, there's not much you can do about it."

"Mastro Natale," I said, "I saw that Spaniard in the piazza in front of the church and instead of just walking away I stopped to talk to him."

"Do you find that man attractive?" he asked, looking straight at me.

It was difficult to answer. "I don't know," I said. "Maybe I do, but I don't want to hurt Antonio. I'm really fond of Antonio – I don't know why I stopped that day."

"You shouldn't have. Now he's after you."

"I don't want to see him ever again," I said, distraught. "I'll make sure I have everything I need here so I don't have to leave the house all the while the men are out at sea fishing. I swear to God I will." And I crossed myself several times in a row.

"I believe in you," said Mastro Natale. "That's why I came."

"You tell him too, Mastro Natale. Tell him I'll stay in the house the whole time." He stood up, his beautiful eyes gazed at me intently once more; it helped somehow to look into those eyes. He started toward the door and when he reached it turned around and said, fingering his beard: "But try not to think about it too much. Just do your work like the others."

After he was gone and I'd closed the door behind him I crouched down beside the hearth, put my head in my hands and burst into tears. I couldn't figure out why I was crying – I was simply filled with desolation that I'd have beaten myself to get rid of. Finally, after an hour, I fell asleep exhausted. Antonio found me there sound asleep, my eyes red from weeping. He sat down beside me in silence, his head bowed. Then he began to stroke my hair and tell me not to worry – he'd go out fishing but he'd be back in time to take me to the piazza for the festival of the Assumption to see the fireworks and he'd buy me a necklace, a bracelet – anything I wanted if I just wouldn't cry any more.

156

When the fishermen cast off from Otranto and rowed out to sea only women were left in our street and life changed. They cooked for themselves and their children, did their usual tasks, but no longer kept to a schedule. Even their cooking was different; they prepared things quickly so they'd be free to visit each other and get together in a circle in front of Filomena's house. My sister came to see me every day and the other women came too. They admired my embroidery and gave me advice and time passed without any particular novelty – at least in the daytime. I say this because for me the nights were not the same as usual. I mean in my dreams – true they vanished in the morning, but they left me wondering about the darker side of the soul. One night I dreamed I was in bed making love to Antonio. He was holding me tight and kissing me, but then all of sudden it wasn't Antonio holding me; it was the Spanish officer and in my dream I was perfectly happy with this new state of affairs. When I woke up I wondered if I was to blame, if a person could commit a sin even in dreams.

The moon was unusually beautiful during that time and after supper the women sat at their doors to enjoy the cool of the evening. This too was something they could only do during high fishing season because ordinarily they'd be busy putting up lunches for the men to take with them in the boats the next morning. Wives without husbands, they were taking life easy, relaxed and good-humored, often telling each other stories about their girlhood in a wistful melancholy tone.

So the days passed until only one remained before the Feast of the Assumption, but the fishermen hadn't returned. A strong tramontana had stirred up the sea; the waves rolled in from a distance and broke foaming over the rocks while the few boats left in port were battered against the wharf at regular intervals. The clouds hovered low and dark over the land.

I had gone out into the cortile to draw water from the well. As the wind puffed out my shirt sleeves and ballooned my skirt, mischievously billowing it up and away, my sister arrived. She was doing all my marketing so I wouldn't have to leave the house.

"To the devil with this wind," I said, thinking about the festival. "Isn't the tramontana ever going to end?"

She shrugged her shoulders and we both went into the house.

"Here, you can cook yourself a nice meal tonight," she said, putting a sack of mussels on the table. But I had no interest in eating. I just wanted the storm to end and Antonio to come home. I was tired of playing the part of the shut-in bride waiting for her husband to return. I'd had enough; I was bored to death with the whole thing. So that morning I'd tried to relieve the tedium by unraveling a knitted garment and arranging bits of leftover yarn in rows on the table. Then I'd set about making them into tiny figures.

"What's this?" said my sister when she saw them.

"Well, take a look. Can't you tell?"

"But this is stupid," she said. "Can't you embroider instead?"

"Embroider, embroider, always embroider!"

"You're much too fond of yourself, my dear sister."

"Listen," I said, "if Antonio doesn't get here in time, will you take me to the festival?"

"Take you to the festival?" She was dumbfounded. "But didn't you swear you wouldn't leave the house until Antonio came home?"

"Just five minutes – we'll walk through the piazza, look at the lights, then come right back."

"No." Then after a pause, she added: "I don't know how you can be thinking about the festival while Antonio's out there being tossed around by this tramontana."

Idrusa VI

It was Assumption Day evening and still the fishermen hadn't returned. As usual every year there was a procession and people flocked to the cathedral piazza, where a huge banner hung from one of the windows of the government palazzo. Once long ago that banner had displayed an image of Marie d'Enghien dressed in robes of silk and wool, seated on a throne with her feet on a satin cushion; later there'd been an image of Duke del Balzo Orsini, he too in silken and woolen robes against a green background. But after the Spaniards arrived he'd met the same fate as Marie d'Enghien, and was replaced by King Ferrante of Aragon. Actually, during the struggle with the barons the duke's image had come and gone for a few festivals but he finally had to surrender his place to a King Ferrante embroidered in silver thread, who made a fine effect and gave a solemn touch to the facade of the municipal palazzo. For Assumption Day, as for the Feast of Saints Cosma and Damiano, the nobility set aside a special idea and kept it in play during the entire festival: this was the notion that all men are equal. In the piazza you'd see ladies dressed in brocades buying candles from ordinary women and joining common people in the walk from the cathedral down to the port to watch the fireworks. No more valets with daggers in their belts blocking the way and forcing commoners to take alternative routes or step down into shops to clear the street. On the contrary, ladies and gentlemen seemed to take pleasure in mingling with us – it put them in an excellent mood.

I went out the kitchen door into the cortile. The night sky was perfectly clear, as it always is during the tramontana. I could hear the noise of the festivities from afar, rising and falling with the wind, but our street was absolutely still – everyone had gone to the piazza.

"Better go to bed early," my sister said when she left.

"Right away," I'd answered, but then I'd gone out into the cortile. I didn't feel like going to bed. The distant sound of the festival touched my heart with confused longings for things that had no place in the fishermen's world. I sat down on the side of the well in the middle of the cortile. Once my eyes became accustomed to the dark I could see the rectangular outline of the separate paving blocks, like an unbroken stone spiderweb reaching from the edge of the cortile on one side to the back of the house on the other: two whitewashed walls that stood out clearly in the moonlight. As I gazed at the pattern of paving stones the straight lines began to waver and the stones themselves seemed to move. I continued to stare at them till they appeared to move up and down while staying in the same place. The whitened wall of the house reflected the white light of the moon. The only dark spot was the tiny kitchen window, a rectangular shadow, clearly defined except where the pots of geraniums and basil on the window sill blurred the line between black and white. While I remained still, staring straight ahead, I could feel the dampness of the night settle on my shoulders. As time went by a triangular portion of the cortile passed into shadow, then grew larger, darker and deeper while the window lengthened in the play of light and shadow. Only one part of the cortile, still touched by shafts of moonlight and outlined by a curve of darkness, remained cut off from the rest of the night. The leaves of the geranium and basil plants began to quiver in the wind, making trembling shadow designs a few inches to the right of the window. I sat there unmoving on the edge of the well, watching as side-by-side the light retreated and the darkness advanced and the paving stones steadily and silently passed from one to the other.

I was thinking about going to bed when I heard steps approaching in the street. "Could it be Antonio?" I said to myself. Now the steps were right outside my door. "He's back!" I thought all at once. "He's come to take me to the festival." I jumped up, ran into the kitchen, and stood there waiting in the middle of the room. The steps halted and there was a knock at the door. I rushed to undo the bolt. As the door opened a crack a man appeared, wrapped in a cloak all the way up to his eyes. I let out a scream.

"Don't be frightened," said a voice I'd heard before. The reflected moonlight coming directly through the window brightened the room enough for me to be sure who he was the minute he took off his hood. I don't know how many minutes passed as we stood there facing each other without speaking, until with sudden haste I turned to light the lamp. When I looked around again, the officer had thrown his cloak over a chair and was coming toward me. Still neither of us spoke. He took my hand and began to kiss it on the back and on the palm. I tore it away. I wanted to scream, send him away, call for help. But I did none of these things – not a single word came from my lips.

"I knew you were alone," he said.

I finally managed to speak. "Go away," I stammered.

"It's sad to be all alone on a holiday evening," he answered, taking a turn around the room with a rustling of his silken and lace-trimmed clothing.

I repeated: "Go away or I'll scream."

"Nobody would hear you. They're all at the festival. Anyway why should you scream? Sit down, let's talk a bit."

"I'm not sitting down," I said and began to move back, to get away from him, until my shoulders touched the wall.

"You're beautiful, but thorny as a prickly pear," he smiled. Again he began to walk about the room with an easy manner as if he'd been coming to my house every

161

evening, all his life. Finally he sat on the corner of the table, letting one leg swing back and forth.

"Why do you want to stand there in the corner? Here now, come on over and sit down."

I didn't budge.

"You like festivities," he said, "but your husband isn't here so you can't go. Maybe you even asked somebody to take you. You did, didn't you? But they've shut you in your house as a punishment. Isn't that right?" and now he was laughing as he talked. I looked at him in terror.

"I don't want you to stay here," I murmured. "Please, please, leave me alone."

Instead he replied, "You're the most beautiful woman I've ever seen in Otranto." He said it so softly, so sweetly that it was really extraordinary. "Come on now," he added, "come over here. You're not afraid by any chance?"

I moved toward the table.

"I don't even know your name. What is it?"

"Idrusa."

"Good. Mine's Manuel." Then: "Before the oil is gone from this lamp, Idrusa, who knows where we'll be, you and I."

He'd used the familiar form of address. I should have run into the street and called someone. I could have escaped, maybe even by the back door and the cortile. But instead I stayed, just like the other time in the past, when I'd encountered him in the piazza in front of the cathedral.

"Hear that?" he said, listening intently. "They're starting to shoot off the fireworks." I lowered my head. I could feel my heart beating.

"The streets are so well lighted tonight that nobody needs to carry a lantern." he said. "You can see perfectly." Then, speaking softly, his voice insistent: "Come here, there's no reason to be afraid." But I didn't move. He was the one who moved – toward me.

162

"What kind of nonsense are you thinking?" he said. "When I saw you for the first time I'd only just arrived at Otranto, with Don Felice's escort. But you weren't in your husband's boat. Who were you with?"

"Colangelo," I answered, " with him and his wife."

"That Colangelo gave me a dirty look," he said, laughing. "You'd have thought he didn't like me. All the fishermen look at us that way. Why?"

"People here don't like foreigners," I answered.

We went on talking for a while. He asked questions and I answered, but soon I began to forget what he'd asked. All at once I became aware of two eyes a few inches from my face; they focused on my forehead, then on my mouth, then my neck. At that point in a quick precise move he knocked over the lamp. As the light went out he seized me violently in his arms, seeking my mouth with his. Then slowly and calmly, his hands began to undo the laces of my bodice.

I was very very happy that night; it was like what I'd been waiting for all my life. But happiness comes only when it's least expected and never lasts for more than a few moments.

We separated at dawn. He opened the door gently, looked up both ways at the sky, then said: "It's cleared off."

That year the summer had been cool and when he left I went back into the cortile and sat down on the wall. The tramontana had given way to settled air, quite unusual in summertime. I thought: "Now the sea will calm down, the boats will come back and Antonio will be home." Crows were already cawing and flying overhead and I could hear the noise of a pulley and the splash of a bucket hitting the surface of the water in a well. "Antonio will want to make love," I thought. From the street came the sound of footsteps as some of the women started out with eggs to sell, then more footsteps as others returned from the market with their

163

baskets full of chicory. When I finally looked out it was already late. The sun was beating down on the pavement where naked toddlers were rolling around and playing. In contrast little girls four or five years old were sitting on the ground and murmuring to each other, all in a row with their backs against Mastro Natale's house. The hours passed quickly and as noon approached I began to be afraid. The idea that Antonio was coming chilled my very bones. "I'll tell him everything," I thought. "He'll beat me, he'll kill me." I couldn't work. I did nothing at all, just wandered about the house and once in a while sat down. By evening I wasn't afraid anymore. When I went to bed all I felt was profound melancholy. I remembered the happiness of the night before and I knew it would come back to my mind every time I heard anyone even mention happiness.

Idrusa VII

The next day the sound of excited women's voices from the street announced the arrival of the fishermen.

"Hurry up," said Filomena, appearing at my kitchen door. "We're going down to the port."

"Are they back?" I asked, frightened.

"Just coming in."

I joined the crowd of women hastening to the port. The boats were coming in slowly, in groups of four, leaving a clear wake that disturbed the regular pattern of the waves.

The groups were a short distance apart and as they neared the shore each woman called out in turn as she recognized her man. When the first boats touched land the last ones were rounding Rocamatura Point, their oars dipping rhythmically in and out of the flat greenish water. But the fishermen weren't calling out as they usually did. They weren't waving to us or shouting back and forth between the boats. Instead it was the women who were talking, trying to satisfy their curiosity.

"What's going on? You'd think it was a procession."

"What's the matter with them? Wasn't the fishing any good?"

"What are you talking about. Look at all those fish."

"They must be tired. The sea's been rough the whole time."

"I should say so. Look at their faces."

"Come on, let's go down to the boats."

"Yes, let's go."

I'd been lost in my own thoughts as I walked along and when I looked for Antonio's boat I was surprised it wasn't already in since he was usually among the first. The women all began to talk at once and squeal and mill around and greet the first men to disembark. Then all at once the commotion stopped. I couldn't tell why because my thoughts were so far away I hardly knew what was happening. I saw the first fishermen on the pier; they were just standing there doing nothing as if they were all out in the piazza on Sunday morning after high mass. They weren't looking at the boats either, despite their cargo of mullet, pike, and bream – some even had spiny lobsters. Mastro Natale, who was in charge, didn't even give the order to begin unloading. He stood there too, just looking at us, as though he'd forgotten his authority. "Natale!" called his wife, as all the women gathered around him.

"Greetings," he said hoarsely.

"What's wrong?" asked his wife.

"Heavy seas, bad luck."

"We could tell even from here," I said. "Constant high winds."

Mastro Natale gazed off at the cathedral, his eyes sorrowful, then looked straight at me for a moment without talking. "Something's happened to Mastro Natale," I thought.

165

Then he said, "The day before yesterday at dusk the sea turned ugly and the waves were rolling in all the way to the Saracen Tower. There was lightning off toward Castro and with two opposing winds the boats couldn't go anywhere. We brought them together on the other side of La Palascia, where there's some shelter." He stopped, wiped the sweat from his forehead with his handkerchief and began again: "It was a hellish evening. No boat could've made it to Otranto alone; it just couldn't be done. The only thing to do was wait it out."

We listened without a word.

"A man alone at sea is helpless," he said looking at me again. "He can't row against the force of the tramontana; he can't go where he wants." At that the women came in closer to form a circle, looking at me respectfully, the way they'd look at the governor. The silence lasted until I myself broke it with a cry: "But what *is* it? What's happened?"

Mastro Natale turned toward me, hesitated a moment, in doubt, then said: "Antonio didn't want to wait with us at Palascia. He said he'd promised you he'd be home in time for the festival to take you to the fireworks. He said it just wasn't possible for him to stay there with the rest of us."

I made a terrible effort to grasp ideas that kept fleeing out of my head.

"I didn't want to let him go," he went on, "because that was no kind of sea to set off for Otranto in, not even for a fisherman like Antonio. 'The sea has its own laws,' I said, 'and there's no breaking them.' But he answered: 'I can't wait here. You know I can't,' and he left us. We saw him round the point at Palascia, but then we couldn't see him any more behind the rocks."

"Go on," I said brusquely, as though giving Mastro Natale an order.

He lowered his eyes: "We found his body this morning, caught in the algae offshore near the Serpe Tower. The boat had gone down."

My mouth moved but no words came. There was a great void in front of me. The only thing I could make out was Mastro Natale's face looking at me. "That was no kind of sea to set off for Otranto in," he repeated. His voice hung in the air and I hadn't the strength to hear anymore. Indeed I must have blurted out those very words. I had no thoughts, no body; the void kept getting bigger and I kept waiting for something, for an answer that didn't come and I was seized with terror at still being alive. Then I found myself at home. "Let me see him," I kept begging even though no one would give me my wish. He was in the mortuary of the cemetery, wrapped in a cloak, but I didn't see him and that was why I couldn't be persuaded he was dead. You have to see the dead. In my mind I continued to see other returns from big fishing trips when the men disembarked proudly from their boats full of shiny fish and began to tell all about it. Not Antonio. Antonio would go straight home and shut the door behind him. He didn't want me to see him before he had cleaned up, smoothed his hair and changed his vest and breeches. When he opened the door again he wanted to make love at once. Now that he was dead nobody else knew these things – only me, and if I were to forget them it would be as if they never happened, as if Antonio had never been here in this world.

The women, dressed in black from head to foot, their faces veiled in black, sat along my kitchen walls reciting the fate of the dead under Filomena's direction: "A gust of wind came in from the sea, came in and brought ruin to my house. Had it been closed inside a barrier it would have flattened everything. Now he can never come home again, not at Easter, nor at Christmas, not even for carnival time. And it might as well rain at Easter and the skies could be gray at Christmas."

But unlike them, I didn't break into sobs and shrieks, and they looked at me in wonder. Nor did I pray. All I did was think, "If I could just die right now, just die all at once, now this minute, it would be all over." I jumped up, unable to stay still, to sit and listen to them any longer and dashed toward the cortile, but they grabbed me, forced me to sit back down and continued their funeral chant: "Oh galley, my galley with silver oars, angels are singing in heaven and in the church the priests." At this point they all screamed in unison, raising their arms and waving their kerchiefs in the air. Then the chant ended and they sat quiet and still. Now the night I'd spent with Manuel had lost all its magic and everything was different. If I even looked at the table where Manuel had sat, or at the bed, I was lost. Whatever the cost I desperately wanted to go out into the cortile.

"Here, take a few sips of milk," said my sister. "You can't go on forever without eating." When it was time for the burial, outside the city at the Monastery of San Francesco, a monk made the graveside speech. He said the only remedy for misfortune was to think of the goodness of Our Blessed Lord in taking Antonio's beautiful soul to live with him in heaven so he'd have the happiness of paradise up there, whereas the earth was nothing but a vale of tears. When he finished and the women were beginning to sing in chorus, I took hold of Mastro Natale's arm.

"Come with me. I have to talk to you."

"Easy now," he said, not moving.

"No, I *must* talk to you."

"Now my dear? Right here in the cemetery?"

I dragged him off in a corner away from the others.

"If Antonio had come back, I'd have told him what I'm about to tell you."

Mastro Natale waited, looking at me in quiet surprise.

"I've wronged Antonio," I said.

"What did you say?"

"Yes, I've wronged him. The night of the festival, while he was dying – I spent that night with the Spanish officer."

He furrowed his brow, said nothing for a moment, then spoke: "You're delirious, my girl – it's the grief."

"No, it's true," I answered.

We stood facing each other among the graves while the women were chanting the litany for the dead. Suddenly Mastro Natale grabbed both my arms in his strong hands: "You're delirious. Nothing happened. Nothing. Do you understand? Nothing at all!"

For an instant all I could hear was the old man's heavy breathing as he continued to look me in the eye, determined to fix his idea in my mind.

"No, that's not true," I said brusquely. "You've got to believe me and you have to despise me."

Mastro Natale was breathing as if he couldn't get enough air. "Hush, Idrusa. Antonio's gone and you don't know what a good man he was. You don't know what you've lost."

Finally I burst out weeping, for the first time since it happened and the force of the tears was so great it took me away from everything.

Mastro Natale wiped his brow with his handkerchief and said, after a minute: "Let's go back now and pray with the others."

The men had finished filling in the grave and everyone was gazing quietly at the fresh earth. A few minutes went by like that.

"Come on, I'll take you home," said Mastro Natale. I knew I was looking at the earth, only at the fresh earth, but I couldn't bring myself to move because moving meant starting to do something again. But what could I do?

At the door of my house Mastro Natale said, "Go up and spend a few days at the Monastery of San Nicola di Càsole. Ask for Father Epifani. Do you understand?" This said, he pressed my hand and went away.

Idrusa VIII

For the next few days the women brought me the traditional meal prepared for bereaved families, then watched to make sure I ate it. You have to eat in bad times, they said, because trouble weakens the blood. After that I went to look for Father Epifani. In fact I made a habit of going up to the monastery quite often. I'd take the long route between the walls of the vegetable plots, stretching my neck to gaze up toward the plateau and the olive grove surrounding the monastery, or if I happened to turn around I'd look down at my house, so tiny seen from up there. Finally Otranto disappeared from view and the breeze picked up. The first time, Father Epifani received me in the monastery garden where he was watering zucchini and pepper plants.

"It's been so dry lately," he said. "Day after day with no rain. Zucchinis need water."

His habit smelled of incense and its hem kept getting caught among the plants.

"Look father," I said, "I'll bring the water from the well and you do the watering. All right?"

"Very good indeed," he answered. "You're a fine girl."

As he watered the plants he hummed an Ave Maria and I went back and forth with the bucket. Then at a certain point I stopped, rested the bucket on the ground and sat down on a stone.

"So now what are you going to do?"

"Now I want to tell you my story," I said.

"I still have the peppers to do," he replied. "Here, be a good girl and help me out a little longer." We went about it together. When we finished he sat down on another stone next to me. There was a nice breeze and white clouds were puffing up like rising bread dough in the sky.

"What's your name?" he asked.

"Idrusa."

"Idrusa? Do you know what it means?"

"What it means? I don't understand."

"It means you are like a racing mare dripping with sweat."

"I'm like what? Names mean something then?"

"Yours does. It's Greek like mine."

"And what does yours mean?"

"Oh dear Jesus," he said, joining his hands. "It means bright and full of light. How could it fit a poor monk like me? Tell me, are you married?"

"I'm a widow."

"Poor girl, so young."

"I'm not a poor girl at all," I said. "I'm full of sins. Do you want to hear them?"

"You?" he said, hardly convinced.

I told him everything. He had a curious idea about sins. He said that when a sin, a big one, had eaten up a piece of someone's soul the person could replace that piece, make it better than it had been in the first place and this was why God had left sins in the world.

"Why do you yourself think you wronged your husband?" he asked.

"I don't know. It was just one of those things that happen without any warning."

"One of those things that happen to people who have lots of imagination," he said. "You see, for people with lots of imagination life's always a very risky business."

At that I nervously picked up a stone, and noticing a scorpion on the wall some distnce away, I took aim and hit it.

"You've got a good aim," he said. Then: "You know, Idrusa, almost everybody has times when they live the way they should, body and soul together, everything in proper order. But living like that for an entire lifetime – well, that's pretty hard to do."

"But what about me, Father Epifani, what should I do now?"

"Well let's see. You told me you do embroidery. You know how to mend nets. All right then, get to work embroidering and mending nets."

"But that's not what I meant," I said irritably. "I don't have any purpose. That's what I'm trying to say." The only answer Father Epifani had was to ask me where in Otranto you could buy cotton string to repair nets, if they had it brought from Lecce or if it came from across the sea. Still, from the way he looked at me I could tell he'd understood perfectly. Father Epifani was one of those people who always understand what you're saying. In the period following Antonio's death I changed my habits. Besides embroidering, I mended nets for fishermen to earn a living and when I finished work, I'd go off by myself down to the sand dunes by Rocamatura. Lying on my back with my hands behind my head I'd look up against the light at the olive leaves hanging above me in a tangle of branches with sky and clouds showing through. I could see the tops of some of the leaves as well as the undersides of others.

Winter came, then another torrid summer. The coast was a white stretch of sand and stones without a single blade of grass left and at night in the moonlight it looked like a dead star. Or had I myself turned into a white stone under the moon? My sister said I'd never been so unsociable. "Other women lose husbands at sea," she went on. "Who knows how many, all up and down the coasts of Italy. And they manage to accept their fate. You have to have sense enough to keep hold of yourself. What's the meaning of all this lying around on the sand in the sun, as if you were a fig set out on a rack to dry? You've got to just go on doing what you've always done and little by little things will take care of themselves." So she said and continued to say. She couldn't understand I only had one fear – that I'd forget Antonio. When we made love Antonio used to say to me: "I'll never forget you, not even when I'm dead," and I'd laugh. Those were only words to me, the same old words. People are always saying after they're dead they'll go on thinking this or loving that. Instead when you're alive it doesn't work this way – new things chase away the old ones. There isn't much room in our hearts. And what about Manuel? What if I were to see him again? What would happen then? Beside myself with anger I rolled about in the sand. There was no use trying to figure it out.

Thinking that hard about things always left me defeated in the end and with a splitting headache besides. For instance, one morning in August shortly after the end of the strict mourning period I got up with a sudden urge to take a dip in the sea, to dive in and swim under water. What can I say? I did go dive in and with my skin tingling from the cold water and my nose full of the pungent smell of algae I began to swim. Every once in a while I closed my eyes and slipped under the surface, every inch of my body immersed, taking mouthfuls of water and then coming up to spit it out, opening my eyes in the light and reaching upward with my arms. I shook my head, feeling as if I'd come back to the surface after spending a year at the bottom of the sea. Soon I began to weary of staying home and I'd seize any occasion to go where I could watch fancy ladies dressed up in brocades out taking a walk. On Sundays after attending mass in the cathedral instead of in San

Francesco, the church near my house where I used to go,
I'd give in completely to the urge to wander lazily
through the streets. I'd go all the way to the piazzella
where the street vendors' stalls were full of earthenware
jugs, black and red terracotta pots, little ceramic
horses and brass lamps that shone in the sun. Then a
sharp anxiety would take hold of me, as if I were
hoping for something. I'd keep looking around without
really knowing what for. Or sometimes I'd take a
different route and go toward the walls, where sentries
closed inside their armor walked back and forth from
one guard post to another. If I came upon a Spanish
officer my heart would begin to beat furiously. Outside
the walls I'd press on to the marshes where the bunches
of tall rushes swayed back and forth, their plumes
caressed by the rhythm of the wind.

"You'll get malaria," said my sister. Or else: "Now
what are you up to? Why are you always going out?"

"First you complained because I didn't go out. Now
you're complaining because I do."

"It's just that you never do anything with moderation.
Where are you off to now?"

"Just for a walk, to see what's new."

"How do you mean what's new? Have you forgotten
you're a widow and young widows can't be always
wandering the streets? Be careful, you're going to get a
bad reputation."

I knew this of course, but things were different now.
At first after Antonio died all I had to do was look at a
chair in my house and there he'd be, sitting in the chair.
Or if I looked at a door he'd open it. Not now. It was
more like he stopped by to visit from some far off
place and couldn't stay very long. But one thing was
sure: it's only after someone dies that we can see him
inside us the way he really was. "Who knows," I thought,
"maybe I could have learned to love Antonio and after a

while we'd have made a perfect couple." But now that it
was all over no one would ever know.

"Why don't you go to see Father Epifani anymore?"
said my sister one day.

I didn't reply. How could I tell her I'd stopped going
when I found myself in the prey of a furious desire to
see Manuel? Could I say to her that when you're in love
your best conversations are with yourself, when you're
out for a solitary walk?

"You're full of whims, you are," said my sister. "What
do you gain by getting tired of everything so quickly?"

One day I happened to come out of Vicolo dal
Crismatico into the big piazza where the fishermen's
smaller children were running around naked, playing and
squealing. The piazza's a place a widow should cross
rapidly with eyes down. But when I heard Manuel's voice
a few paces away, speaking to his Spanish comrades, I
stopped dead and looked at him. He'd seen me too and
was coming toward me. It was late Saturday afternoon,
just before sunset. Instead of turning around and going
away, I said, "Good evening," and thus began the second
part of my life.

Idrusa IX

September was windy that year; every evening the
tramontana banged the doors and shutters of houses. I'd
watch the passing shadows until late at night, and inside
myself I was a little mad. "Someone's coming," I'd say
now and then. "Who is it?"

One night I started in surprise. He was there at my
door. In an instant my lips were trembling in antici-
pation. We kissed so hard we couldn't breathe and then
Manuel pushed me down on the bed and threw himself
on top of me, holding me passionately. We remained in
an embrace all night long and every once in a while

when he'd begin kissing me again I could have died of happiness.

We spent many nights like that, consumed by love.

Sometimes Manuel embraced me with a fury; sometimes, breathing heavily, he'd say: "Look at me, look at me now," but I'd always keep my eyes closed and wouldn't talk. Or he'd get up during the night and look at me in the lamplight, filled with desire but at the same time detached – in a state that was half excitement and half icy distance. He'd sit on the edge of the bed on top of the sheet, making the straw mattress rustle. I'd wish I was a lady so we'd have a mattress stuffed with cotton wool that wouldn't make any noise. The head of the iron bed with its brass knobs was doubled by the lamplight. In front was the real bed, the real brass knobs and behind it on the whitewashed wall a sort of grate against which Manuel's head moved this way and that. On warm nights the smell of the sea came in through the open kitchen window and the light from the starry sky fell on the rumpled sheets. He would talk as he sat there gently caressing my breasts and my belly. At first he only talked about me. He said I was very very beautiful, white as new feathers on a seagull's breast; I wasn't like any of the other fishermen's women – I was like those wild sweet-smelling carnations that grew in the hills. He said I was intelligent too. He could talk to me about any subject at all because I would understand and this never happened with my peers. As time went on he began to talk about the women, the many women, he'd been with in different countries of the world. He said there were women and women: some appealed to you for certain reasons, others because of something entirely different. He knew all about every one of them and told me what he knew with the kind of pleasure a person takes in describing as best he can the houses or the roads he saw on a long trip, or the dinners he ate. I was amazed at all this but no less happy, beause he wasn't referring to me.

"But did you love them?" I asked once.

He looked directly at me, and said, "Of course."

"Like you love me?"

He laughed. "No, not like you."

He lowered his eyes but quickly looked up again, smoothing back his hair in his graceful aristocratic way: "The nights here are really hot," he said. I wanted to continue the conversation we'd begun but I didn't have the courage.

We spent long hours in each other's arms, hours during which I was simply carried away and lost all idea of the world around me. But Manuel, despite his poetic lovemaking, was alert any time he wanted to be. For instance if the clock in the church tower struck he'd always know whether it was for the seventh or the ninth hour after sundown. A part of him was forever detached and aware. This too was a source of amazement for me.

Idrusa X

Those months of love passed all too quickly. Summer came and then winter again with storms that moved in from the sea over the rocky coast and gave the night sky an air of catastrophe. I'd wait for him wrapped in a shawl and huddled in front of the brazier. Manuel came faithfully to our encounters. Although as he sat down his manner was lazy and careless, his lively spirit shown through like coals under ashes, and watching him I thought how there's something mysterious in every creature. That's how so many different things can come together in harmony. I loved him and for me such happiness was like a plant that's forever green.

If he was late he'd excuse himself, saying: "There were fishermen in the street," or even: "I was afraid somebody would see me – I don't want people to talk."

Then I'd quickly forget my long wait by the brazier sitting with my legs crossed and drawn up under me. Sometimes he'd go away for ten days or even two weeks. Then he'd say, "Well my dearest, we won't be seeing each other for a week or so."

"Why do you have to go away?"

He'd put his hand on the back of my neck, stroke my hair and say: "It's good to be apart every once in a while. Then when we see each other again the pleasure's even greater – it's like everything's new, like starting over again."

I couldn't make sense out of this kind of calculation.

"You mean you don't mind leaving me?" I asked.

He considered my question with a twinkle in his eye: "I mind and I don't mind. There are some things you women can't understand. As far as this matter's concerned, you're all immature."

Manuel and I had been meeting at night for a year and a half, or nineteen months to be exact, and those months had gone by in a flash. But at the same time they seemed as long as an entire life. A life, however, from which something was missing. Like this for instance: Manuel was always talking about love, but he never talked like he was *in* love. The exact opposite of Antonio in this respect. It was one night in January, when the fire in the brazier had gone out and I was sitting there alone and cold, listening to the wind whistle under the doors that I first asked myself how this life I'd begun with Manuel might end. So many details now readily came to my mind, details I hadn't thought about before, insidious memories. My present life reminded me of one of those country paths that twist and turn as they lead from one farm to another, from one property to another, before they arrive at their destination. As you walk along one of them you think how a shortcut straight across the countryside would take you directly where you want to go.

I jumped up, moved away from the brazier and went out into the cortile in the cold. All at once, looking up at a sky full of stars, I was struck by the thought that it might have been better never to have known Manuel. Love had reached the stage for me where it was beginning to bring unhappiness. The next day I blamed it all on the fire going out and the cold and loneliness of the night. I spent the whole day working on the laundry; then in the evening I carefully did my hair and changed my dress to be ready for Manuel. When I heard his step I closed my eyes as though in fear. When I opened them he was already upon me, kissing me avidly.

"You're trembling. What's wrong?"

I stood still without speaking.

"Look at you now. You're like a frightened little doll. But so pretty! Do you have any idea how lovely you are, how beautiful?"

He began to call me pet names with his usual charming gestures. "If you'd been a woman, Manuel," I thought, "you'd have been a real flirt."

"Want to sit down?" I said and then stumbled over the chair. Good God, I was dazed! But he quickly jumped up again and began to handle me, taking off my clothes and nibbling my breasts.

"Damn these clothes, Idrusa," he said. "I'd like to find you already naked when I got here."

He laid me down on the bed and threw himself on top of me, covering me with his whole body in a fury of kisses and I was simply lost, holding him tight to my breast. At such times love once more overcame all my fears, just as the smell of the spicebushes on the plateau overcomes the cold winter air.

But it wasn't always like that.

When the season changed Manuel began to come late at night after the Big Dipper had appeared behind the Serpe Tower. Sitting down, he'd begin to tap the tips of his fingers on the table.

179

"God almighty," he'd say sometimes, "what can a man do with himself in a town like this to keep from dying of boredom."

He'd sigh and say, "Isn't there anything to do? My dear Don Felice Sancio Ayerbo of Aragon, can't you invent something? We're here to defend the coast from the Turks. The Turks aren't coming. Great. Send us to Lecce or Brindisi to organize something. There's always something that needs organizing in this world."

"Would you like to leave?" I'd ask him.

"Try to imagine, my dear – for months all I've had to look at is the same 120 faces. What more can I say?"

I'd get up, go to the well and get water to make him a cold drink. When the bottom of the bucket hit the water with a plop, I'd jerk the cord to fill it and then begin to pull it up. "Does he still love me?" I'd wonder, bending to look down toward the bottom of the well. Some evenings Manuel didn't appear. "He's busy," I'd tell myself, "or his friends are keeping him." In bed I'd stare wide-eyed into the dark, troubled by a curious anxiety for the morning light to return.

In those days I began to believe that when Manuel didn't come to see me he was with another woman, maybe someone from his own class. I set about imagining the scene in detail, and my brain did a splendid job of it. By now my fantasy was as true as two and two make four. I was sure of it: in a salon of one of the Otrantini palazzi Manuel was conversing with the beautiful woman I'd invented and at a certain point he'd lure her away from the other guests for a long private talk during which they'd look into each other's eyes and set themselves apart from everything around them. They'd go on talking, perhaps for an hour, as though carried away by the subject they were discussing. But in reality I alone could see into the depths of their souls and I knew all that talk was just an excuse to gaze into each other's eyes, to lean toward each other smiling, to

brush shoulders or arms and feel the unexpected thrill
of closeness. Such is the secret accord between a man
and a woman who feel mutual attraction. Maybe Manuel
was telling her about a coot-hunting expedition,
describing the hunters advancing slowly through the
swamp, knee-deep in water. But meanwhile his eyes were
saying: "What marvelous shoulders you have, what eyes.
Keep looking at me that way, keep it up, you delightful
female." And she did, despite her apparent concern for
the mortally-wounded birds floating gently with wings
spread like water lilies in the marsh. "What a dis-
tressing sight, yet it must have been beautiful too!"
she'd exclaim in her excitement. I envied that woman.
Endowed with the frivolous graces of beautiful ladies
she could gradually make a conquest of Manuel,
charming him in lively conversation where they
competed on equal terms like two knights showing off
their prowess in a tournament, sparring with the points
of their swords. I'd had nothing like this.

Or sometimes I'd imagine I was walking along the
edge of the old borgo, past the three huge old prickly
pears surrounded by a low stone wall with grass growing
on top of it. In my mind I suddenly saw Manuel holding
the woman passionately. Her round white arms reached
out from the wide sleeves of her closely fitting bodice
to wrap tightly around his neck. One day I really did
take the path of the three prickly pears, as we called it.
It had been raining and there was still a bit of drizzle
in the air. In Otranto the rain made everything a
different color: the red earth turned dark brown and
whatever had been merely green become brilliant green.
Walking along by the prickly pears I ran my hand along
the grass on top of the wall. It felt wet and soft. The
last raindrops were going drip, drip, drip on the thick
leaves of the prickly pear – all at once first one cloud,
then another, parted. A minute later the sun came out
and the drops on the leaves began to sparkle. I stayed

and waited for a while, as if expecting something. I was almost annoyed the couple wasn't there, and I was denied the bitter pleasure of discovering them and seeing Manuel confused and embarrassed. But in real life when you've imagined something step by step, if it actually happens it's quite a different matter. So it was for me. I did come upon Manuel in the piazza just as he was crossing it with a lady at his side. A small woman with a rosy little face, she was all clad in silk and lace and walking happily along, aware she was pretty and in fine form. I caught my breath. But not Manuel. He was anything *but* confused and embarrassed at seeing me. Quite the reverse, he waved as if I were an old friend he was used to encountering daily in the same place. He even smiled.

"Who was she?" I asked that night.

"A lady from Lecce," he answered.

"She's pretty," I exclaimed, full of anger.

"Yes, she's pretty," he repled calmly.

"Have you known her long?"

"Oh, for a while."

"You've got something going with that woman," I said.

He burst out laughing. "You're prettier," he answered, running his fingers through my hair and bending my head from one side to the other. "To begin with, you're wild and you give me a damnable desire to grab you and hold you the minute I see you."

I jumped to my feet. When he talked like that about me and about love, like somebody recalling a kind of pleasant game, I felt belittled and almost offended.

"My little cat," he said, grabbing my arm.

"Let me go!" I yelled. I could have killed him at that moment.

"All right, all right. I mustn't fool around with pretty ladies from Lecce. Can we stop talking about that now?"

When he left I thought he didn't love me, or rather maybe he'd never loved me, but he'd keep coming to see me, maybe for months or even years and in the end there'd be nothing between us except the habit of meeting. I felt very bad about this, to be sure, but those feelings were nothing compared to my ferocious urge to imagine the days and months ahead as it seemed they were bound to be. Later on he'd be transferred to Naples or Taranto and he'd say with his usual aristocratic charm: "Unfortunately my dear, this time I really am leaving for good." Alone all day long, sitting in the cortile with no more will to work, I'd have given anything to know whether things really would turn out the way I imagined. Because if they did, it was certainly worse than if he'd already deserted me – much more offensive. "I've got to know," I concluded to myself. "I've got to make the effort to find out."

Assumption Day came and I put on my best dress and went to the service in the cathedral, which was filled with people from every walk of life, seated according to rank and family connection. For example, in the central nave as far back as the column of the Holy Spirit there were chairs and seats covered with damask and decorated with little golden doves' wings. These were for the nobles. Just behind, filling four rows of benches, Spanish and Neapolitan officers were saying their prayers with their eyes fixed on the beautiful ladies directly in front of them. Finally, in the back were the fishermen and the ordinary workmen from the city. As for the women, we sat on either side of the nave, separated from the rest by the aisles. "He's there," I said to myself, looking toward the center, persistent in my desire to catch sight of his head in the crowd. Suddenly an idea came to me, took hold of me. Like the wind if you happen to be on an open road during a storm: it grabs you and pushes you along and forces you to run even though you don't want to. As soon as the service was over I went outside in front of the cathedral to wait, and when he appeared I walked straight up to him.

"Shall we walk down to the port?"

He looked at me horrified: "The two of us together? Have you lost your mind? What will people say?"

"But everybody's talking about us already," I answered.

He winked at me: "Words are feminine; deeds are masculine." He went on, "It's one thing to say it my dear, quite another to see it. And what a time to be seen! Today's a holiday and half of Otranto would be watching you."

"I don't care," I answered proudly.

He shrugged, turned toward the piazza, saying: "Where do you want to go?"

"To the port and then you can take me home."

We started off. The air was full of golden light and the streets were like white rivers leading down to the sea. For a moment I dreamed of being Manuel's bride. Here we were, returning slowly to our house after attending mass together. I glanced at him: he was walking beside me uneasily, like someone who isn't quite sure what route to take and looks around lost. Then, abruptly, he spoke, and not without a certain ill humor: "So what's this, Idrusa, something new?"

Instead of answering I said, "I wonder how wide the streets of Naples are and how many different kinds of people you can see there. It must be marvelous!"

"Yes, the streets are wide."

"People here – we're much too quiet. It's too bad, there must be so many things to see in the world."

We'd reached the port. The boats were pulled up on the beach on their sides while on the shaded part of the pier we saw the fishermen, all dressed up in their Sunday clothes and standing in little groups. They turned their heads every now and then, to glance around in quiet serenity. This was their way to relax on a holiday morning until it was time to eat, then go to the tavern, where they'd stay and drink till late at night. When we passed their eyes fell on us with such a direct look that I felt a great haste to turn into Vicolo del Crismatico. Not until we were in the house did Manuel heave a sigh of relief and resume his usual joking manner, the manner I'd once found so enchanting.

"Brave as a tiger!" he said, gazing at me with curiosity.

At that, for the first time in two years I asked him with confidence what I wanted to know. I did so as I folded the veil I'd worn to mass, as though my question was a futile one.

"Listen, Manuel, sometimes I wonder what you'd do if a woman wanted to stay with you for always, for life, even marry you, maybe have children, eh?"

"Those things are so frightening I can't even think about them," he answered laughing. But, suddenly serious, he narrowed his eyes and looked straight at me: "Because unlike me, you'd like to get married wouldn't you?"

"No I wouldn't," I retorted brusquely. "Not for anything. I've never even thought about it."

"No, all joking aside," he said, "you'd be a perfect wife. You'd be great at bringing up children, even though you'd give them a good smack now and then when you got irritable," and he burst out laughing.

There it was. I'd managed to get him to come right out and say what he thought. It happened in an instant, like when somebody dies in a war.

Manuel was leaning against the doorway: "Well, my sweetie, see you Monday. I really have to go now."

I gave a start, then accompanied him to the gate of the cortile. He took the shortcut toward the piazza. Although it was the hottest part of the day I went out into the vegetable garden, where I walked back and forth from the cortile gate to the garden wall. It was an

August noon and the sky looked like a vast piece of blue
silk that would never fade. I went over to the pepper
plants and roughly tore off dry leaves, then picked a
ripe pepper. When I reached the carnations I went back
to get a bucket of water and splashed it over their
roots. What else was there to do? I sat down on the step
to the garden gate. The sun was scorching. What could I
do with myself? Everything I'd wanted was gone.
Finished. I might as well die.

Idrusa XI

Those were long days. I wandered through the house,
went out into the cortile, then came back in again, then
went out the front door into the street. One day I came
upon Mastro Natale cleaning sea urchins.

"These are from Palascia," he said, offering me one.

"Why from Palascia?" I asked. "Are urchins from
Palascia different?"

"They don't have sand like the ones from the point,"
he said, "and the meat is redder. They call them the
archpriest's urchins and they sell at two pennies more a
dozen because they're so rare."

I didn't know anything about sea urchins from
Palascia or from the point because Antonio scorned
any kind of shellfishing and always went out to sea when
he took to his boat. Mastro Natale split a sea urchin
in half, turned it over to clean it, then placed it carefully in the basket. "What's the matter?" he said.

"Nothing," I answered.

"Come on now, what is it?"

"You're spying on me," I said. "All of you fishermen,
you spy on me and you despise me – the women too.
Because I go with the Spaniard. That's true, isn't it?"

He held out his arms like the priest at the *Dominus
vobiscum*, then picked up another urchin and began to
clean it.

I passed my hand over my forehead, rubbing it irritably.

"Were you out fishing last night?"

"Yes, shellfish."

"Did you sell your catch?"

"Early this morning. The Spanish troops in the garrison buy all our fish. They go crazy when they see them in the boats – they aren't used to anything fresh."

He stood up, stretched his legs. "You ought to see them when they go for a swim," he said. "They squeal like women when they first go in the water. Then as soon as they get warmed up, it's like the sea belonged to them. But if it gets a little bit rough they urinate in fear." Going back to cleaning sea urchins, he repeated, "What's the matter?"

"God help me," I said with a sigh.

"God has nothing to do with things like this," he answered. If I'd stayed there any longer I'd have fallen down at his feet and wept, just like that other time in the cemetery. I walked away abruptly and went back in my house.

Monday evening I was worried about how things would go with Manuel. I put on my best dress and started to braid my hair and fasten it on top of my head with a tortoise shell comb the way I'd seen aristocratic ladies do. But halfway through this process I suddenly recalled our first night of love – the moon in the cortile, the sound of his steps, the happiness of that dawn so long ago. I resumed combing my hair, studying myself in the mirror: "Yes, I am beautiful," I thought, "but what's the use?" When I heard his step on the pavement I told myself: "Chin up," and pretended to be humming a tune.

"So we're happy tonight?" he said as he came in and placed his silk cape on a chair. I continued to hum while he glanced at me out of the corner of his eye: "Greetings my sweet," he said. "What a splendid sight you are this evening. Come over here and let me look at you."

Instead I moved quickly away, stopping at the door to the cortile.

"Hey, where are you going?"

"I feel like a bit of air. Can we sit over here?"

He did as I wished. Sitting beside me he alternated between holding me around the waist and stroking my side: "Such ideas this evening."

I felt an angry joy at leaning my head on his shoulder then picking it up again just at the wrong moment, while he grumbled.

"Look, the North Star," I said pointing it out.

"So I see," he said.

"By October you can't see it from here."

"Is there any particular reason why we have to discuss stars tonight?" he said. Then: "One of the many nice things about making love is it keeps women from talking." He began to move his hand around under my clothes.

"Settle down," I said. "I don't feel like it this evening."

"What?" he said, amazed. "How come?"

"Because I don't feel like it."

"So what's this new state of affairs?"

"So," I thought, "last time he really didn't understand a thing." Behind the pretty words, the grace, the seductive charm, there really was nothing to him – in place of a heart and soul Manuel had only fancy talk. Thus for two years we'd been making love and all the while I'd been alone: there was a void between the two of us. At first I hadn't seen it but it was there just the same.

"Why this sudden change? We've always gotten along perfectly well."

I jumped up.

"All right Idrusa, stop it now." He picked me up roughly and carried me to the bed; my heart was in my mouth. He threw himself on top of me. Curses on him: his kisses still moved me. But at the same time I found myself thinking about what was happening to my body, something I'd never done before. His kisses both excited and disgusted me and I tried to free myself from that desperate pleasure. I couldn't look at him because I didn't know what I might do – maybe scream, "I hate you Manuel!" I kept my eyes closed and my head thrown back until he stretched out beside me and quietly fell asleep. Then I opened my eyes, raised myself up on one elbow and begin to study him in the flickering lamplight that played over his face. "Who knows what you were like when you were ten?" I thought. "Or twelve? Or maybe if you hadn't grown up surrounded by people dressed in silk and satin, people who never did any real work but thought they could do anything? Maybe you'd have been different altogether." Then I remembered the procession for Saints Cosma and Damiano, when the Spaniards' boat came up beside Colangelo's, pitching and rolling in the rough sea and Manuel began to stare at me and wouldn't stop. "If only I hadn't gone out in the boat that day, or if only Colangelo's boat had been on the other side of the saints...."

An idea struck me like a bolt of lightning: "Antonio would be alive. He'd be here right now. He'd be sleeping on his left side the way he always did, with one hand closed in a fist on the pillow. When he woke up his hand would open, then come to rest on my neck." I looked at Manuel again, thinking, "So much time gone by and so many things I've done and this is the way it has to end." Then I came back to my first thought: "You're proud of your noble grace aren't you Manuel? Somebody like you can go to bed with anybody he wants and whenever he wants. You're a gentleman, a Spaniard too, and I'm just a fisherman's daughter, poor besides and alone.

How could things have been any different between the two of us? Why didn't I ever think of this before?"

At dawn when Manuel began to get dressed and I was lying naked on the bed with my hands behind my head watching the rectangle of the window brighten and change color from one moment to the next, I was surprised at the contrast between that night and all the others. I thought about how certain things shouldn't ever be done by calculation even though they could be, which meant for the first time in my life I'd spent a night as a prostitute. He pulled his cloak together and turned the silk purse hanging from his belt so the right side was outward. He was always careful about his dress.

"Aren't you coming with me as far as the vegetable garden?" he asked.

I swung my legs off the bed, stood up and slipped on my dress.

"The weather's turned nice," he said.

"There'll be a tramontana," I answered.

In the garden the clear morning air smelled of the sea and wild fennel. It was cool on my throat, my arms, refreshed my whole body, still sluggish from sleep. When we reached the garden wall he said, "Oh, I forgot to tell you. I'm leaving today. I'm going with four other men to Brindisi to carry a message to the viceroy from Don Felice Ayerbo of Aragon. There's talk of Turks in the area. Some say they might invade Albania. Well, we'll see." He interrupted himself, then said, "I'll be riding an Andalusian stallion. God, what a splended animal."

I didn't ask him as I usually did, when he'd return. He himself brought it up: "I'll be gone for a while. I'll probably be back with the new moon. About a month."

Silence.

Then he spoke again with enthusiasm: "If you could see that stallion. Full of the devil he is." He passed his hand through his hair, then patted me. "Well, keep your spirits up." I stared back at him, but he was already distracted. "It should be a quick trip with a mount like that," he said. "I'll bring you a present. Let's see now, an embroidered kerchief? No, maybe a shawl. Would you like a shawl?"

Silence.

"It's not easy to guess women's tastes. You say 'a shawl' and they think, 'why not a roll of lace?' Best to find out. Is there something you'd like, little one?"

"No," I said, barely audibly. At that moment I had an unmistakable revelation that all love between the two of us was finished.

"Well, I have to be going," he said. He looked at me, and added, "Come on now, chase away last night's storm clouds. Remember making love's the only serious thing in the world." He kissed me: "Be good now, take care of yourself for me." He descended toward the port with a spring in his step till his slender figure disappeared around a turn in the street.

I neither wept nor tore my clothes. I stretched out fully dressed face down on the bed and dug my fingers into the pillow, then relaxed them, then dug them in again and went on like this for several hours until I finally fell asleep.

I dreamed I was in the old olive grove of the Monastery of San Nicola di Càsole, where there are always a lot of noisy crows among the branches. But in my dream there was only a heavy silence. Two of the monks' goats were scampering about and pawing at the roots of the olive trees raising red dust. I was sitting on a porous stone at the edge of the grove where I could see the trees on one side and on the other a vast desert of sand and stones. It was late evening. It would soon be dark and it was a long way home, but for some reason I couldn't move – I couldn't get up. If I called out, someone from the monastery would hear me in that vast silence, but I couldn't make a sound. Suddenly I heard a rapid pounding far off, as if a hundred millstones were grinding grain behind the monastery. But the pounding increased abruptly and came so close the goats ran away in terror. A herd of wild horses appeared, racing madly toward me – Andalusians with angular heads held high. Whinnying furiously, they whipped their black tails in the air. Now they were almost upon me; I could see their muscles working as they ran. I told myself, "They're going to crush you, trample your head under their hooves – get up, don't let them kill you – quick now, up!" but I absolutely couldn't move. I was glued to the stone. My sister's voice dislodged me: "You sleep in your dress? Idrusa!"

I roused myself.

"Are you awake Idrusa? Yes or no?"

"Yes," I said softly.

"I'd like to know if there's any other woman along the whole coast who goes to bed in her dress."

I sat up.

"But what *are* you doing? It's almost noon."

She gave me a long look, then remarked sadly, "Maybe it was a mistake to let you live alone after the tragedy."

"Why?"

"Because you don't know how to live. Every day you get into some new scrape and you're still in mortal sin."

"So goes the women's refrain, doesn't it?" I answered. "I'm a sinner, one of *that* kind.... They'd like to get together and stone me."

"Don't exaggerate. In any case that Spaniard has certainly cast a spell over you."

"I'm not going to see 'that Spaniard' any more," I answered crisply.

"You aren't going to see him any more? Praise God," she sighed. Then she thought for a moment and added, "You scare me, Idrusa. When you decide to do something new you always scare me."

Idrusa XII

"What a lot of names he has," I thought. "Don Felice Sancio Ayerbo of Aragon!" I'd heard Manuel talk about him so many times, describing him as a trusting old man always ready to bless God, the king of Aragon and all humanity itself. "His is a lively old age," Manuel would say. "You can't help liking him."

When I presented myself at Palazzo San Marco, headquarters of the Spanish command and asked to be announced to Don Felice, the officer on guard first looked me up and down, then began to talk and talk, until he worked himself into a fit of irritation. He said I'd have to explain the purpose of my visit, and nobody could see Don Felice without first giving the reason why they wanted to see him, and Don Felice, a most wise and glorious man, was *adelantado* of the Spanish militias and therefore didn't have time to waste with women from Otranto. At this point, quick as a cat, I fled from the room and before the officer could cope with his astonishment I was knocking on Don Felice's door and pushing it open a crack. Inside I saw a man sitting behind a big black table; he was heavy but strong with a high forehead under a mass of wavy white hair. He raised his eyes from his papers and looked at me gravely.

"Good evening," I said, breathless, entering the room.

"Good evening," he answered quickly.

At that moment the officer arrived behind me in great disarray: "She came in on her own," he stammered.

"So I see," answered Don Felice.

"She got away from me," said the officer regarding me with hatred.

Don Felice shook his head: "Let her talk, no need for you to stay." The other bowed and disappeared behind the door.

"Well now, what is it?" said Don Felice, barely glancing at me with an official expression.

I blurted out, "I want to ask your lordship to send the officer Manuel Lopez y Rojo away from Otranto."

He frowned, "And why is that?"

"Because if you don't send him away, I'll kill him."

His frown disappeared and he began to look at me with greater interest.

"But who are you?"

"Idrusa, daughter of Michele de Castellis, fisherman."

"You're expecting a child."

"No sir."

"He promised to marry you."

"No sir."

"He's deserted you."

"No sir."

"Well then, what is it?"

"He's offended me."

"And what's that supposed to mean?"

"That it's worse than if he'd deserted me, believe me sir."

My answer didn't satisfy Don Felice.

"That may very well be true," he said, "but we can't dispatch everyone who offends us to the next world. There are offenses and offenses, for goodness sake."

I answered with determination, "He has wounded my very soul and even if mine is only the soul of a common woman I can't let it be trampled on, because it's the only thing I've got."

Don Felice studied me and furrowed his brow for a moment. Then, as his expression returned to normal, I said, "That's why I can't have him here in Otranto any more. And please excuse me for entering without permission. I've told you everything, sir – I've warned you. And please do pardon the intrusion."

Before he could open his mouth to reply I bowed,
turned on my heels, fled into the street and kept on
running all the way to the sandy beach at Rocamatura.
There I stretched out flat on my back and didn't move
for hours, thinking of nothing. I was almost at peace.
At night I went home.

The next day a Spanish soldier knocked at my door
and said he had an order from Don Felice Ayerbo to
take me to the palace.

Don Felice received me in a beautiful room. "Here's
our wild woman," he said when I came in. He was
wearing a close-fitting skirt of knight's green, striped
tights and dark colored shoes. Circling his ample waist
– he was a heavy, florid man – was a silk sash fastened
with enameled clasps bordered with gold. A purse, also
of silk, hung from the sash. He wore no weapons or
head covering and an abundance of white hair, carefully
combed in the old-fashioned way, fell almost to his
shoulders. He had pale eyes, aristocratic manners and
despite his heavy body, a light and graceful step. I noted
a curious thing about Don Felice's face. When you first
looked at him it was the face of a fat old man, with
puffy cheeks and scores of wrinkles around the eyes, but
if you watched him for a while the face itself seemed to
light up and the eyes took on a youthful sparkle.

There was a sound of bells coming from the window.
"I was trying to figure out which church they're coming
from," he said, approaching the balcony. "You have so
many churches in Otranto!"

"They're the bells of the Church of the Forty Saints,"
I said, thinking, "He's saying these things to put me at
ease."

"Come over here and take a look at Otranto spread
out below us."

I moved closer. It seemed like a different city, from
up here. There was the piazzella, the cathedral, the

curve of the port where the colorful boats and sails contrasted with the blinding white of the houses.

"I liked this city of yours right away," he said, "as soon as I got here two years ago. I liked it because it's a fishermen's town, a city of strong men who are as ancient as the earth. You see, my little one, if you enter the garden of a villa and find that not a single weed has been allowed to take root in the plots of grass and flower beds and not a single dead leaf has been left to rot in a corner, you sense the invisible presence of the skilled and watchful heart that created such harmony. The people of Otranto, men and women who know how to keep their own counsel, resemble that master gardener. You understand what I mean, don't you?" Well, of course I understood the words he was saying, but what they had to do with me or why he'd sent for, that was another story. Maybe he wanted to cheer me up because he felt sorry for me, or maybe it wasn't even that. Besides at times he didn't seem to be speaking to me at all. He just stood there talking aloud to himself. Apparently he loved to talk and it was enough just to have someone there – it didn't matter who.

We were still at the window and he told me he had six children, all grown up now, one of them a girl who must be exactly the same age as I was. He told me about his estates in Spain where poplars grew in the red clay soil, and where his wife was living with the six children. He said he liked to open the window at dawn to let in the first light and imagine his children bathed in that white light – it pleased him to build a palace of light for them.

He had a curious way of talking, Don Felice, with so many wisps and curves and turns of phrase it made me think of the warbling of birds. A single word or phrase was quickly followed by a hundred others all inter-twined. Never in my life had my ears heard anything like it.

When he bestirred himself and moved back into the room hung with tapestries, he pointed at a chair.

"Sit here," he said.

I obeyed.

"Teodoro!" he called.

The old servant appeared in the doorway and looked me over from head to foot.

"Bring us some marzipan and sweet Alezio wine."

"Yessir," replied the servant and with a final glance at me, bowed and went out.

Don Felice said suddenly, "When two people are in love they say a lot of things that sound like nonsense to anyone else but them. Sometimes after talking such nonsense for a long time the two get married. Other times they break things off. That's the way life is, but it's no reason why a person should think about committing murder."

I said nothing.

"I've informed myself about you," he added. "They've told me you're twenty two years old and a widow. Is that right?"

"Yessir."

"You're young," he said, "and beautiful too. If you'll listen to a bit of advice from me, let Manuel de Rojo go his own way. What do you care where he is? That fellow's had a hundred women. You, on the other hand, can easily find a worthy young man, a handsome fisherman from Otranto and begin building dream castles all over again. You know at your age life's a garden of wonders...."

His fancy way of talking was now beginning to annoy me. I jumped to my feet: "I don't care for your advice," I said grimly.

"Don't go running off again. The marzipan is coming."

At that moment Teodoro appeared with a loaded tray and as long as we were eating and drinking neither of us returned to the subject.

"Because, my dear girl," he said finally, "love isn't a sanctuary lamp that always has to be kept lighted no matter what. You say, 'I'll kill him' – come now my dear, aren't you exaggerating? One really ought to keep in mind the fact that the world wasn't created just for lovesick hearts. What would be the use when all is said and done? Let's be reasonable – the good Lord demands something more from us than that. Do you have a mother?"

"She's dead."

"A father?"

"He's dead."

"Don't you have anyone at all? No relatives?"

"A married sister who lives in Minervino."

"Does she resemble you?"

"No, she's completely different."

"So much the better. And what does she know about all this?"

"She knows it's over."

"You didn't tell her what you told me?"

"No."

"Good. You know what we're going to do now? For a few days, nothing. He's away. Before he comes back we'll decide. For now, you must destroy the whole structure of this thing in your mind – porch, nave, the entire temple must go. Understand?"

"Oh come on now," I thought, "enough of this kind of talk...what's it supposed to mean anyway?"

"I see you liked the marzipan," he said. "I'll have Teodoro bring you some more one of these days. And do come back to see me, won't you? Then you can tell me how you're working things out inside yourself."

Idrusa XIII

Don Felice did send me marzipan, but that wasn't all. One day Teodoro arrived with a beautiful piece of silk.

"The master says you should spend the next few days sewing a new dress with your own hands so you can wear it when you come back to the palace."

"But why?" I was dumbfounded.

"Because my master is a good man. A real gentleman. He helps anyone in need and now he's helping you. To tell the truth though, I'm not always pleased about these things. It depends."

"What about this time?"

"Oh well, this time he's doing the right thing. Yes indeed. But some of those lazy do-nothings he gives a lot of money to! He'll say, 'I'm giving them a bit of a boost to help them get on their feet again,' but types like that don't care one whit about getting on their own two feet."

The women of Otranto were dying of curiosity at all these comings and goings from the palace. They stood in their doorways, some with babies in their arms, watching my door. I knew what they were saying: "What kind of widow is she anyway? She didn't even cry when her husband died, and now she never stays home."

One day Mastro Natale's wife Filomena told me exactly what she thought: "You've changed a lot since Antonio died, maybe too much. If you go on this way nobody can hope for anything good from you. Why are you doing it? Why can't you live like the rest of us? Oh Idrusa!"

I really didn't know what to say.

I set about cutting the silk and spent hours stitching, fitting and making ruffles trimmed with ribbons and lace. I worked at a furious pace, but with a mind distinctly divided: one part of me wanted at all costs to hurt Manuel, or even his whole aristocratic race, but another part wanted to do some really great thing, I wasn't sure what, for humanity in general.

When Don Felice saw me all dressed up with my hair carefully done he was speechless – I think it was the first time he looked at me as a man looks at a woman. He remained silent for a moment, then suddenly got to his feet, drew himself up to his full height and exclaimed: "Life is full of poetry."

Then he spoke of Manuel, saying that if I really loved him he could talk to him, maybe even persuade him to marry me.

"Don Felice, I want you to send him away from Otranto."

"Saints preserve us," he answered, " what do you care where he lives?"

"If he's not in Otranto any more, for me it will be as if he'd died or caught the plague."

He shook his head and fell silent – extraordinary for a man who loved to talk as much as he did.

After that he sent for me every now and then; it was clear he liked my company and I hoped to persuade him to do what I wanted. Sometimes he was in a good mood and talked about himself. He said he'd built his wife and children a house in far-away Spain. It had one floor partly under ground and two upper stories. That was enough for them; they didn't want anything more. But the tower – the tower he'd built a little at a time to please himself, something after his own heart. He said for a sixty-year-old man like him, everything life had given him had gradually retreated from the center and made a frame around him. He had become the painting in the frame, and his aging heart had lately begun to beat in a new and different way. He said these things with emotion, and as he spoke his great honey-colored eyes even seemed to fill with tears.

"Is this possible?" I said to myself.

He had a weakness for the Holy Scriptures and his speech was full of references to the Bible. Even with regard to the story about the tower and his sixty-year-old heart he told me that the Parable of the Laborers in the Vineyard showed that God agreed with him. Weren't the laborers who came last to the vineyard paid as much as those who came first? The servant Teodoro, coming and going in and out of the room always nodded his assent when his master said these things, and I looked at both of them in wonder. They seemed to me to be a remarkably curious pair. One day Don Felice's oldest son arrived in Otranto to pay a visit to his father. He was a scrawny youth, short of stature, with thin lips and ears that stuck out. Teodoro couldn't stomach him because he was always so harsh and irritable with Don Felice – typical, I thought, of the way children treat sentimental fathers. Don Felice's response was to burst into speech with twice as much enthusiasm. After a few days his son left.

Once Don Felice invited me to dine with him. Before sitting down he made the sign of the cross and in a solemn voice asked God to bless me, himself and our food. This done, he looked lovingly at his plate of fish surrounded by salad greens and served in the Catalonian style with blancmange, then sat down a bit removed from the table because of his sizable paunch. I watched as he ate – all that white hair circling his forehead made him look like a great peaceable lion. It was clear he was happy to have me with him. At one point he said, "Do you know the story of Ruth?"

"Ruth? I've never heard of her."

"Well, as the story goes, Ruth was from the land of Moab and she came to Israel as a widow with her mother-in-law Naomi. She was, the Bible says, quite beautiful."

"But why are you always reading holy books?"

Don Felice smiled: "They're full of wisdom and poetry. Those patriarchs who slept on the good moist earth knew how to pray and how to love with greatness. They were men of fulfillment."

I don't know why, but I had to laugh. "So what happened to Ruth?" I asked.

"She set about gleaning in old Boaz's field. One day Naomi said to her, 'Bathe and anoint yourself, then put on your best dress and go to the threshing floor. After Boaz has finished eating and drinking and gone to sleep among the sheaves of grain, go and lift his blanket and lie down at his feet. Then he will tell you what to do.'"

"But why did she anoint herself?" I asked.

"Because the oil was perfumed."

"What happened next?"

"Ruth obeyed. In the middle of a starry night Boaz found the girl at his feet. 'Who are you?' he said. And she answered, 'I am your servant Ruth. Spread your blanket over me,' The fragrant essence of the night entered old Boaz's nostrils and spread quickly, violently, throughout his body. Suddenly he took fright at the distant stars shining through the palm fronds, at the vast plain of the earth stretching to meet the sky, and his old heart began to beat very fast. Then out of the night came her voice once more: 'Naomi sent me because you are my kinsman.' And he said, 'You have surpassed your own goodness, daughter, because you haven't gone in search of young men, be they rich or poor. May the Lord bless you.' And so saying, he spread his blanket over the girl."

I had listened carefully to the story and all at once it came to me what it meant. "How come her mother-in-law sent her to that old man?" I objected. "And why should the Bible be telling stories like that?"

Don Felice started, taken aback; then he made a sweeping gesture with his fork. "To Ruth and Boaz was born Obed and Obed begat Jesse and Jesse begat David the King," he said solemnly. He must have felt a sudden pain as he spoke because his face flushed red and he looked confused.

"He's not well," I thought. "He might even be having a stroke."

"What is it, Don Felice?" I said. "Shall I call Teodoro?"

"No, no," he answered, staring blankly into space. After a minute or two his face gradually regained its normal color and he turned his gaze to me.

"I'm quite well," he said. Smiling at me, he repeated: "Quite well indeed. Go ahead and eat, my little one." Then as though continuing a thought: "You, I, all men would like the world to be pure but nature won't go along with us and we all end up sullied in one way or another. Hence, the Bible, being a wise book, doesn't hide these things."

"Well, well," I thought to myself.

"I'm old," he added, "and since I haven't many more years to live, God allows me to be sincere – with myself as well as with others. Do you see what I mean, Idrusa?"

"You always mention God, no matter what you're talking about," I said, and he smiled again.

But the most incredible thing was that after a minute or two he turned to his plate of spiced freshwater tench with great relish, paying special attention to the pine nuts in the sauce, which he picked out and ate one by one. All in all a different man, a jovial dinner companion.

When dessert finally came it was a torte made of rich ricotta, beaten eggs and Neapolitan fruit pastry, all with a sugar crust flavored with rosolio liqueur. I began to think I'd made my point and one day soon Manuel would be called to the palace and Don Felice would stand there in the middle of the room, his legs wide apart, his belly sagging between them, and make a nice little speech about how a change of air would be useful to an officer of Manuel's caliber and a transfer to such and such a place would be best for all concerned, with God's blessing.

That was, in fact, what happened one brilliant sunny day while the branches of the palm trees in front of Don Felice's palace were swaying in the breeze as I arrived. It was one of those days that often follow a strong tramontana, when the wind has swept the whole world clean. Don Felice had sent a messenger to inform me and I was hurrying to thank him. But just before I reached the stairway I saw Manuel coming down the last flight of steps. I wanted to flee but he was quicker than I was.

"Oh no you don't," he said, grabbing my arm.

We looked at each other in silence for an instant, each studying the other's face.

"It *was* you, wasn't it?"

"Yes."

"Why?"

"So I wouldn't have to see you in Otranto ever again."

"This I've understood, but why?"

"You don't know what love means, Manuel. You've never known. For you it's as if love simply didn't exist anywhere."

"So, when I was away a month ago, you'd already thought about getting rid of me."

"Yes," I said.

"How about that. And you appealed to Don Felice...oh my, you're really going to make your way in the world, aren't you."

"You don't understand at all," I said, in despair. "You've never understood."

He shrugged. "We've had some wonderful times together, Idrusa. But then you had to get ideas about marriage, children, cooking pasta for me, and so on." He looked me up and down intently. "We're really elegant today, but ill humor doesn't become you."

When he talked like that I felt like the whole world wasn't worth an empty cockleshell.

"I hate you, Manuel."

He answered me calmly: "This is the last time we'll see each other, Idrusa, and we'll both remember this occasion, so let's try not to say anything stupid." Though I tried, I couldn't hold back a sudden desperate sob.

"Here, here now," he said. "Things like this always end sooner or later – that's only the rule. No need to take it too hard. Above all, let's not make it into a tragedy."

"The horses are ready, sir," said his servant, approaching him.

"Is everything packed up and loaded?" asked Manuel.

"Yessir."

"I'm going to San Cataldo," he said. "No telling whether it'll be as windy as Otranto or if there'll be as many northerly storms."

For me it was like the world had turned upside down and after all those nights of love, holding each other until dawn, Manuel and I were now just two strangers. The past had broken away and left us – it was gone, vanished forever.

"Well, goodbye Idrusa. Good luck," he said.

"Good luck," I barely murmured.

We looked at each other, said no more. When the carriage began to move I almost cried out, called to him: "Manuel, don't go! I still love you," but I got hold of myself. "No, no not that!" I thought, and rushed up the stairs.

"Well, well," asked Don Felice, "are you happy now?" His eyes, the eyes of a little boy grown old, twinkled with good humor. It was strange because at that moment I should certainly have been pleased and he displeased, but I was so mixed up I really couldn't quite figure out why the opposite had occurred.

Idrusa XIV

Moving quietly about my house among the chairs, I did my sewing and ironing, making sure every seam, every crease, fell exactly right. If not I'd undo what I'd done and start all over again. If the hem of a sheet wasn't perfectly straight I'd even spend a quarter of an hour retouching one spot. I shook out the fringes of my linens, then carefully straightened them with my fingers, one bunch of threads at a time, as though my life depended on it. I cleaned every corner of the house and wiped down all the walls. When I came to a window I'd take a damp cloth and wash the dust from every geranium leaf. If they were crinkled I'd open each one with dogged persistence and give it as much attention as if it were a sacred chalice. I performed all these tasks to perfection and with the greatest calm, simply because my heart was so completely, almost pleasantly, empty. And so the days passed. At night when I could no longer work I went to bed early, but even then no specific thoughts took form in my head – images appeared and disappeared by themselves like white clouds blown by the scirocco into shapes of faces, horses, pillows or flowers, which quickly vanish in the sky.

There was no more reason for me to sit with Don Felice in his room with the balcony, but every now and then he sent for me, and like a sleepwalker I went and presented myself at the palace.

"You shouldn't go," my sister kept saying. "There's another danger waiting there for you."

"Danger?" I had to laugh. "What danger?"

"Why do you think he wants to see you?" she insisted. "Why does he send you clothes and bracelets? Why do you always make the same mistake, my child?"

"Oh I suppose he's fallen in love with me," I answered, bored.

"And you keep going to see him?"

"Of course I do."

"Idrusa, that's not very nice."

I shrugged.

"Listen my dear sister," she said, "can't you even live for a little while without committing a sin?"

"The only thing all of you ever talk about is sin. Don't you know anything else?"

I wanted to destroy myself, I really did, and she didn't understand. I remembered when I was little we used to play a game down by the port. The idea was to see who could hit the live oak with a stone from farthest away. If I didn't win I'd get so angry at myself I'd plunge into the water and hold my head down until I felt I was drowning. Only the nausea from swallowed sea water brought me back to the shore. Once Colangelo, Assunta's husband, noticed; he was a little boy then and used to play with us.

"Hey, you're really stupid," he said. "You know you could die doing that?"

"Of course I know."

"So you *want* to die?"

"What business is that of yours?"

"But you're a girl. Look, you're shaking?"

"I am *not* shaking!" I screamed and would have dived right back in the water if he hadn't grabbed my arm. We began punching each other so hard that day that Mastro Natale had to separate us. "But where does a tiny little girl get all that strength?" he said.

I wonder how it would have turned out if all this had happened to someone else. Would she have become Don Felice's friend? I did. I knew all there was to know about his life and the lives of the patriarchs. Often while he talked I thought about other things but my mind always retained some trace of those long stories full of oddities, although I could never quite understand where they were going. They were strange people, those patriarchs, always mixing up their own sins with God's plans, just like Don Felice.

He educated me, taught me fancy manners, dressed me in wonderful silks and brocades. There was something really great about Don Felice – he was a good man who saw to it that those around him lived well, which is a rare quality among gentlemen, at least those I've known on this earth. Still he must have realized that I spent time with him merely to keep from thinking about the broken pieces of my life and to have the silks and brocades I loved so much. All this was as plain as day. He could have recognized it and still taken me in his arms, but he didn't. He didn't see the obvious. He told me I was an angel and when I was near him he actually felt a rustling of two tiny wings lifting his soul and carrying it upward – at that point he almost always ended up speaking in Latin – he had a passion for Latin. At times I was even picking it up.

Anyhow, for my part, I can only say I was no longer the same person or at least I didn't seem to be. I was as unstable as the ripples in the sea. Spanish and Neapolitan officers who frequented the palace would see me fanning the brazier and fall in love with me, sometimes desperately. I began to understand that men love not being loved, even though they don't realize it. The more distant you are the more they want to be near you. I wondered why I hadn't arrived at such a simple conclusion before. At that my thoughts would turn back to Manuel, to the extraordinary love we might have lived and I'd entertain a whole lot of ideas that were now absolutely pointless. Then I'd decide to do some sewing let's say, or put some lace edging on a petticoat and instead I'd get up and go down to the sandy beach at Rocamatura: the only habit that remained of my former life was this practice of lying on the sand a few feet from the waves and staring through the wild fennel bushes, watching life go by. And I would have kept it to

my dying day, I think, if something hadn't happened to
Otranto that changed everybody's habits. One morning
when the tramontana was stirring up heavy seas this
something appeared on the horizon: the Turks. Don
Felice insisted I should get into his coach at once and
leave with him for Lecce, or even Brindisi.

"I'm not budging from here," I said. "So save your
breath, Don Felice. I'll do exactly what the other
Otrantini women do, and their fate will be my fate."

"Then I'm not going either," he answered, determined.

"You must go, this isn't your land. It's different for
you."

"Eh? What's that? You don't yet know who I am, my
little one. But you'll find out soon enough. You've set
yourself up for a magnificent spectacle, let God be my
witness!"

He was the only Spaniard who didn't flee Otranto,
and as for the spectacle – he kept his promise.

Idrusa XV

The day of the attack on the Porticella we women took
the small children and went to stay in the cathedral, on
the archbishop's orders. Thus the naves came to look
like the streets of an encampment and mothers with
little ones gathered in the chapels. The archbishop
came to visit each chapel in turn, telling us that things
don't always follow the same course, or go according to
our poor plans, but seemingly chance events are always
the result of God's will. Therefore, he said, anyone who
insists on explaining them by reason alone is falling
into the devil's trap. The children, huddled together on
the floor at the feet of the various altars, stared wide-
eyed and full of wonder at the archbishop, then turned
to each other and burst into tears. Even nursing babies
shook their little heads and pummeled their mothers'
breasts with tiny hands instead of taking the nipples

offered to them. All the little ones were nervous. The
doors of the church had stood open for thirteen days,
and the brilliant August sun, which came through the
windows as well, shone on the red, green and yellow
pieces in the mosaic floor; it brightened the trees in
the Garden of Eden, the Scorpion, and the Scales,
reaching as far as a point halfway between the Tower of
Babel and Noah's Ark.

The second day after the doors were opened the first
of the dead was carried in, his head dangling like a egg
plant. They presented him to the Madonna, who stood
quiet and peaceful under her golden crown, then laid
him on the table in the sacristy with his feet pointing
toward the door. The dead man's wife tore out locks of
her hair and flung them on the corpse while old women
prayed in mournful voices. With every day that passed
more dead arrived in ever increasing numbers and all
ended up on the sacristy table, feet pointed toward the
door. They were so bloody and dirty the women cried out
to see them – some fainted and fell to the floor. Eventually Father Epifani gathered together the younger
women without children and after looking us all over
finally spoke directly to me: "Do you think you could
manage to clean them up so they'll look decent and
proper? And not be too long about it?"

"I think so," I said and from that moment on it was
my job to wash the faces of the dead and prepare them
for burial. They arrived and departed quietly, like
creatures from another world. After Canon De Pasca
raised his arms inside his wide sleeves to give the
benediction, Father Epifani, aided by a lay brother,
wrapped each one in a cloak, and took him off for
burial.

"These, Idrusa," he'd say, "are happy now."

It bothered me to hear him talk like this. For me
happiness was sitting at the foot of a tree or beside the
sea.

One evening Assunta came up to me by the sacristy door and said she wished she were dead.

"Now, now, get hold of yourself," I answered.

"Aren't you scared?" she said.

"Well, sometimes I am. Who isn't?"

"What exactly are you afraid of?"

"Oh well, that depends."

She burst into sobs. "You don't have any children. You don't understand. What will happen to my Alfio? Will they cut his throat?"

"But didn't you hear what Father Epifani said," I answered. "He made it very clear. They take little boys back to their country, dress them up like Turks, send them to the mosque five times a day and then make soldiers out of them. Soldiers get paid and after a while any one of them can buy his freedom if he saves enough money."

"Do you think it's true?" She thought for a bit then began to cry again. "My little Alfio a Turkish soldier!"

"So what does that mean anyhow? Only God knows how things really are. But all this is only talk – Don Alfonso is going to liberate us."

"Do you honestly think he'll come?"

"Of course he will. It's only a question of days, maybe even hours."

Actually I no longer believed Don Alfonso would come – nobody did. But during those days everyone tried to convince the others he would and so we kept talking about him.

"You're a good woman, Idrusa," Assunta said suddenly. "I was wrong before when I judged you harshly."

My sister had also come to stay in the cathedral. She and her husband had left their farm the day the Turks first appeared. Once when I was sitting with her and Assunta in the Chapel of Saints Cosma and Damiano, cutting and sewing bandages for our wounded, a Neapolitan stranger came up to our group. From the way he was dressed he seemed to be in the governor's service.

"Which of you is Idrusa?" he said.

"I am," I answered.

"Come with me. Captain Zurlo wants to see you."

"He wants to see *me*?"

"Yes Ma'am."

"Now what have you done?" asked my sister, horrified.

"Who me? Nothing. What would I have done? I've been washing and dressing the dead."

My sister turned to the stranger: "Why do they want her? What's happened?"

"I have orders to take her to the palace. That's all I know."

I put my bandages down on a bench.

"Oh no, you never do anything, do you?" said my sister. "And yet the things that always happen to you never happen to other women."

"Oh come now," I answered, annoyed. I went out the east door with the messenger and we walked along in silence. On the stairway of the palace we encountered Teodoro, Don Felice's servant. He looked scared to death.

"My master's dying," he said.

"What happened?"

"He was wounded in the chest when he was up on the walls."

"On the walls?"

"Yes, he wanted to be there; he wanted to die."

"But why?" I asked, starting up the stairs without knowing what I was doing. I didn't even wait for an answer to my question.

"Who knows why? Just all of a sudden he didn't want to live any more."

Captain Zurlo and Canon De Pasca were standing at the foot of the bed, as Don Felice, breathing with difficulty, struggled to talk. His wide-open eyes focused first on one then on the other, as though he was trying to say something with a look. Finally he stammered: "David says...."

"Don't tire yourself, my friend," answered Captain Zurlo. "God is close to you now; it doesn't matter."

Don Felice sighed two or three times, then raised his head: "*Transibo in locum tabernaculi admirabilis* – I will go to the house of the Lord," he said and fell back on his pillow. "I'm going." At that I moved closer and he saw me. For a moment he looked at me in silence, moving one hand about the bed as he clutched the sheet in his fist. Several minutes passed before he managed to whisper, "Idrusa."

"Don Felice," I said.

We looked at each other in silence. Meanwhile Captain Zurlo had called the canon over to a corner to talk to him.

"Did you see?" said Don Felice and fell back again.

It was clear he wanted to say something but he didn't have the voice left to say it. His heavy breathing echoed through the room in widely spaced gasps, almost a death rattle. Finally he tapped his forehead two or three times with his finger, nodded yes, and calling on all his strength, he spoke: "Our head is little, too little." He fell silent for a bit, let out a long breath, then said, "Too little to know what happens on the other side, but I'm telling you...." Again his voice gave out. "I promise...as soon as I can...I'll be with you always."

Watching from the corner, the canon shook his head. Don Felice closed his eyes, while I made an effort and kissed his hand, all bathed in cold sweat.

In that same instant we heard a burst of mortar fire and Don Felice reopened his eyes but he said no more.

"They're firing mortars, blast them!" exclaimed Captain Zurlo, leaving the room. The canon, attending to his duty, took a book in hand and turned the pages

until he found the right one. Then he sat down and in a
low voice began to recite the prayer for the dying.

Don Felice, his eyes closed, was breathing in heavy
wheezes.

"He's dying," I thought. Then, "Why can't the soul
simply fly away all at once? Why does it have to be
pulled back and forth like this for hours?"

Captain Zurlo returned and, standing at the foot of
the bed, gazing at Don Felice, he said, "He was a fine
man." At last he turned to me: "You can go on back to
the cathedral now."

I took one last look at Don Felice. In a few short
moments his face had gone white, his cheeks hollow –
but then all at once I saw him again as I'd first seen
him, sitting at his table in Palazzo De Marco, raising
his white head to ask me in astonishment: "And who are
you?" I heard his voice as it had sounded that day, along
with his present death rattle – then both were swallowed
up in the litany for the dying, which the canon and
Teodoro were reciting at the foot of the bed. I
remembered him again – on the balcony of Palazzo De
Raho when the bells of the the Church of the Forty
Saints were ringing and his honey-colored eyes had
looked into mine as he told me how he wanted to build
a castle of light, outlining it with his arms. He'd been
happy. Once more that faraway voice was swallowed up
in the litany for the dying and I couldn't stand it
anymore. One step at a time, I backed out of the room
to get away from that horrible dirge, then found myself
in the street. I could see the doors of the palazzi, the
corner of Vicolo Santa Rosa, the cathedral piazza,
Father Leone standing in front of the cathedral talking
to a fat little man with a mustache – but I saw it all as
though far off in a dream. As I walked back I seemed to
be following a very old memory, along a street I'd taken
years before.

My sister was standing behind the east door anxiously waiting.

"What happened?"

"Don Felice is dying."

"A stroke?"

"Anything but! He was hit while fighting on the walls."

"On the walls? As old and fat as he was? Had he gone completely mad?"

"Don't talk like that," I said.

"That man ruined your reputation and now I'm not supposed to say anything, is that it?"

There in the silence of the church, without even knowing how it happened, I burst out laughing and crying at the same time. "Oh yes," I screamed, "this is really the time to be thinking about reputations."

My sister gave me a frightened look and went away without another word.

Idrusa XVI

Alfio and the other little ones his age had fallen asleep, all tired out from climbing up and down on the church pews all day.

The four lanterns kept burning at night flared up now and then in a draft and transformed the figures of saints in the frescoes, with their capes and staffs and crowns, into so many bearded ghosts lined up along the walls. Every now and then a child whimpered in his sleep.

"Now I can go out," I thought and was already on my way toward the main door, walking past the chapel where the women lay sleeping on sacks spread out on the floor. As usual Father Leone too was asleep. I had already gone out another night without him noticing. I found myself in the piazza where three streets came together, streets lined by the most beautiful buildings in Otranto. All was still. Wrapped in my shawl, I went down Vicolo del Crismatico, but then all at once I stopped, afraid I'd meet someone. The other time I'd gone out I'd come upon Colangelo right here in this street. He'd certainly been out of his head that night, had no idea what he was doing. If not, why did he suddenly start kissing me that way? "I'm a swine!" he'd shouted at the end and dashed off who knows where. Anyway I turned back and sat down in the cathedral piazza, just outside the door. Low clouds dragged across the sky, thinned out, then closed in again and thickened. Every once in a while a star or two seemed to pass hurriedly by, then disappeared just as quickly. Suddenly the moon came out, white as chalk. It frightened me. No, I thought, there was no hope left. It was plain as day we were done for. But it wasn't that in itself. It was another thought that filled me with wonder. Here we were – me, Antonio, Manuel, the chairs in my house, my cortile, the well bucket, all of us caught in a net, even Don Felice, who used to walk about on the rugs in his reception room with his belly sticking out in front of him – and the candelabra in his palace, everything....But a single tug at the end of a cord would be enough to send us all one by one sliding into a vast sea. Was that how it was in the end? Nothing left of anyone? Three Neapolitan soldiers went by in silence, with tired steps.

"How are things going on the walls?" I asked.

"Bad, damned bad," one answered.

"Two or three days," said another, "and we'll have nothing left but our breeches."

When I went back into the cathedral Father Leone was awake.

"But how did you get outside?" he asked, dumbfounded.

"I went out while you were sleeping. I was hot."

"While I was sleeping? Was I sleeping? Dear Jesus I'm so tired I can't tell whether I'm awake or asleep. Quick my dear, come inside."

The women were beginning to wake up and walk around, murmuring back and forth from one chapel to another, holding their babies in their arms. I entered the sacristy. Father Procomio and Father Epifani were pouring what little goat's milk could still be found into various jugs for the children.

"Good, you're back in time," said Father Epifani. "But where were you?"

"Out," I answered.

"Wandering around in the streets?"

"Not very far."

"Any news from the walls?"

"Oh yes, the latest word. Pretty soon now we'll all be done for," I answered.

He continued pouring out milk, passing me a bowlful. "Here," he said, "do me a favor and drink a little milk."

It was still warm from the goat's udder. It tasted good.

Three days later, the twelfth of August, a Friday, we heard a racket so loud we thought the main walls of the cathedral would come down. The naves filled with the smell of smoke. Then Antonio De Raho came rushing in shouting, "Bolt the doors – the Turks are coming!"

In the midst of the general uproar the Basilian monks bolted the doors with iron bars. A little later the old archbishop appeared, clad in his pontifical vestments. He made his way through the central nave and sat down on his throne, just to the left of the principal altar. When the Turks broke through the main door and invaded the church he sat there motionless, tall and thin in his gilded robes, crowned with his miter of white silk striped with gold, holding a huge cross in front of him, clasped tightly in both hands. The Turks rushed forward in a shouting mob and bounded up to the steps to the altar but there they stopped short at the sight of the archbishop. The feathers on their zarcolas waved back and forth as they stood staring and shaking their heads. Maybe they couldn't believe it was really a man sitting there in purple robes and gazing upward. He remained still for a moment longer, continuing to gaze at the gold cross, then slowly got to his feet and turned his eyes from the cross to faces of the Turks, looking at each one in turn. Finally he held out his wizened hand and cried in his feeble voice, "Unhappy wretches, fallen into eternal darkness!"

The Turks looked at him wide-eyed – a moment passed before they got hold of themselves. But when they did, they stabbed him and burst into wild yells. As we stared petrified at the wounded archbishop we saw one Turk yank off his miter, put it on himself and swagger away through the nave wagging his head like a puppet.

"Stay together, don't move," the friars kept repeating. "Don't cry." Oh yes, "Don't move," indeed. But when I saw a Turk tear Alfio out of Assunta's arms and heard the little boy screaming in fear, that was enough for me. I leaped at the Turk in a fury and grabbed Alfio away from him

"Idrusa my dear," shouted Father Epifani.

Two or three Turks jumped on me, one on top of the other, as I held Alfio to my breast, speechless with terror. They finally got him away and one of the *delli* came at me with a dagger in hand. Beneath the wings of his zarcola I could see his eyes staring at me with burning intensity and I looked right back at him without flinching. He paused, his dagger raised, until his enraged face dissolved into a grimace that could have been a sob of joy. He sheathed his dagger. "Beautiful, beautiful," he grunted in our language, taking hold of my shoulders. I felt his hands on my neck and I staggered, but then, quicker than a cat, I covered his eyes with one hand, seized his dagger with the other and plunged it into his chest. From where I had slid down on the floor I could see his eyes above me for an instant, astonished and full of questions. Other Turks nearby burst out laughing and then the astonished face vanished. Above my head I saw a vast red sky and all noises faded away. Instead a profound calm settled over me under the weight of that red sky. From an immense distance a single voice reached my ears: "God bless you, Idrusa. God bless you, little one." It must have been Father Epifani – it seemed to be. But I couldn't answer. I was already far away, so very far away from that voice.

PART III

Nachira I

The cellar still smelled of wine, but there was no wine left, only the faintly sour odor absorbed by the stone of the walls, treacherous for an empty stomach. Besides, God help us, it was pitch dark wherever we looked – we could have been drowning in the air. It must have been one of Lanzillotto Fragà's winecellars; he'd been a member of the council long before the Turks ever came to Otranto.

"Nachira, where are you?" said Cola Mazzapinta in a low voice.

"Here by the stairs," I answered.

"We have to get out of here, Nachira. We'll starve to death if we don't."

"Where can we go? The minute we come out they'll grab us."

"But we can't stay here."

"We *have* to."

"Listen Cola," I answered, "now that the war's over things are different. A man has to think about saving himself. There's simply no point in dying now."

My legs had gone to sleep so I stretched and tried to find a better position, but there was no way to be comfortable on that moldy floor.

"How many of us are there?" asked Cola Mazzapinta.

"Ten or so, I think, counting the ones at the back. Cristoforo Rio was the last to come down. He said the Turks had rounded up all our men in the piazza, then counted them and taken their names and locked them in the castle courtyard."

"What are they going to do with them?"

"We'll find out," I said.

221

"Are you saying they'll be killed?"

"We'll find out."

"Good Saint Basil, is that all you can say?"

"Why? Have *you* got a better answer?"

We heard a scraping sound, then feet coming down the stairs.

"Oh, oh, what's that?" whispered Cola.

"You down there," came Gaetano Calò's voice from the stairs, "it turns out we've been stupid. Know what I saw?"

"What?" asked Cola.

"There's a little window here behind the stairs. I looked out and saw how stupid we are."

"All right, so what did you see?"

"I saw Don Donadeo Colussi and Don Antonio di San Pietro rushing back and forth like arrows, carrying papers in their hands. So I called Don Antonio over and asked him what he was doing. Know what he said? He told me he was paying the ransom and they were putting him aboard a ship bound for La Valona. They'll take him there, then let him go free. So what are we doing down here?"

"But those folks are rich," I said. "What are we supposed to use for ransom? Different kinds of cheeses?"

Nobody said any more. A faint whistling broke the silence, growing gradually louder until it was almost a howl. Probably the wind. Those in the back of the cellar began to come forward one by one, feeling their way along the walls. Somebody stumbled – there was a thump, then a, "Goddamn stones!" Time passed slowly, very slowly. None of us had any idea what was in store for us. Or why we were even born in the first place. And to think we'd all gotten married and drunk to each other's health on our wedding days and there'd been music and dancing and merrymaking. And we'd had children too, as if we were going to be around for centuries, certain we'd know how to take care of everything and nothing would go wrong we couldn't set right. Beside me Mazzapinta let out a sigh so loud we turned around. Life is like the sea, I thought: when the water's calm you can look down through it to the rocks at the bottom with the seaweed curling and straightening, little fish darting and shimmering, sea urchins gripping the stones and all sorts of tiny things moving gently in the current. But if it gets riled up into waves and foam everything disappears and death itself can rise out of that same stretch of water.

"There'll be a tramontana tomorrow," exclaimed Mazzapinta.

At that Cristoforo Rio said, "I've got a notion the Turks will cut off our heads."

Silence again.

After a bit Gaetano Calò said, "What if we slipped out of here at night? Near Palazzo Colussi there's an underground passage leading outside the walls. Remember? That's how Fanciullo made it back in during the seige when he returned from Naples."

"But if they catch you before you get to Palazzo Colussi they'll kill you," said De Raho. "We could surrender at dawn instead and ask to work."

"It looks to me like they'll be cutting off our heads," repeated Cristoforo Rio.

"For Christ's sake, will you stop it!" swore De Raho.

"Palazzo Colussi's only a minute or so from here, two alleys away," said Gaetano Calò.

"But then there's the piazza. Any piazza's bad business – like nets are for tuna," said De Raho and added, "Listen Gaetano, I was in the cathedral when the Turks burst in and my wife cried out to me, 'Antonio there's no need for you to die now. You've got to do your best to stay alive!' She was the one who made sure I got out through the sacristy in the confusion. She told me to take refuge in a cellar. But tonight I just don't see any way out of all this."

"Well I do," said Gaetano Calò. "I'm not staying here like a cornered rat."

"Same here. I can't stand it any more," said a voice in the dark.

We were all edgy because we didn't know what to expect and now the fear of death had got hold of us all, a fear we'd never had during the seige.

Above us in the street we heard footsteps, the heavy tread of armed men.

"They come and go like they owned the place," said De Raho.

"Why did we put up such a fight?" sighed Gaetano Calò. "What good did it do? Now those bastards are just making themselves at home in our houses anyway."

At that Mazzapinta bestirred himself and spoke up in a definite voice like he was making a proclamation: "Captain de li Falconi (he's dead too, God rest his soul) said if we didn't resist, the Turks would be in Lecce in two days and from there they'd go on to Brindisi."

"Oh sure, the logic of war," said Gaetano Calò. "Don't make me laugh. But what was the use? Are we any better off?"

"That's about enough of this kind of talk," answered De Raho irritably.

For a while nobody spoke. We crouched there listening to every little noise from above and waiting anxiously for nightfall. Then the noises stopped and a profound calm took their place – even more frightening – like the world itself had stopped. Night had come. At this point we separated into two groups, groping along carefully, stumbling over one other's legs and asking, "Hey, who's that?"

"All set then, everybody?" said Gaetano Calò at last. Three men stood ready to go out with him.

"May God protect you," I exclaimed.

"Good luck if we don't see each other again," said Gaetano Calò.

"Good luck!" we answered in chorus.

They went up the steps on tiptoe and disappeared. The six of us who were left remained quiet, straining our ears to listen.,

"If their idea works," said Mazzapinta, "they'll make it to safety in two hours. If not it's only a matter of minutes...."

I remembered the walls – the smoke, the dust, the scimitars, the Turkish hats – and the sound of Cola Mazzapinta's voice as he shouted from the main tower: "When Don Alfonso comes, we'll chase you back into the sea, you heathen pigs!" But now Mazzapinta was sitting next to me, rubbing his leg every once in a while where a musket ball had grazed it.

I was half-sitting, half-lying down, with my head against a stone so cold and hard it was driving me crazy. I shifted my position, peering left and right, trying to estimate the size of the cellar. It was probably big enough for thirty casks, maybe even thirty-five, a nice winecellar.

"Well, mates," said De Raho suddenly, "I'm not afraid of the Turks themselves – you know what scares me? Their god, that's what. He must be a demon. We're going to have to deal with him, I'm afraid."

"How do you mean?" asked Mazzapinta.

"The Turks will say to us: 'First honor our god. Then we'll see about you.' So what do we do then?"

Nobody had an answer.

"See what I mean? That'll be the hard part," said De Raho.

"Oh well, for now let's try to get a little sleep," answered Mazzapinta. "We'll need clear heads tomorrow." The wind was whistling. We could feel the heavy gusts against the walls, followed by total silence. Then renewed gusts all over again and in the background a thin sound like distant wailing. I remembered a day two years ago. I was out at sea with Colangelo and the wind was tossing our boat back and forth like it was trying to pick it right up – and all the while there was this series of faraway whistles. That was the time a two-hundred pound swordfish suddenly hit the prow of our boat, then dived under head first and began to lash about with its tail, raising great clouds of spray.

"Keep a tight grip on the rudder," I said to Colangelo. Then I grabbed the trident and stood up in the prow. The swordfish kept diving and resurfacing and shaking its fleshy tail like it was the only big fish in the sea. Colangelo was holding the rudder tight in both hands, leaning backward and biting his lip. The fish disappeared underwater and that looked like the end of it. But no – out he jumped on the other side of the boat, shooting straight up like a puppet on a string.

"Look out. With this sea, he'll capsize the boat!" shouted Colangelo.

I was about to tell him I was just waiting for the right moment to use my spear but the biggest wave yet splashed over the boat and drenched us both. The fish dived again but as soon as his tail went down his head popped up. "All right then, die!" I shouted standing up straight in the the prow and sinking the points of the trident into the vital spot just below his gills, where the barbs held it fast. He stopped moving but then suddenly jumped halfway out the water and looked at me. Yes he did, he looked right at me, his round eyes staring into mine, like he was asking me something. At last he turned belly up and sank back into the sea.

Sitting there in Lanzillotto's Fragà's winecellar, I saw the eyes of the swordfish moving forward from the back of the room, staring at me like they did that day. Then they faded back into the dark, only to appear again, and then again, and all the while weird squeaky noises were coming out of the walls.

"De Raho, you hear that?"

"Hear what?"

"Don't you hear those noises in the walls?"

"Mice," said De Raho. "There must be a drain back there somewhere."

"I saw a pair of eyes looking at me, like they were asking me something."

"But you were snoring," he said. "Well, better take it easy now, and quiet down."

I was hot. I touched my forehead; it was burning up. "I've got a fever," I thought, and suddenly a lot of dancing figures appeared in the back of the cellar. They were wearing raggedy reddish-yellow cloaks and moving up and down and back and forth. I closed my eyes, then opened one again – they were still there. "Go away, go away!" I wailed until I fell into a black void and forgot everything.

"Nachira," De Raho woke me up brusquely. "Have you had enough sleep? It's daylight outside."

I stood up but I was so weak and dizzy I had to lean against the wall.

"I guess I was delirious," I said.

"Forget it. We've got to go up now," he answered.

Mazzapinta and the others gathered around.

"All right now," said Mazzapinta, "the minute you see a Turk, everybody down. Got it?"

"Where are we going?"

"You were asleep, so you didn't hear anything," said Mazzapinta. "Just follow us and do what we do. Understand?"

Nachira II

We went up the steps on tiptoe. The alleyway was deserted but the houses, their doors wide open or smashed apart, were evidence the Turks had already made an extended visit and cleaned out whatever they wanted. We

advanced very slowly, walking on the balls of our feet
like we were leaving church during the sermon. We
stayed together, hugging the walls of the buildings.
There was a lot of noise in the direction of the main
street and the piazzas, and as we turned the corner we
saw three Turkish soldiers coming toward us. They were
moving in a careless lackadaisical way and from the
look on their faces they were thinking about a nice soft
bed.

"Everybody down!" shouted Mazzapinta and we all hit
the ground like we'd been struck by lightning. The three
Turks stopped a couple of feet away and glanced at us
without interest. They mumbled something to each
other and then one bent down slowly and touched our
breeches to see if we were carrying knives. After that he
motioned for us to get up. We did so quickly and he
made a second gesture that seemed to mean, "Start
walking." It was the first time we'd seen Turks up close,
without muskets or scimitars, without feeling we had to
kill each other.

"Well, well, how about this now," I said to myself in
amazement. "Turks right here in front of us. I wonder
what they're thinking?" But we couldn't tell. They just
looked like three ordinary men, dead tired and annoyed.
If anyone had described Turks like this before, just men
wearily dragging one foot after the other, looking
almost melancholy, I wouldn't have believed it. At that
point several mounted officers appeared from the
opposite direction. They were dressed up in fancy
uniforms with those typical hats made of Turkish
brocade and worn slightly askew to show off. Their
horses, held to a slow trot, tossed their heads back every
now and then. When they reached us the officers spoke
briefly with our escorts, but we couldn't make out a
single word of their cursed language. Nonetheless after
a bit we realized from the way he was acting that the
soldier who had checked us for knives was describing

228

how we'd hit the ground. Then the officers began to look us up and down with a certain curiosity as if we were something really amusing. All at once as one of them was talking, the others burst out laughing. Finally they spurred their mounts and trotted away, their scimitars dangling against the horses' flanks.

"Damn them," mumbled Mazzapinta.

"Quiet," hissed De Raho. "There might be one who knows our language."

We set off again two by two, the Turks at our side. The sun shone so bright the sky itself seemed happy. Perfect weather to go down to the port and start out on a day's fishing. But one glance at the town was enough to change that impression. It brought a lump to my throat to see Otranto reduced to such a state: its walls crumbling, gates broken down, streets stained with blood. Turks were wandering in and out of the gates; here and there someone sprawled on a doorstep, fast asleep.

"They've turned it into Istanbul," said Mazzapinta.

The light was so brilliant I couldn't focus my eyes – something that never happened before – and my head was spinning. It must be the fever, I thought, because it wasn't just my eyes. My whole body was in a sweat, hot and cold at the same time.

We passed the Church of the Forty Saints. There in front of it, where a shadow traced the outline of the facade, five Turks were sitting in a circle, in that cross-legged way they always sit. They were eating and they were young. It was obvious the pleasure they took in their food and the patch of cool shade – they were happy just to be alive. I'd never thought of Turks doing such things and I found myself amazed once more.

We came out in the main street near Palazzo Colussi. Here there was only minor damage because the bigger structures had withstood the bombardment and if it hadn't been for the stones and the debris and garbage in the streets anybody might have thought the city was like it used to be.

"Look over there," blurted out Mazzapinta in a choking voice. Right in front of Palazzo Colussi, their arms thrown out wide, lay four bloody corpses: Gaetano Calo and his three companions. We stopped to look. They seemed to be closed inside a solitude as wide as the whole world, yet small enough to pinch the heart.

"They didn't make it," exclaimed De Raho.

I crossed myself, and my comrades watched me, terrified, then rapidly glanced at the three Turks, who merely motioned us to move on. At that my comrades also quickly crossed themselves.

"May their souls rest in peace," said Mazzapinta.

"Peace," we answered in chorus.

We walked along glancing back as long as we could still see them. Little by little the corner of Palazzo Colussi hid their heads, their shoulders, their arms. Only their legs and bare feet remained visible, white and forlorn on the paving stones and finally they too disappeared from view. The three Turks, still placid and sleepy, didn't stop us from looking backward. All they cared about was that we stayed in pairs while they followed, just as if they always went for walks this way.

"Poor Calò," said Cristoforo, "he didn't want to stay in the cellar like a cornered rat."

We arrived at the main piazza. The cathedral doors were wide open and Turks were going in and out, their cloaks turned up and tucked into their belts, but wait, there were horses coming out of the cathedral too.

Mazzapinta raised his puzzled eyes to heaven. "They've made it into a stable!" he said.

He shuddered then, and added, "Horses eating off the altars."

In the meantime we'd reached the Cortiglio, the east wing of the cathedral, where the archbishop's chapel was. No horses here, no noise either. I was struck by the way the Turks calmed down and stopped talking as they approached. When they reached the door to the chapel they stood still for a moment with bowed heads, then dropped to the ground.

"Here's where they've put their god," said Mazzapinta.

Some of the Turks looked at us as if they'd like to tear us apart. Others passed by indifferent, not even glancing our way.

"Hope they all drop dead!" said Mazzapinta.

"Shut up. Somebody might understand you," repeated De Raho.

All at once the street was filled with the sound of screams: out of Vicolo del Crismatico came a heavy cart drawn by two horses and filled with Otrantini women, sitting all in a heap, hanging onto each other or to the planks that formed the sides of the cart, their clothes torn, their hair tangled – they looked like a bunch of mad women. One of them fell backward into the bottom of the cart, another hung over the side trying to jump out, but a Turk following on horseback pushed her roughly back inside. He reminded me of a herdsman driving goats in from pasture trying to keep his flock from scattering as they cross a road. The cart lurched and began to rock back and forth – it was overloaded and going too fast. The driver was whipping the horses recklessly and singing at the top of his lungs. He was blind drunk and his song was only for his own pleasure, like he was off somewhere in the middle of the countryside. Even the strips of his turban were coming loose above his flushed face. When he passed us, Mazzapinta and I lunged at him but the soldiers grabbed us by the arm.

"Hold it!" shouted a man in our language, placing himself in front of me. I looked at him in shock.

"Stay where you are," he repeated. "Are you crazy? Do you want to be killed?"

Raising one arm, he turned toward the soldiers, said a couple of words in Turkish, and they moved away from us. The lurching cart rapidly disappeared in the direction of the port, leaving us standing there feeling stupid. Where were they taking the women? To La Valona? And when would we ever see them again?

"Go on acting like that and you won't last long," said the stranger.

"What's it to you?" yelled Mazzapinta.

"Cola, he's right," I said.

"But who is he?" muttered Cristoforo Rio. "I know I've seen him somewhere."

"Who are you anyway?" I repeated, but even as I said it my memory cleared as if a veil had been snatched away: he was the renegade Christian who'd tried to get us to surrender.

"I'm the one you shouted down when I wanted you to listen to reason," he replied unruffled. He took us to the archbishop's place and as we went up the long marble stairway he said, "Priests used to live here, didn't they? Now it's one of the Turkish headquarters."

"Used to?" I thought. "It's hardly been two weeks."

They took us to a huge room on the second floor, where the archbishop customarily ordained new priests. Although still adorned in crimson and gold it was now full of worktables where some Turks sat writing while others moved about in their midst. To see them, it hardly appeared there'd been a war at all. In fact, they didn't even resemble the cursed pagans they were. They might as well have been clerks in chancery. "Just look at this," I thought, astonished. Every now and then one of the men working at a table wiped the sweat from his face, stood up with a paper in his hand and went over to talk to someone at another table. But from the bored expression on their faces you'd say they were merely repeating things they both already knew and didn't care a fig about. Nearby another stood perfectly still, so quiet you couldn't see whether he was reading or asleep on his feet. Still another raised his head from his work-table and spoke abruptly and emphatically, as if he were the boss. His neighbors looked at him but no one responded.

The renegade Christian went over to speak to this same man, then quickly returned to us. "Wait here for now," he said. "The Turkish officer who's supposed to take your names will be over in a minute or two."

The six of us stood there together, not moving, all dead tired. As for me, I was still dizzy from the fever.

"Where were you holed up anyway?" asked the renegade.

"In the Fragà winecellar," answered Cristoforo Rio for all of us.

"Last night a whole family came out of a cave," said the renegade. Then he began gazing around and finally he yawned.

About an hour went by like that – if they'd only give us a bench, we thought.

All at once Mazzapinta spoke up: "So you've become a Muslim?"

"A matter of chance," he replied.

"And you're not sorry about deserting your faith?" Mazzapinta persisted.

"One faith's as good as another," he remarked with a faint smile on his bloodless lips.

"But you do believe in God?" asked Mazzapinta brusquely.

His answer was a curious one. He said if God really and truly existed, He'd be something so beautiful and wonderful that even we who believed in Him wouldn't be able to imagine what He was like. It wasn't until he'd come to this conviction that he'd put off his priest's habit.

"Priest's habit?" repeated Mazzapinta, dumbfounded.

"That's right. I was the Archpriest Giovanni. I used to live in Calabria." He waved an arm: "A long long time ago."

At that moment a Turkish youth maybe twenty years old, who happened to be passing, fixed his black eyes on us in a sort of excitement, then began to gesticulate and after screwing up his face like he wanted to talk but couldn't, said in our language: "Now...you...us...peace." He waited, gazing at us bright-eyed.

"If only there could be," I said.

He placed a hand on his chest, fingers spread out, then said, "Chalîl-beg."

"Good health to you," I answered, pleased.

He smiled. "How about that," I said to myself and once again nothing in the world seemed to make any sense.

Meanwhile Mazzapinta had walked right up to the renegade. "How about the devil? Do you believe in him?"

"Oh well, that's another question!" he exclaimed with a superior air.

And full of the devil he was – like Satan was wrapped around his soul. As for me, I thought it would have been better if Mazzapinta'd kept his mouth shut, but he always had to talk. But I didn't say a word. I rather liked that Chalîl-beg with his open smiling face, his youthful enthusiasm. Young folks are like that – the minute a feeling gets hold of them they get all carried away.

"He thinks we've converted to Islam," muttered Cristoforo Rio.

"That remains to be seen," I answered. Then I had an idea. I went up to Chalîl-beg and said to him very slowly and clearly: "We – us – food – very hungry." He looked at me for a minute, both curious and puzzled, his little eyes wide. Then his face lighted up and he waved his hands a couple of times as if to say, "Wait a minute," and rushed off down the stairs.

At that very moment, two Turks were coming up those same steps, naked above the waist, heads bowed, hands tied behind their backs. Two others escorting them quickly presented themselves to the head clerk, the one who'd raised his voice to speak to the others before. Now he listened, frowning more and more angrily as they talked, until he himself burst out shouting in their cursed language.

"Those two are going to be whipped," explained the Calabrian.

"Why?" asked Mazzapinta.

"They were found making love to two women in the cortile, right in broad daylight."

"*Our* women! Damn them!" yelled Mazzapinta.

The Calabrian said, "It's written in the Koran that one must only make love in total darkness so the man cannot see the woman's shame nor the woman see the man's shame."

"Hear that?" said Mazzapinta to me. "They're scum, that's what they are."

By now it was almost noon. The hollow feeling in our bellies, made worse by our long fast, was terrible at mealtimes. It was as though our stomachs still remembered their former routine. If one of us yawned, then right away another did and within a few minutes so did all the rest, each in his own way. Take Mazzapinta now – he'd open his mouth very wide and end with a great sighing, "A-a-ah!" He simply couldn't be any place without making himself heard. Finally the Turk we were waiting for came over. He too sat down at a table and while he looked at his papers he listened to the renegade telling him about us in a quiet humble voice. Once he'd heard the story, he had us line up in front of his table to be counted – we were six. He studied each one in turn, making comparisons and trying in the space of a minute to figure out the differences between us. Finally he began to ask us our names. As soon as we told him he ran a brown finger down a list of names on a paper in front of him and then began adding ours at the end. When he came to Mazzapinta he said, "How many Cola's are there in this town anyhow?" He spoke our language well. He asked us where we'd been for a day and a night after the Turks breached the walls and entered the city.

"In Palazzo Fragà, in the winecellar," answered Mazzapinta for all of us.

Then he wanted to know if we went there before or after the Turks came into the city.

"After, of course," said Mazzapinta.

He stared at us, "Why 'of course'?"

"Because it wasn't right to hide before," said Mazzapinta. "It would have been cowardly."

A flash of humor passed over the Turkish official's face, as if he wanted to smile but restrained himself. "We've run into a Turk who's not such a bad sort," I thought. "I guess pagans can be good folks as well as anybody else."

"When you came out of the cellar, did you try to flee?" he asked.

"We wanted to surrender," said Mazzapinta. "May the devil take my soul it that's not true."

"How much ransom can you pay?" asked the Turk.

"We don't have any money," stammered Mazzapinta, "but we can work. We'll do any kind of work you give us."

He was an odd one, that Turk, neither young nor old, maybe in his forties. At Mazzapinta's words he fell into a sort of distraction as if they'd reminded him of something else that had nothing to do with his duties, something far away from this room and all of us. From the look on his face it was not anything very cheerful. He said, "Don't you have anyone who can pay the ransom for you?"

"All six of us are fishermen," answered Mazzapinta.
"We make our living from the sea."

"The sea doesn't pay very well," sighed the Turk
quietly and wrote something on the paper. Then he said,
"You men go join the others now. We'll deal with all of
you at once."

When he heard this the Calabrian called two guards
aside and ordered them to escort us to the castle. So we
paired off and started down the stairs, worried and
thoughtful. We had just reached the bottom when
Mazzapinta turned to me. "Look!" he said.

There at the foot of the stairs stood Chalîl-beg
holding a great big barley loaf, wagging his head and
winking. He came up to me, gave me the loaf and said,
"For all."

"God bless you," I said, and he burst out laughing.

The guards didn't interfere. They were curious fellows,
those Turkish guards, always peaceable and sleepy.
When all is said and done they were better than the
Spanish soldiers. If they hadn't been pagans we'd have
had nothing to complain about.

Chalîl-beg didn't want to leave us, especially me. He
must have liked me as much as I liked him. "If we really
were at peace," I thought, "we could sit down and have a
good talk and once he'd learned our language I'd
explain to him that his god is a bunch of nonsense
somebody dreamed up with no basis."

"You...where?" asked Chalîl-beg.

"To the castle," I replied, "down, down," and I
pointed down under ground.

He stopped smiling, gazed at us and said: "You –
good men. No fear."

We looked at him in silence. Then Mazzapinta spoke
for all of us. "Goodbye," he said, and Chalîl-beg ran
back up the stairs.

Nachira III

We retraced our steps through Otranto, but now there seemed to be something entirely new in the noontime air, something foreign rising up from the earth itself and filling the streets, the piazzas – like during a plague when you may be perfectly healthy but you know the pestilence can strike from one minute to the next and it'll be all over. When the castle came into view De Raho said, "This is going to be bad. They'll be wanting something, those Turks, but what?"

Anyhow at least we won't be alone," I answered. "There'll be Mastro Natale to give us advice."

Since all the Otrantini men had been crowded together in the three cellars of the castle, they took us to the middle one.

"Well here we are back in a cellar again," said Mazzapinta, "just like a bunch of mice."

To be honest about it, when we went down the inside stairs of the castle and saw those men, young and old, all packed together and holding their arms out and calling, "Here come the others, more coming," I could sense the shadow of death itself moving about unseen among those crowded bodies.

"But where've you been?" they asked.

"Hiding in the Fragà winecellar."

"How about that, and so they came after you."

"We surrendered. We were dying of hunger."

"But there's nothing to eat here either," said someone. "So what happened then?"

"A lot," I said. "Is Mastro Natale here?"

"Yes," somebody said, "over there sitting under the arch."

We made our way through the crowd, climbing over men sitting on the floor, till we reached him.

"Mastro Natale, what can we do?" I asked.

"Wait," he answered. The old man was thinner and paler, but his eyes were still alert and determined.

"If we'd had money we could've saved ourselves," I said. "It's easy to work things out when you're rich."

In the evening a rumor went around that Akmed Pasha was coming to talk to us in person and we'd have to be very careful because he was a cruel and ignorant man, given to fits of rage. In fact, it was by robbery and destruction that he'd become pasha in the first place. He'd started out as nothing more than one of the sultan's stable boys. Because Otranto was contaminated with cadavers and the streets were still bloody the pasha had had his tent pitched on top of the Minerva Hill three-hundred paces away from the city and there he remained, sitting crosslegged on his rugs while his courtiers fanned him with peacock feathers.

They ordered us out of the cellar and we found ourselves assembled in the main courtyard. There in peacetime Spanish and Neapolitan soldiers used to walk miles back and forth, turning sharply left or right to the sound of a fanatical voice bellowing out orders so loud you could hear it all the way to the piazzetta. When they finished marching they'd emerge from the courtyard with dull eyes and sweaty faces, completely worn out from that totally useless effort. We'd been standing there maybe half an hour when we heard coach-wheels on the paving stones; then there was a roll of drums and the pasha appeared. He was a short wiry man with dark skin and a big nose; he wore a short red skirt with a black border and a white turban on his head.

"Is *that* him?" asked Mazzapinta in amazement.

"Eh, well yes," I said.

"What the devil, he looks like a worm."

"Careful," I said, "the Calabrian's still here."

"He's going to translate," added Mastro Natale.

The pasha's courtiers were lined up behind him perfectly motionless, heads down and hands clasped on their belts so tight you'd have thought they were tied. After giving us a hard look, the pasha began to speak and the Calabrian translated: "Your captains and governors are pigs. That's why you've ended up this way. It is written in the Koran, 'A tree grown in barren earth bears fruit like the earth it grows upon.' And that's why things have turned out badly for you."

Because we were so fascinated by the very sight of him, the courtyard remained perfectly silent. Only the pasha's rough common voice rang out, the voice of a stable boy. Meanwhile the Calabrian kept translating in a quiet soothing tone as if trying to comfort us. The pasha drew his tiny little body up as much as he could, glaring at us with defiance, shaking his skirt and shouting: "Your leaders have reduced you to slavery but *we* want to help you. We're ready to give you back your women, your children, your houses, without even asking for money. We only want one thing from you – renounce the wrong-headed faith your leaders have tricked you into believing and embrace the one true religion, the faith preached on earth by Mohamet, God's only real prophet."

At this all the Turks made a sort of bow, while the pasha picked up his little ivory staff and waved it in the air, yelling at the top of his voice: "Do you see that gate?" He was pointing to the entrance to the smaller courtyard where the guards were: "Any man who wants his freedom, anyone who wishes to return to his wife and children, step forward and go out through that gate. March!"

Several minutes passed; each one seemed longer than an hour, the suspense was so terrible. We all looked at each other. Nobody moved. May God forgive me, but maybe if somebody else had come forward I might have followed. But I wouldn't have been the first, not me.

"Hurry up, make up your minds," said the Calabrian, a sour look on his face, "don't balk like a bunch of mules. Let's go."

Nothing happened. Life itself seemed to have come to a halt inside us. The Calabrian began to shake his head as if to say, "Chin up, now. Don't do anything silly."

Then the pasha flew into a rage: "You want to remain Christian? You refuse to follow orders?"

In the ensuing silence one voice was heard.

"We do want to remain Christian." It was Mastro Natale. The pasha listened to the Calabrian's translation, than once again drew himself up, puny though he was, stuck his long nose in the air and began yelling at such earsplitting volume the Calabrian could only wait quietly until the din ceased. After that he translated, saying conquered infidels could not be allowed to live, and therefore we would have to be put to death. They would have to cut off our heads and thus destroy our entire race of pigs. Without even waiting to see how we took this news the pasha abruptly turned around. His courtiers quickly fell to their knees, then just as quickly stood up again, raised their arms to heaven, lowered them again, touched their own eyes, then stood aside for him to pass.

We found ourselves once again in the cellar. How could any of us even think straight anymore? I squatted down and took my head in my hands. It was still burning up with fever.

"Friends, we couldn't do otherwise," said Mastro Natale out loud.

Very little light came in through the two tiny iron-barred windows. They were about ten paces apart and so close to the sea the water used to come through them and flood the cellar during winter storms. That day we could hear the waves so clearly we might have been aboard a Turkish galleon.

The renegade Calabrian came down and stopped on the bottom step: "Listen to me, men of Otranto," he said. "There's still time for you to change your minds – you have until dawn. And you don't have to really change your minds inside, just saying so will be enough. What are words anyhow? Nothing, that's what. Why are you so afraid of a few words?"

At first nobody answered, but after a minute or two Mazzapinta cried out in exasperation: "All the same, the ones with money for ransom – you don't care if *they* stay Christian, do you? But not us – you're sending us to our death."

The Calabrian held out his arms like the priest at the *Ite missa est*, and sighed.

"And what's that supposed to mean?" persisted Mazzapinta.

"That's just the way things are," answered the Calabrian.

"All right, that's how they are," repeated Mazzapinta, his face so red he looked like he was choking.

The Calabrian went away.

"Now he'll go make the same little speech in the other cellars," announced Mastro Natale calmly.

I believe we were all thinking the same thing – feeling the place somehow wasn't real, or our companions either – it was all a bad dream. Except for one group in the back carrying on a heated discussion and shouting, but maybe they hadn't yet decided whether to stay or leave. Their voices echoed in my feverish head until all at once I began to shake uncontrollably, and I felt like there was cold water running down my back.

"But it's true," said De Raho, all excited, "if we had money we could remain Christian and live. There's no help for the poor in this world. It's a beautiful world but it's all wrong and we're going to die a stupid death simply because we're poor."

"No it's not a stupid death," burst in Mazzapinta. "Somebody comes along and says to you, 'All right now, you have to throw out all your beliefs!' And you answer, 'Oh no I won't by God. I'm keeping my beliefs.' And so you have to die. But that's not a stupid death."

Just then Father Leone da Faggiano got up and began moving about in our midst, saying we should prepare ourselves properly for the next world. Lowering his voice to a quiet paternal tone, he told us to reflect carefully and ready our souls for the coming encounter with God and the court of heaven. Easy to say! As for me, I couldn't stop thinking about my wife Nicoletta, wondering, "Where is she now? What's she doing? Is she crying?" All women cry when there's trouble. Idrusa's the only one who doesn't. She didn't even shed a single tear when her husband died – but she's different, eccentric.

I suddenly remembered the day I went to Nicoletta's house to ask for her hand. It was Assumption Eve. Since it was a holiday the whole family was sitting in a circle in the farmyard, their hands in their laps, their eyes a bit dreamy – the way hardworking folks look when they find themselves idle. The older ones sat there in dignity, knowing they were superior; the young ones – Nicoletta and her brothers and sisters – were glancing curiously at each other, all keyed-up and ready to laugh, waiting for something that wasn't there, at least not there on the outside. It must have been inside their heads – waiting for life, I'd say. When Nicoletta's father saw me coming and said right away, "Sit here Nachira," motioning toward an empty place beside Nicoletta, I was sure they were going to give her to me and I was so happy I couldn't talk for a little while. I just sat there speechless in my best clothes, my hands in my lap like the rest, looking around embarrassed, but at the same time wanting to prove my worth. I'd have liked them all to need my help; I wished I were a paladin who'd be able to save them by facing great dangers to myself. I was thinking about all this when Mazzapinta said, "Our children will return to Otranto. When the city's liberated the release of prisoners will be part of the conditions."

Meanwhile Father Leone, who'd completed his rounds, came over and began to count everyone and set up an order for us to go to the back of the cellar and confess to Father Epifani, who'd absolve us from the burden of all our life's sins. "Listen," said Father Leone, "we all have sins on our conscience. Now's the time to get rid of them, to offer the suffering God has sent us in exchange for his forgiveness. Because, my brothers, God in his infinite wisdom has arranged events for the good of our souls. When we weren't even giving it a thought he'd already foreseen everything and all we have to do is follow his sacred will. *Mamma mia*, brothers! Think of the magnitude of divine mercy!" It was odd, but the more he talked about the liberation of our souls, joining his hands and getting all worked up about the supreme happiness we were certain to regain in the next world, even though we were losing it in this one – the more he carried on, the more life on earth seemed so beautiful and wonderful that it ought to go on for years and years.

As for me, I was overcome by a fierce desire for a glass of wine. Maybe it was the fever. Anyway that idea stayed in my head and I simply couldn't get rid of it. "If only Antonello was alive," I thought, "he'd figure out some way to bring in a jug of wine, even here. What a man he was, that Antonello." I stood up but began to stagger because of the fever – it was hard to breathe and my guts were trembling. Mazzapinta got there just in time to catch me as I fell. When he eased me down on the floor and my back touched the stones I was shivering as if he'd plunged me into cold water.

"Father Leone," shouted Mazzapinta, "this man can't move. Call Father Epifani over here."

"Mazzapinta," I begged, holding on to his hands, "listen, I...."

"What is it?"

"I don't want to die. I want to live."

"Eh? Me too. Stay still now."

"I want to drink and go down to the sea. I want Nicoletta," I sighed, all agitated.

"Oh, oh. He's delirious," shouted Mazzapinta, "he's out of his head."

I kept sweating and sweating and a furious anger took hold of me. The thought that I'd come into this world simply to be killed drove me into a rage. Finally I lost consciousness. When I came to, I heard a voice so sweet it went right to my heart: "Nachira, are you all right? Can you hear me Nachira?" Father Epifani's eyes, pale and gentle and melancholy, were looking down at me. There was still some light in the cellar and the setting sun touched the wall beside me, directly across from one of the windows. I looked at the sun, at Father Epifani, and said, "Father, God didn't give me the same strength he gave the others."

"But you're having an attack of malaria," he answered. "Maybe something can be done for you. We can say you weren't in your right mind and couldn't decide."

I grabbed his arm: "Father Epifani, I should just be killed. Tell Mazzapinta to do it. If he doesn't, I assure you I'll become a Turk for a glass of wine. I'm dying of thirst."

"Wait Nachira, wait a minute and don't think about anything." He ran back toward the stairs while I tried to make myself as small as possible. I curled up like a snail so as not to feel that terrible heat and cold in my back. Alone in my corner, I watched as men stood up, sat down, moved about restlessly but talked very little.

Only a phrase or two reached me now and then from far away.

"We have to hold out," said Mastro Natale.

"I've got a notion we'll starve to death first," answered Cristoforo Rio. "Why don't they give us anything to eat?"

"What do they care?" said Mazzapinta. "They know they're only going to cut off our heads anyway."

After a while Father Epifani appeared again. He bent over me, his hand behind my neck trying to raise my head, like you do when you try to get a little kid to drink.

"What's this?"

"Wine," he said.

"Wine? How did you get it?"

"Never mind. I gave them the silver crucifix from the crown and they gave me wine. Go ahead. Drink it all."

The sun went down and all at once it was night there in the cellar. The only light came from above, where the windows were now only tiny blue rectangles. Either from the fever or the wine I fell asleep, and when I awoke it was pitch dark. It must have been after one o'clock because the moon, in its last quarter, had come out. I felt better, less feverish, calm, like a new man. Looking around I noticed they'd lighted an oil lamp at the foot of the stairs and I could see my companions stretched out on the floor almost on top of each other, or sitting with backs against the walls. Here an arm stirred, there a leg – like a litter of rabbits trying to find room in a burrow.

And yet there was at least one man in Otranto who'd forgotten about the war that night – he was singing. It was a song in a foreign tongue that came softly in from the street, marvelous to hear.

"It's a Turk," said Mazzapinta, suddenly sitting up.

"He must be on the rocks on the other side of the port," added Mastro Natale, who had already been sitting up.

"Lucky him. He can afford to sing!" said Mazzapinta bitterly, but he kept listening. The clear ringing voice was beautiful in the silence of the night.

"He must be very young," said Mastro Natale.

The song mounted up and blended in with the night, the moon, our sorrow. Maybe the Saracen was pleading for the stars to come down and touch his hands and felt sad because they stayed up there in the sky.

"It's a love song," said Mastro Natale.

The answer was hoofbeats on the cobbles of the guards' courtyard. We heard footsteps too, coming from the same direction. But the Saracen went on singing his melancholy song as though his heart were about to break. The smell of seaweed came in through the windows, the smell of our own sea.

"Hey," said Mazzapinta, seeing that I too was sitting up, "so you've come around, have you?"

"August nights are short so it'll soon be dawn," said Cristoforo Rio.

"There'll be a tramontana. So much the better," answered Mazzapinta. "It won't be so hot climbing up the Minerva Hill. That's where they'll be taking us."

"We'll be a regular procession," I said.

"Wait and see how many of us are still left," said Mastro Natale. "The night may have calmed your fears but it's frightened some of the others. And the Calabrian will be back underfoot ready to start all over again with his pack of filthy lies."

We said no more about the Calabrian, or about the tramontana, being in that frame of mind when everything's suddenly boring. The night, which ought to have been short, seemed to go on forever. The patches of moonlight on the walls stayed in the same place as though the moon itself was standing still. I was sure this night would never end. If anybody stirred and raised an arm, it grew eerily longer and didn't even look like an arm any more. And that shadow at my back? It was Father Epifani watching me. When I spoke to him he made as if to search for something on the floor.

"Father, I'm going with the others," I said.

He nodded assent and, wringing his hands, whispered, "How many more will resist? How many will there be?"

Nachira IV

After a while morning did indeed come. It was the fourteenth of August, Assumption Eve. "The day I went to ask for Nicoletta's hand," I thought. Because when you're about to leave this world it's funny how many things you remember. At the same time it's like you've got to figure out a problem and even though all the numbers are there in front of you, you just can't get it right. A bit later came the sound of dozens of feet on the cellar stairs. We quieted down at once, stunned and dismayed. Turkish guards carrying coils of rope began tying our hands behind our backs while their commander watched the operation from the stairs, his head high, like he thought he was wearing a crown. After that they made us go up into the courtyard, where we saw the prisoners from the other cellar being brought in too. Their faces sagged from lack of sleep; their eyes were dazed. Then one of the Turks began to move about in our midst holding a tablet with Turkish writing on it. The renegade Calabrian, who was acting as interpreter, walked beside him looking to left and right and repeating: "Anyone who's willing to believe what's written here will be spared. Anyone who refuses will die."

"Don't weaken, my friends!" shouted Mastro Natale. "We're men of honor."

"You there, quiet down," answered the Calabrian. "No talking. Each man has to decide for himself." He raised his voice so all could hear: "Anyone who's willing to believe what's written here," he said, pointing to the tablet, "step forward and proceed through the gate to the other courtyard." A few minutes passed, ten maybe, or twenty, who knows. Then one man stepped out from the group and walked slowly, head down, toward the gate. We all watched, tense and silent. Then a few more came forward and hurried out as if they were running away. My eyes sought out Father Epifani. He was standing in the first row, a look of anguish on his face.

"Worthless scoundrels," said Cola Mazzapinta.

We looked around at each other – there were still a lot of us, hundreds.

The Calabrian began to make his rounds again between the rows. Snake that he was, he probably thought that given enough time others would weaken. Now he was saying, "Anybody who wants his wife and children back move up and go out the gate. You can go home, eat and drink, go back to work at whatever trade you like. Do you hear? Home with your wife and children again!" He sounded like a merchant crying his wares in the marketplace, and just as merchants always find somebody who'll stop and listen, so did he. A small group broke ranks and approached him.

"Is that really true? You'll release our wives and children to us?"

"Why not?" answered the Calabrian. "Akmed Pasha has given his word."

"I'm going," cried Salvatore, an innkeeper from the old borgo. Throwing his head back, he raced off toward the gate. About twenty others followed.

At that Antonio Primaldo, a wool-trimmer, a quiet old man who'd never been known to raise his voice, stepped out of line and quickly made his way to the empty space in front, his head jerking angrily, his

shoulders bent forward by the ropes binding his hands
behind him. His voice was full of passion as he shouted:
"That's enough with being cowards! We've fought for
the king and now we'll fight for the honor of our own
souls. Long live the Holy Christian Faith!" The guards
jumped on him and began to pummel him with their
fists and hit him on the back with the blunt sides of
their scimitars. The rest of us began yelling and
struggling to break free of the ropes. Mazzapinta
succeeded and ran to help Primaldo, who'd collapsed
from the beating and because of his age. Turkish
reinforcements arrived, some on horseback, spurring
their mounts madly forward right into our midst. They
quickly restored order, but the Calabrian's job was
finished. Pale and motionless, his back against the
wall, he stood watching us through narrowed eyes, the
skin of his face periodically twitching in anger – the
anger cowards always feel towards people who carry out
their duty no matter how hard it may be. No more men
left the group. After exchanging a few questions and
answers, the guards began to count us. Since I was in the
front row I heard their commander tell the Calabrian in
our language: "There are still a lot left."

"Blast it," answered the Calabrian, "this business is
going to take forever. We'll be at it till nightfall."

"Good reason not to waste time – we'd better get
started right away," said the Turk.

They counted the first fifty – I was among them – and
marched us off, five in a row, toward the Minerva Hill.
The round ball of the sun, still reddish, was rising over
the sea as we climbed slowly upward, roped together. I
glanced at the cathedral tower because I'd have liked to
hear the bells ring but they remained silent. It was hard
going – my heart felt like an orange with all the juice
squeezed out. A flock of sea crows flew over and I
lifted my head to watch them. Then I closed my eyes.
When I opened them again we were almost there. God

help us, we were climbing the slope where the oleanders
grew, close to the top of the hill. I wanted to cry out,
"Wait – stop – there's lots of time left – let us have a
little more! What would it cost you?" A heavy silence
hung over us; our hands were tied, our mouths closed and
the sun was beating down on our backs. We stopped in
the clearing. The pasha was sitting crosslegged on a red
rug in front of his tent. The executioner, wearing a
golden crescent on his cap, was ready. A grasshopper
was hopping about at my feet – lucky grasshopper – it
could go right on hopping. Then I raised my eyes – my
heart was pounding – I saw a bright light shining over
the countryside and the red and white oleander branches
reaching toward the sky. Those oleanders on the
Minerva Hill were the last things I saw in my life. Who
would ever have thought....

Aloise de Marco I

While the bells of Otranto rang out in a holiday mood
men and women dressed in a thousand festive colors
advanced from every corner of the city toward the
cathedral piazza, moving at a lively pace that gave
them all a youthful air. As they laughed and talked
among themselves the bright October sun played over
land and sea so cheerfully it seemed the world had
suddenly paused for a moment of exceptional
happiness. With so many men in warrior's garb, the
ladies stood out – their fresh complexions, finely sewn
dresses, and brocade cloaks rendering them more
beautiful than ever, and so proud they appeared to be
the very personification of the conquering soldiers'
glory. Here and there, however, a local nobleman
walked along observing the joyful throng with the
haughty regard of a philosopher contemptuous of such
glory, while Neapolitan officers rode through the
crowd on slender frisky horses adorned with golden

fringes, and made even livelier by the unusual atmosphere. It was the beginning of October 1481 and the people of Otranto were flocking to the cathedral for a solemn Te Deum to celebrate their liberation by the militia of Don Alfonso of Aragon on September thirteenth of that same year. Not since the days of my youth had I seen a holiday in Otranto, the yellow tower draped with banners – the dragon, the crucifix with its golden inscription, "*Recordatus sum virtutis eius* – I remembered his valor," the red bars of the House of Aragon – not since my family had moved to Naples when I was twenty. Thus ten years had passed, during which the distance from my native city as well as the life of capital and court had transformed Otranto into one of those interior realities that are closer to facts of the imagination than to a sum of real things. The fishermen's tiny white houses down by the port, accomplices to the events and fantasies of my childhood, survived in my heart as a precious intermittent life linked with moments of solitude and profound reflection. When Duke Alfonso assembled his troops to free the city from the Turkish occupation I found myself torn between the peaceful ease of Neapolitan life and the gentle tug of nostalgia for my youth. I opted for the second and joined the expedition.

That October day I was making my way toward Otranto's main piazza with Giovanni Francesco Caracciolo, commander of the Brindisi garrison. All at once, looking up at the belltower, which rose beside the cathedral in the brilliant sunshine, he burst out laughing: "Ha, ha! That was a real spectacle. I can still see him up there, bobbing and bowing and showing us his rear end."

"Who?" I asked, curious.

"The muezzin. During the seige he climbed up to the top of the belfry every evening for the call to prayers. That meant a whole lot of deep bowing to right and left, always facing away from the northwest, where we were. So I'd see him from behind while he was busy waving his arms and when he set about bowing and prostrating himself I'd get an excellent view of his backside. One day Don Alfonso told one of his artillerymen, 'Blast that bat off his perch for me and I'll give you a gold piece.' The artilleryman snapped his fingers, gave the command and began firing from a knoll west of the borgo about thirty paces from the walls, first at random – one ball falling short, another overshooting – so the muezzin wouldn't know he was targeted and stay up there. Once he had him zeroed in, he turned to Don Alfonso, 'Now if your excellence would care to watch, I'll knock him off,' and then he fired his mortar. The ball hit the Turk right in the middle of his back, sending him into the air in a thousand pieces, which fell to earth off toward the walls a good distance from the belfry." Gian Francesco burst into laughter again. "The rest of the Turks must have had a good day's work picking up all the pieces."

Meanwhile we'd arrived at the cathedral piazza.

"You aren't planning to go in, are you?" asked Gian Francesco in astonishment.

"We have to. The new archbishop will be preaching."

"Brother Serafino?" He snickered. "Brother Serafino's no preacher. After the first three words you can guess everything else he's going to say."

Those of us who had commanded troops during the seige knew Brother Serafino well. He was a member of the order of San Francesco della Scarpa who'd been named archbishop by his holiness the pope on Don Alfonso's recommendation because of service rendered to the militia during the campaign. He was a rather young man, tall but heavy with the kind of soft opaque liquid fat one associates with sickly people. Under bushy eyebrows his dull colorless eyes stared out of his round face with the sad afflicted air of an ox, creating the impression he was totally incapable of rapid decision.

"Oh well, poor fellow, he's a hard worker completely dedicated to saving souls – anyhow a friar who's really religious," I answered.

"Saving souls?" Gian Francesco snickered again. "You know how he thinks of souls? As a bunch of sheets that have to be protected by prayers and genuflections from the world's dust and dirt. If their pure whiteness gets besmirched they have to be separated into three distinct categories: souls saved, souls that still can be saved, and souls already damned. That's all he knows about souls and all he cares to know – since he's only interested in what will profit heaven."

"Nonetheless saving souls is his life's purpose," I said.

"So it is, strange as it may seem," he remarked. "But you can't call it virtue. Virtue's no better than sin if it doesn't include a whiff of something more – intelligence or imagination or...well *something*, I don't know what. Do you remember when that wounded soldier was in such a bad way and Brother Serafino plopped himself down beside his bed and didn't budge until the man died? Stayed there maybe ten hours straight, like a watchdog."

"Without eating," I put in. "With no rest."

"Yessir, without eating or sleeping. But what do you suppose was in his heart? Fear, that's all. Fear for the man's soul, that breath of divinity he'd so carefully cleansed of all impurities, fear the devil might contaminate it at the last minute with – oh no! – maybe even a happy memory! As for the poor wretch's wounds, the possibility he might escape death – all this didn't concern him one bit! Not a bit. Such matters have no bearing on the inner material he considers subject to salvation; thus they don't count at all – they're nothing. You see what I mean?" We walked along for a few minutes in silence among the crowd before he spoke again: "I remember when I took an arrow in my shoulder back in Minervino. I was standing by one of those haystacks the Turks piled up in the fields and set on fire when we arrived, to warn their cohorts in the city. Well, my men took off my armor and carried me to a hut in the village, laid me on a bed with a servant who sat on the floor beside the bed. Weak from loss of blood, I fell into a state of semi-consciousness. I could hear the firing of mortars, but it was muted as though at a distance. Evening came and I opened my eyes and looked up at the first shadows of night moving across the sky, bringing with them that feeling of catastrophic sadness you always get if you happen to be in bed at twilight. It can drive you insane if you let it. So I started to think about the women I'd made love to in the recent past, and would you believe it? They readily took shape in my mind, distracted as it was and drifting towards eternity. I saw one leaning in through the window, her breasts escaping from her low cut dress, another in the act of undressing, tossing her dainty shoes into a corner, moving barefoot about the room as she undid her skirt and lowered it to the floor with both hands, then stepped prettily out of it, leaving her legs bare – enough to take your breath away. I could see into my memories with miraculous clarity, one image flowing into another – unbelievably lucid and accurate. 'But just look how rich my life has been,' I thought, and at that realized time had passed and it was fully dark. The servant sitting cross-legged at the foot of my bed had fallen asleep. Suddenly there was a knock at the door. The servant roused himself, took the lantern and went to answer it. As he came back into the room with the lantern in his right hand he lifted it above his head to get a better view and looked me over from head to toe as if searching for the answer to some problem he had to solve.

'Well, what is it?' I asked.

'It's Brother Serafino,' he said. 'He wants to hear your confession.'

'At this hour?' I raised myself up as best I could and shouted at the servant: 'Tell Brother Serafino I'm sleeping.'

He went out, then came back again: 'Brother Serafino says to wake you up.'

At that point I lost my temper. 'Tell Brother Serafino to quit worrying – I'm not planning to die tonight. He can come and hear my confession tomorrow if he really insists on it.' The servant exited but returned at once to report that Brother Serafino wanted to see for himself. He appeared now in the doorway, fat and pale as though his flesh were melting and said, 'I wish to bring you the benediction of the Lord, Don Francesco.'

'Thank you, Brother Serafino,' I had to say. 'How come you're up and about at this hour?'

'I was passing through and wanted to see how you were,' he replied.

I'm certain he wasn't passing through at all. He'd come on purpose, obsessed with saving my soul. 'I'm happy to see you're feeling better. I'll leave you to yourself for now but with your permission I'll come back tomorrow morning.'

'Go to bed, Brother Serafino,' I answered. 'You look terrible; you're in worse shape than I am.'

He sighed, bowed his head and said, 'War is one of God's ways of testing us – it can lead the soul astray.' He paused a moment in thought, then added, 'My friend, the world is full of sin. It's an awesome thing. If you think how someone can go to hell just for missing a single mass that's enough to scare anybody. But during war a man can die from one minute to the next. What would happen to his soul if we didn't provide for him in time?' As he spoke these concluding words he trembled, almost shuddered. My servant, still holding the lantern, looked at him intently. 'Well, as far as I'm concerned you don't need to worry,' I answered. 'I have no intention of dying.'

Brother Serafino managed a weak smile, but his eyes remained anxious, as if to say, 'You seem to be a thinker, my friend. This is the greatest danger for the soul.' Finally his pale puffy lips began to whisper a prayer. Approaching the bed he made a grandiose sign of the cross and concluded, 'May the Lord bless you and illuminate your soul.'

'Thank you kindly, Brother Serafino, and good night,' I answered.

The room was empty once more but the spell was broken and my delightful memories had vanished. When morning came he arrived punctually to hear my confession."

Gian Francesco fell silent. We were at the exact center of the piazza. Around its edges a small crowd of working people stood quietly watching the arrival of the local gentry for the service. They were peasants from inland and fishermen from tiny villages along the coast, who had come to fill the void left by the Turkish massacre of the population of Otranto.

"Well, well," Gian Francesco continued, "our fat monk has made himself a career out of all this. Who'd have ever thought one day Brother Serafino'd be giving us his ring to kiss?"

Even from the piazza we could hear the preacher's grave and monotonous voice as we headed for the side door in order to enter at the middle of the left nave. Leading up to this entrance from opposite sides were two stairways of about twenty steps each, whose edges were either worn smooth by the piety of the faithful or else pockmarked by the violence of gunfire. All three naves were packed with people. At the foot of the altar in front of the central nave stood Duke Alfonso's armchair and prie-dieu, made conspicuous by their red-embroidered, damask upholstery. Behind the duke sat the nobles and barons of the realm, as well as the military commanders, constrained by their dress uniforms and by having to sit in the front rows. They were so still they could have been statues except that now and then the corners of their mouths twitched or a face reddened because its owner couldn't unbutton his collar to get a bit of air. They expressed the investiture and the cupidity of power in every aspect: their capes, their skirts, their hands folded in noble repose, their rigid necks.

"We should be up there with them," I said.

"So we should but it's much better here," answered Gian Francesco with a malicious smile.

Archbishop Serafino cast his eyes over the mass of humanity spread out at his feet and spoke in a weighty serious tone. At the moment the two of us entered the cathedral he was describing the martyrs' last night in the cellars of the castle and from the assurance in his voice you'd have thought he'd been an eyewitness.

"And then they knelt on the bare stones of the cellar," he was saying, "and struggling against the flesh, they began to pray in chorus. Thus they passed the entire night in prayer and singing, and in graciously comforting one another for the temporal death that would gain them the crown of martyrdom. Indeed *vera et copiosa messis tantum e coelo est* – a true and abundant harvest comes only from heaven. From that point forward no more thoughts of earthly life crossed their minds; instead, as if already admitted to the ecstasy of paradise, they saw the angel choir smiling in heavenly exaltation. And even as their souls were entering the celestial court, Our Lady the Virgin Mary, comforted by their holiness, produced a remarkable miracle. In the cathedral hung an image of the Madonna, called the Madonna of the Crismatico, which Luke the Evangelist had painted with his own hand shortly after the death of Our Lord Jesus Christ.

My faithful ones, you must already know that this painting had once before been the object of a portentous miracle performed by the Holy Virgin. On a certain sunny morning long, long ago a mysterious boat appeared far out to sea, a small boat with neither oars nor crew. It came directly into the harbor and landed gently on the gravel beside the pier, right before the fishermen's eyes. In that boat was the Madonna of the Crismatico, and the Otrantini carried the image to the cathedral in a solemn procession, happy the Virgin had granted them such an unequivocal sign of her love. Now while the holy martyrs were praying in the cellars of the castle the night of August thirteenth last year, the Madonna's image detached itself from the wall of this temple." He stopped and pointed toward the apse, "From that wall over there, can you see? And then the painting took flight toward the heavens. The martyrs noticed a streak of light in the starry sky and, smiling at one another, they blessed the Virgin for once again giving a ready sign of her predilection for the people of Otranto."

Duke Alfonso sat leaning casually forward, legs apart, folded hands hanging loosely between his knees. A vigorous dark-skinned man with brown hair and an aquiline nose, he was listening amiably to the archbishop but at the same time seemed to be thinking, "Well, Serafino, you've fulfilled your duty to the troops and now I see you also know how to make the most of your brain. Good. Getting you named archbishop reflects credit on me – you're going to be an asset." The congregation listened ecstatically, drunk with faith – the preacher held their souls in his hand.

"So now my beloved faithful," he went on, "reflect a moment in your hearts. Think of those eight-hundred men marched off in groups of fifty with their hands

tied, marched up the Minerva Hill to be decapitated
one by one by their heathen captors – oh haughty and
horrifying deed! Yet out of such travail God created yet
another portentous miracle – in fact the first to bend
his neck to the axe, a man called Primaldo, was already
marked by divine predestination. He remained standing,
headless as he was, despite the Turks' best efforts to
push him over, and fell only at his own will, when the
last of his compatriots had been decapitated. Afterwards the bodies of the saints, left unburied there on
the hill as a meal for vultures and wild beasts – clear
evidence of pagan impiety – remained intact and
uncorrupted for months, giving off a divine light visible
at night from afar. The Turks, astonished at the
mysterious flickering, thought there was a fire burning
on the hill. I tell you this on the authority of men who
were present so that in your hearts and souls you may
understand the power of holiness."

The sermon finished, his arms in their full sleeves
came to rest, and Archbishop Serafino left the pulpit
and knelt down in his enormous red satin cassock in
front of the altar to chant the *Te Deum*, surrounded by
prelates in white surplices, like pinnacles around a
huge red cupola. A ray of sunlight filtering through a
travertine window sparkled on the lace of the moving
surplices as the measured chant of the faithful rose
gently from the naves.

At the end of the ceremony when the crowd began
moving out through the three doors like waves of a
great river flowing into the piazza, people's faces wore
a strange dazed look. Each in his own way was picturing
those momentous events, events which had been
followed by many other vicissitudes of war, matters of
life and death – all brought back to the present by the
archbishop's sermon, made so distressingly real they
displaced the careless happiness of an hour before.
Friends moved closer together in little groups to talk

about it, first in low voices then little by little in a louder, more normal tone. While some exclaimed in amazement so intense they no longer quite seemed rational, others looked around at the buildings decorated with banners and garlands of flowers, at the distant deep blue of the sea and the green of hills that appeared to have been put there as a feast for the eyes. Gazing at all this they struggled to escape an atmosphere so infused with heroism it threatened to choke their sense of peaceful well being.

One livelier spirit noted that saints were indeed rather curious creatures: they sang before they died, saw paradise from their knees, and remained erect without heads, whereas all other mortals would have succumbed to a resounding terror at the sight of the executioner's axe. Then Gian Francesco remarked that none of all this had been proved anyway and he was of the opinion those Otrantini saints, poor wretches, had been good and scared the last night and it probably never even entered their minds to sing hymns. As far he was concerned the greatest damage to noble historical deeds occurred when people like Brother Serafino started to admire them. To which Matteo di Capua replied that it wasn't Brother Serafino's fault since three-fourths of the human race were so starved for unusual events that when anything extraordinary happened they got right into the spirit of it, and without such occasions their very souls would waste away.

The discussion grew more animated since most of those present weren't too pleased with Gian Francesco's and Don Matteo's comments and besides they showed little respect for the sanctity of the martyrs. At that moment Duke Alfonso approached the group. Still glowing from his victory and satisfied to find himself in his own element surrounded by soldiers and beautiful ladies on a splendidly sunny day, he was particularly happy to be there in Otranto, which had surrendered only after an arduous seige lasting months. "Well my friends," he exclaimed with brutal enthusiasm, "the archbishop views things in a manner appropriate to his sanctity. But as a soldier I can tell you if we kicked out the Turks we owe it to those tough dogged fishermen and peasants who fought with their fists against swords and held out stubbornly for two weeks, giving us the time to prepare our defenses."

The duke's sound and simple explanation seemed to chase a nightmare from the piazza and serenity returned of itself to the faces of all those present. We continued slowly toward the castle in a procession behind Duke Alfonso. There were twenty of us – barons and soldiers among whom the Duke stood out in his long silk cloak trimmed with silver. He was bare-headed and carried no weapons, a tall man, full of health and vigor. Behind us came the pages in yellow, black and white capes, while peasants and fishermen who had moved into Otranto from nearby villages or inland farms stood motionless along the street watching – tenacious, almost obdurate in their silence.

"The best kind of people," said the duke, pointing to them. "They don't lick anybody's boots."

Then the talk turned to horses. The duke told how he'd celebrated their victorious entry into Otranto by giving aged Ugento wine to his gray Andalusian and how the animal had let out a series of whinnies that implied he was turning into a donkey. As everyone was laughing a sound of fifes and bagpipes came from a side street, playing a march as festive as a cheery thought wafting through the air.

"What's that music?" said the duke. "Let's go have a look."

The multiple instruments became a single pipe to my ears, one great trumpet sound conquering pain and sorrow, the voice of my people reborn, a wedding song – Otranto's wedding feast. We turned into the side street just as the procession reached us. In front were the peasant bride and groom, followed by relatives and friends in their holiday dress with bright-colored plumes on their hats. Each one was completely occupied with keeping in step directly behind the person in front, directly ahead of the one behind, and maintaining perfectly straight rows, two by two, down the middle of the street.

A page dispatched for information reported to the duke that a young man from the San Donato farm was getting married, the first wedding to be held after the liberation of the city: hence the fifes and bagpipes. The duke was delighted with the procession, watching with his slightly crossed eyes, jester's eyes we called them.

"Wonderful!" he said. "My friends, this wedding is a symbol. Yes indeed, because little things, not big ones, signify real change. The truth is we live but one day at a time."

In Otranto, weddings always included a procession and the so-called "handkerchief dance" in the cortile of a farm.

"You know what we'll do?" said the duke. "This evening we'll all go out to the farm and I'll lead off the dancing with the bride."

Aloise de Marco II

The San Donato farm was a low, massive stone building with a few scattered windows so tiny they gave it the appearance of a fortress, all in all suggesting the age-old necessity of defense against Saracen raids. The huge structure housed three families of tenant farmers, each one made up of parents, children and a series of innumerable grandchildren and great-grandchildren, almost a little village in itself. All had turned out in bright-colored holiday garb and lined up in order along the walls of the courtyard waiting for the duke to arrive and begin the dance. They had the patient, calm and collected air they always assumed toward any ceremony, be it mournful or joyful. When we arrived they greeted each one of us obsequiously, even the horses. Then the heads of the three families advanced into the middle of the courtyard, stopped in front of the duke, and in a grave and dignified manner began to pronounce phrases they'd known by heart from childhood, having heard their fathers and grandfathers recite them every time someone dressed in silk or velvet or brocade appeared at the farm. Educated only by their long years of servitude, they consistently regarded us in terms of a single idea: that receiving homage was as much an absolute necessity for us as wearing silks and brocade. Thus when the duke cut their rhetoric short in his brusque and military manner and exclaimed that today we should be honoring the first bridal couple in liberated Otranto the three old men looked at him with suspicion. But the duke lacked sensitivity and imagination, which after all have no place in a soldier's career, so he didn't notice a thing and cheerfully persevered.

"Where are the bride and groom? Bring them out!"

The young couple came forward with that thoughtful attitude produced by a timidity so intense it leaves the mind devoid of any thoughts at all. The bride would have been sufficiently intimidated if any of us had looked at her but with everyone's eyes upon her she was physically unable to raise her own. Her emotion was already so intense that when the duke took a ring off his own finger and offered it to her as a gift she was petrified. For a moment all the farmers remained more or less immobile. Confronted by a scene that didn't fit in with any of the wedding customs followed for centuries, they lapsed into a remarkable silence. At this point, the duke, having decided to make the peasants' joys the business of the day – though he saw these joys from a

prince's point of view – called his pages and ordered
them to make sure everyone had plenty to drink. We had
in fact brought along great quantities of wine and the
atmosphere soon warmed to a festive mood. The duke
proposed a toast to the health of a reborn Otranto
finally free of the Turks, then began to recount the
episodes of the war for all to hear. He told about the
occupation of Minervino as well as Count Giulio
Acquaviva's expedition into the Giuggianello Woods,
and the revenge taken on a Turkish soldier who had
killed one of his pages and who fled into the sea on
horseback when he saw the duke's insignia. As he spoke
he grew more animated, talking and gesturing as though
even now Turkish forces were advancing toward him
through the courtyard. Like all men who have but one
real passion in their lives he was unable to discuss or
interest himself in anything else but that.

Before long the duke and Gian Francesco Caracciolo
got carried away by the occasion and drank a bit too
much, behavior so strange to the farmers it attracted
all their attention and touched the venerable nobility
with a hint of ridicule. I thought of Duke Alfonso's
father, his majesty King Ferrante; a consummate
politician, he would never have allowed himself such a
liberty, would have understood the danger in letting the
tenant farmers see him as a man like them when he was
placed so far above them. The youngest peasants were
laughing cautiously, their faces hardly changing at all.
Was I the only one who realized it? Maybe, because I
was the only one not drinking, and being a native of
Otranto I understood my people better than anyone
else. But did I really understand them? Who, I
wondered, would have expected such a race to do what
they did when they found themselves face to face with
the Turks? Was it a strength in their blood? Could
anyone have guessed how hard it would be to figure out
what goes on in their hearts?

"Are you dreaming, my friend?" shouted a voice in my ear. "You're always off somewhere in your imagination. Have a drink instead." It was the duke himself, handing me a goblet and rousing me from the meditative state I'd fallen into.

"You know I never drink, your excellence," I murmured.

"A man endowed with a noble soul should drink. Otherwise he's fated to sink into gloom – like you."

"I'm not gloomy, your excellence," I answered. "I love the smell of the fields, the rose mallow and wild fennel. I like the tranquillity of these people here."

The duke, made talkative by wine, took my arm: "If you follow this course you'll become a good provincial poet *breviter*, but there's plenty of them already wandering about the kingdom. Look, I myself like the country once in a while. Today for instance. I'm really having a good time here in the open air. But the difference is for me the smell of rose mallow or whatever you call it, won't keep my brain from functioning."

Such talk always rendered me awkward but luckily at that point the duke noticed the bride wasn't drinking. So he went over and offered her the goblet I had refused. She stood there surrounded by other peasant women and tried to avoid taking it, blushing in embarrassment and stammering excuses and thanks, but to no avail. The duke, with the tenacity of one who has drunk a bit more than necessary, kept insisting. Finally he decided she absolutely must have something to eat. He shouted that eating teaches people to drink. The poor woman didn't know what to do.

Finally the moment arrived to begin the ritual dance. In our region it was the custom for the bridal pair to begin the dance with a colored handkerchief in hand, the groom holding one end and the bride the other. That day the duke was replacing the groom but after several turns he suddenly tore the handkerchief away from the bride, waved it around above his head for a few seconds like a sling shot and then flung it into the air, calling out: "No more handkerchiefs – everyone can dance hand in hand now – in freedom. Let this be a sign your servitude is ended. Do you understand, my good men?"

The farmers stared at him in silence, their expression both puzzled and slightly intrigued. Then they all raised their arms and shouted in chorus. Did they perhaps really believe for a moment that their lives would change?

Although the duke had claimed his right to lead the dance to the end he motioned to the groom to take his place and then all the tenant farmers gradually formed couples and they too began to dance: leaping up and then stamping their feet in place, now with hands on hips, now with right arms extended so each man touched his partner's hand. They seemed a little embarrassed, either because of our presence or because they could no longer swing the usual handkerchief between them.

"Beautiful!" exclaimed Gian Francesco beside me, immensely pleased. "You'd think they were calves and heifers who'd learned how to dance."

Then he moved back as if to get a view of the entire scene and stood with arms crossed. Suddenly he remarked, "See? Events in this world are always repeating themselves. Politicians know it and count on it. As soon as they can people will take up their old habits again and do the same things they did before."

"These, however, repeat themselves in the same way eagles do, or swordfish. There's nothing like the pride of the poor."

"So what? They're still repeating themselves. Funny, I find myself thinking of my professor of physics in Naples. He was tall and thin with bony shoulders – loved to go on about phenomena that theoretically should occur in nature but have never been verified because of some particular reason or other – well, he always used to sum up those reasons in the phrase: '*quod fieri non potest sine perturbatione rerum omnium* – what cannot be proved without disturbing the order of all things.'"

All at once we heard the duke's voice: "What's going on here? A discussion? Come now, get into the spirit of the occasion, my friends. Let yourselves go." The duke was all fired up and in a state of totally natural happiness, absolutely incapable of picking up any kind of subtlety.

"You are most extremely magnanimous, your excellence," answered Gian Francesco with a smile and a bow.

"I adapt to my surroundings, Caracciolo. Unlike your friend here. Look at him. I don't know what he's talking about, but his head is always full of bizarre ideas, like all solitary men."

We joined the group. Near me several young peasant couples were dancing with their heads tilted back, their lips parted and their nostrils flared as if they were following the trail of a seductive fragrance through the air. The men's foreheads glistened with sweat from both heat and emotion, while the women's hair, braided and coiled at the back of their necks, bounced up and down with the dance. Up in the sky, still blue in the day's last sunlight, the first stars were coming out in shimmering brilliance. Old folks were holding children by the hand and the little ones, eyes wide and shining, had fallen in love with the dancing couples, and gotten lost in the discovery of a wonderful new dimension.

I noticed an old man seated next to me, his legs slightly arthritic, the palms of his hands resting on the top of a heavy walking stick.

"How about you?" I asked him. "How did you get along when the Turks were here?"

As he smiled the muscles contracted in his face, which was as shiny and dry as a polished nut: "I hid like a mole in a hay shed, sir, up by San Nicola di Càsole. I put it this way: Since God isn't showing himself, we'll have to try to figure out what it is he wants from us."

"And then...?"

"I waited. My son had died in combat and I'd hidden my women inland, in the village. I waited for the king's soldiers to get here so I could come out of the hay shed and go back to the farm."

"Were you sure they'd come?"

"Why shouldn't I be sure, sir? Still, the winter was a fierce one – it was so damp I picked up all sorts of aches and pains, so bad I could hardly move my legs. I sat there in the hay and kept thinking back to my youth – it seemed like now I was nothing but a pebble. Yet, I thought, a lot of pebbles together make a mountain and there's no way a mountain can disappear. When the king's soldiers finally did come and I saw them riding down from the plateau on their horses I wanted to run to meet them but my legs wouldn't move for the pain and I stood there at the door of the shed, choking from the urge to call out: 'Welcome, welcome! May Jesus Christ go with you!' Then I laid right down in the meadow and spent I don't know how long rolling around in the grass with my arms stretched out. I got so worked up I was crying. Finally a couple of Neapolitan soldiers came up to me: 'Hey there Grandpa!' they shouted. 'You're a mess all right, but never mind – you're alive.' Then they picked me up on their shoulders and carried me inland to a farm."

"Are you happy now?"

"Oh yes. God is great."

At that very instant the dancers broke into their traditional song and little by little the old people standing with their backs against the walls of the farm buildings joined in. It was a wedding song wishing the bridal couple good fortune, but it was strangely melancholy and its effect didn't fit in with the pace of the dance, as if to symbolize the sharp contrast between the joy of such a celebration and the uncertainties of the world.

"These people are pure gold," I thought to myself. "They've understood everything." At that my gaze quickly turned to the Minerva Hill and, good God, I seemed to see a crowd of Otrantini dancing up there too – and still more climbing in groups up the slopes, not ghosts but handsome vigorous men who'd made something constructive out of their lives. In my mind I'd entered an unknown world, maybe even a distant future....Gian Francesco slapped me on the shoulder.

"Let's get moving. The duke thinks it's time to leave them alone to enjoy their party. So what do you say to a few more drinks ourselves? There's lots of this good wine back in town!" After a bit he added, "By the way what are your thoughts on this nonsense about the end of the handkerchief meaning the end of their servitude? Are these people really going to believe it?"

I shrugged. Half the Minerva Hill was now in shadow. The sun was setting and the world seemed vast indeed.

How many years have gone by since that night? But then, only the living count the years. And has anything really changed?